Michael was in trouble...

She couldn't shake the feeling. She barely knew him, yet fate had somehow catapulted her into his arms, and since then she'd felt closer to him than any other man. Maybe that allowed her to sense his danger.

Her mind went blank, and a feeling so powerful swept over her that she gasped. The room swirled into blackness, and her skin grew clammy. It was as if suffocating walls were closing around her and it was a struggle to draw breath. She might have screamed if she hadn't been panting for air   Michael's air.

She had to go to him, quickly—if only she could figure out where he was.

Visions flashed before her. The old Lafayette Cemetery...a stone slab...a dank musty enclosure...the small of death. Then she knew. Michael was in a tomb!

Dear Reader,

Our "Decade of Danger & Desire" continues! To help celebrate and to thank you for your readership these past ten years, we've brought you a very special gift—Rebecca York's Peregrine Connection.

Since its original publication in 1986, the Peregrine Connection trilogy has been a favorite of romantic suspense readers—some of the most sought-after books, according to booksellers.

It's our pleasure to make them available to you once again. Whether you'll be reliving the danger and desire, or discovering it for the first time, enjoy!

Sincerely,

Debra Matteucci
Senior Editor & Editorial Coordinator
Harlequin Books
300 East 42nd Street
New York, NY 10017

Rebecca York
In Search of
the Dove

Harlequin Books

TORONTO • NEW YORK • LONDON
AMSTERDAM • PARIS • SYDNEY • HAMBURG
STOCKHOLM • ATHENS • TOKYO • MILAN
MADRID • WARSAW • BUDAPEST • AUCKLAND

To Linda, for sharing our year of adventure

First published by Dell Publishing Co., Inc.

ISBN 0-373-22305-6

IN SEARCH OF THE DOVE

Copyright © 1986 by Ruth Glick and Eileen Buckholtz

Printed in U.S.A.

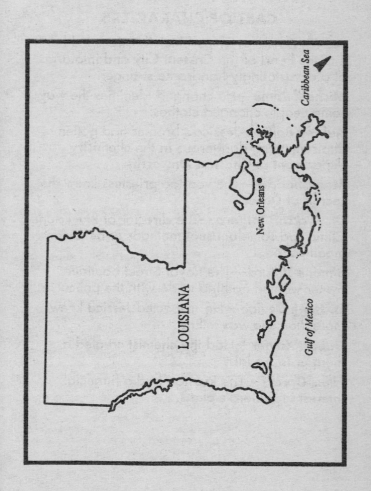

CAST OF CHARACTERS

Jessica Duval—Her psychic vibrations led her into the heart of the Cresent City and into arms of a devastatingly handsome stranger.

Michael Rome—He changed identities the way some people changed clothes.

Aubrey Bollin—Jessica's brother had gotten into something dangerous in the chemistry department at Chartres University.

Moonshadow—The voodoo priestess knew the secrets of Dove.

Dr. Jackson Talifero—The director of Blackstone Clinic had some unusual methods of behavior modification.

Simone Villard—The Royal Street boutique owner wanted nothing to do with the police.

Lt. Hugh Devine—He suspected Jessica knew more than she was telling.

Gilbert Xavier—Had the chemist created a monster in his lab?

Filiks Gorlov—The Russian had a financial interest in Talifero's plans.

Authors' Note

We were delighted when Harlequin Intrigue told us they would be republishing our Peregrine Connection trilogy. They are some of our favorite stories, and we had a wonderful time creating daring women and dangerous heroes and catapulting them into plots swirling with high-stakes intrigue and jeopardy.

With the fall of the Berlin Wall, the collapse of the Soviet Union and the restructuring of Eastern Europe, the world has changed at warp speed over the past eight years since the Peregrine novels were written. Yet, with spy scandals at the upper echelons of the CIA and even a terrorist attack at the World Trade Center, themes of preserving peace and the balance of world power are just as relevant today as they were in the eighties when the Peregrine Connection was written.

When we considered a setting for *In Search of the Dove,* we thought of New Orleans, with its aura of intrigue and romance. Over the past twenty-five years we've had numerous occasions to visit the Crescent City. Eileen and husband Howard honeymooned there. And Ruth and husband Norm have made several trips to the area where they explored the bayou, the French Quarter and the Garden District. One of her most memorable impressions was of the spooky aboveground cemeteries, which became the setting of a major scene in the novel.

And what better place than New Orleans to tell a story featuring voodoo and ESP? Paranormal elements have always appealed to us, and this was the first time we had an opportunity to use them. At first, we had a hard time researching voodoo because all the library books on the subject had mysteriously disappeared from the shelves. But we kept on digging, learning about secret ceremonies and potions for binding a lover or warding off bad luck. When you read the novel, you'll see how strong a part both the rich setting and spooky themes play in our story of Peregrine agent Michael Rome and Jessica Duval and their quest to find the source of the mysterious drug called Dove.

After reading *In Search of the Dove*—and all the Peregrine Connection books—we were pleased with how well the books stood the test of time. We hope you think so, too.

Rebecca York (Ruth Glick and Eileen Buckholtz)

Chapter One

She thought he was fumbling in the kitchen drawer for a can opener, but when he turned to her, she saw his fingers were wrapped around the handle of a stainless-steel knife.

She stared at him in stunned silence, almost hypnotized by the ragged, shallow wheezing of air in and out of his lungs and the wild desperation in his dilated eyes. They might have been symptoms of a physical illness. His grip on the knife was not. He was holding it like a weapon, not a tool.

"Aubrey, no," she whispered, astounded that she had misread him so badly.

"Why did you have to come here and interfere?" he hissed.

"I care about you. I want to help you."

"I don't need your damn help." The words were flung like a slap across her face.

Though Jessica's heart was slamming against the inside of her chest, she kept her voice calm and turned her hand palm upward. "Give me the knife."

"I'll give it to you all right." As he spoke he lunged across the dirty tile floor, the weapon flashing in an arc. She screamed and dodged, slamming her ribs against the edge of the counter. She didn't feel the injury, didn't know that the knife had plunged into the cabinet above her, splintering the wood.

All she knew was that Aubrey's hands were empty and that they were reaching for her throat. He was only a few inches taller than she, but his lanky build concealed a wiry strength. There was no doubt he could choke her to death.

Her own arms came up, gold bracelets jangling as she tried to find leverage against his chest, or shoulders, or face—anything. He laughed, a maniacal sound from the depths of Bedlam that froze the breath in her lungs. She might have wondered at his transformation if she hadn't been fighting for her life.

Her nails raked scratches down his cheek, yet his angry assault didn't slacken. Wildly she kicked at his leg, knocking it out from under him as her leather sandal flew across the room.

When Aubrey tumbled backward to the floor, he dragged her with him, tangling them both in the flowing fabric of her skirt. But she could feel him weakening. With all the strength she had left, she slammed her arm against his nose. There was a trickle and then a stream of dark blood.

He went slack, and she stared down at him, amazed that he was still breathing—and that she was too. Then she leapt toward the telephone, her fingers frantically jamming against the buttons as she punched 911.

"It's my brother," she said, gasping, to the night dispatcher. "He's unconscious."

"What's wrong?"

"Some kind of drug...I don't know. He tried to kill me."

"Give me your location."

She supplied the address on a side street off Jefferson Boulevard.

"Your name?"

"Jessica Duval."

"Sit tight. A unit is on the way."

The trembling didn't start until she hung up. Then her whole body began to shake uncontrollably as the realization of what had almost happened sank into her. Her legs were putty, and she slipped to the floor, pressing her back against a kitchen cabinet. Across the room, the figure on the floor moaned, and she cringed away.

She ran clammy fingers through her short auburn hair. God, how had Aubrey's life deteriorated in only a few short months? Why hadn't she, of all people, sensed something was wrong?

Things hadn't been easy for him since Aunt Edna had died, but over the past few semesters, she'd thought he was finally getting it all together. He'd been excited about his graduate assistantship in the chemistry department at Chartres University here in New Orleans, and he was close to finishing his thesis.

But then his letters had stopped. At first she'd assumed he was just busy, but the silence had continued. When she'd finally called last month, the experience had been unsettling. If Aubrey had been sullen or uncommunicative, she might have dismissed it as one of his moods. Instead, his thoughts had spewed out of the phone like popcorn from an air popper, scattering in a thousand different directions, impossible to follow. When she'd asked if anything was bothering him, he'd instantly switched from giddy amiability to cold rage.

The next call a week later had been the same. By then the bad vibrations were too strong to shut out. Leaving her jewelry boutique in her assistant's competent care, she'd caught the next plane for New Orleans.

A distant wailing noise somewhere in the darkened city grew in intensity until it seemed to fill the inside of her head. Sirens. A memory of grim-faced, disapproving policemen made her fists clench.

Pushing herself up, she half staggered to the door just in time to admit two men in white uniforms carrying a stretcher. One made sure she was all right before joining his companion who had crouched over the limp figure on the floor.

Fingers probed, instruments flashed.

"Respiratory depression. Start the oxygen."

"I don't like his pupillary reflex."

"Brain damage?"

"Maybe he's just toxic."

"PCP?" The drug was associated with unpredictable violence.

"No. Something different. Your guess is as good as mine."

Whitefaced, Jessica hovered over their shoulders, afraid to hear what they were saying, afraid not to hear.

"Do you know what ripped him?" one of the paramedics asked.

"Pardon?"

"What he's *on*."

"I don't know."

"Too bad. He needs detox right away. How long has he been on the stuff?"

"Six weeks? A month?" she guessed.

The paramedic whistled through his teeth. "He's pretty charged up. It must be something more than brain ticklers."

The street talk sent a chill down Jessica's spine. She watched numbly as the men lifted the stretcher and carried Aubrey's unconscious form out to the waiting ambulance. A wave of despair threatened to drown her, but she fought it back. They might not have been close over the past few years but he was her brother, her only living relative, and he needed her now more than ever. Slipping into her sandals and grabbing her purse, she hurried outside after the departing men. She was going with Aubrey to the hospital to do what she could, even though it probably meant making a police report. And, God knew, for her that was the ultimate sacrifice.

WHILE HE WAITED for the light to change, Michael Rome studied the Bryant Hotel. With its pink plaster façade, louvered shutters, and iron grillwork, it was typical of the French Quarter, he thought. When the signal turned green, he ambled across the street, his rattlesnake boots clicking softly on the macadam. A moment later he turned into the passageway that led to the hotel's courtyard entrance—another New Orleans hallmark. There the bright September sun was filtered through the leaves of banana and avocado trees that grew in massive planters. The tropical foliage sheltered a small bubbling Spanish tile fountain.

He stood in the cool shade, thumbs hooked over the pockets of his stone-washed jeans, as if he were a well-heeled visiting Texan debating whether or not to drop some money. The relaxed posture was a deliberately calculated effect, as was the expensive western garb, which included a plaid pearl-buttoned shirt and a wide-brimmed Stetson tilted down on his forehead. From the shadow of his hat, alert gray eyes sized up the hotel, which he knew to be a first-class establishment for discreet rendezvous. However, he wasn't here to make himself comfortable. He was more concerned about possible escape routes if he had to leave its charming confines in a hurry.

A lithe blond dressed in a jungle-print sundress drifted to the open doorway and smiled.

"What can I do for you, sugar?" she asked, not bothering to hide her frank appraisal of the tall, whipcord-lean man who stood in the courtyard. Although his face was too blunt-edged to be called handsome, there was a certain rightness in the way his high cheekbones, square jaw, and uncompromising nose complemented each other. Somehow he didn't look like the type who had to pay for sex.

He acknowledged her smile with a slight dip of his head. "I was looking for Daniella," he drawled. The voice was deep, the accent Dallas. It went with the healthy tan—and probably the roll of crisp green bills in his pocket.

"She's not here right now. My name's Cheryl. Maybe I could help you out." She swayed toward him, bending at just the right angle to provide a view of her creamy white cleavage.

An amused smile flickered at the corners of his firm lips. "No, ma'am, I'm sorry. I was real set on Miss Daniella."

"I'm afraid she's gone."

"Gone?" He tipped back the Stetson and gave her a direct look.

"Last night she was packing like the devil himself was after her. This morning you wouldn't know that she'd ever been here."

He didn't have to fake the surge of disappointment that coursed through him. He considered asking to see the empty room. But that would arouse suspicion. He didn't want anyone to know that someone other than an eager customer was making inquiries about a high-class prostitute named Daniella La Reine.

As if undecided how to broach a slightly embarrassing subject, he hesitated for a moment, dragging the pointed toe of his boot across the flagstones. "I understand she had something special, an—ah, voodoo love potion she uses. Something that, uh—"

"Sugar, you don't want to go fooling with a voodoo potion. I can make you feel real good, without drugs."

"Are you sure you don't have any of that stuff? I'm willing to pay."

Cheryl shook her head. "No. If I was you I'd forget about it, unless you want to go back to Big D missing half your marbles."

"That bad, huh?"

"Yeah."

"Thanks for the warning, darlin'." He stood and chatted for a few minutes more, the conversation light and flirty as if he were considering changing his mind about her offer. In the course of telling him why she was more desirable than Daniella, Cheryl added considerably to the knowledge he had gained from three days of painstaking legwork.

He had a description of Ms. La Reine now. He was pretty sure her "voodoo potion" was really a brand-new street drug called Dove. And he knew she had been a student at Chartres University before deciding that she wanted a shortcut to big money. Perhaps someone there remembered her.

His loquacious informant also had quite a bit to say about the short, nervous man with thinning hair and wire-frame glasses who'd been a regular customer of Daniella's over the past few weeks. Cheryl noted that when he'd left her colleague's room, he hadn't had a particularly satisfied look on his face. At Daniella's prices, she didn't know why he kept coming back.

Michael tipped his hat, keeping his exit as much in character as his entrance. Like most of the people he'd talked to recently, Cheryl would remember the urban cowboy trappings and mannerisms better than his face. But that was exactly the idea.

He was a master at assuming a carefully cultivated persona, and that ability had saved his life on more than one occasion. So had the large hands wedged casually into his pockets. They were like the rest of his body beneath the expensive western finery—firm, tough, and well trained. In fact, they could slice through a five-inch wood block or put a hole in a brick wall.

When he reached Bourbon Street, he stopped at the first open-air bar he came to and ordered a mint julep. For an agent on assignment, liquor was against the rules, but he wasn't going to tell if the bartender didn't.

What a city, he thought, turning to drape himself against the bar as if he were simply interested in watching the passing scene while he sipped his drink. If ever there was a place that seethed with wicked excitement, it was New Orleans. Unfortunately, he wasn't there to enjoy wicked excitement.

Nominally, he was on assignment for the Drug Enforcement Administration. But the top-priority request for his services had really originated in Berryville, Virginia, at a country inn called the Aviary. The inn was a front for a secret intelligence organization known as the Peregrine Connection. While Michael Rome officially worked for DEA, he was also a Peregrine operative reporting to its director, Amherst Gordon, code-named the Falcon.

Only a few highly placed government officials knew of Gordon's existence. He was an old espionage mastermind who had staged his own death in order to go underground. The operations the Falcon now ran, many of which were funded by his own personal fortune, could never be officially approved by the attorney general. Because Gordon didn't have to answer to Congress, Peregrine could do things in days that would take the FBI or CIA weeks to set up.

One of the Falcon's most reliable underworld sources had warned that a new and frighteningly destructive drug called Dove was being test-marketed in the Crescent City. If it made it big there, the sky was the limit. Michael's job was to throw a monkey wrench in the distribution network and make sure that didn't happen. And he didn't have a hell of a lot of time to do it.

THE VOODOO PRIESTESS put a beautifully manicured hand on Gilbert Xavier's arm. Her tawny fingers were graceful and tapered, the nails a deep crimson, the color of blood. A flowing white caftan covered her body from neck to toe, and her thick hair was wrapped in a jade turban secured in the center of her forehead with an ornate silver pin depicting two entwined serpents.

Her dark eyes probed Xavier's countenance. He tried to hold his gaze steady under her scrutiny, knowing that after three weeks on the run he looked more like a hobo than a college professor.

Was he a fool to trust this woman with his life? He wasn't sure, yet something had brought him to her door.

"Things have not gone well with you, Gilbert," she observed as she drew him into her little house. The clapboard dwelling was in one of the city's less prosperous districts. Like its neighbors, it needed a coat of paint and new louvered shutters. But inside, the air of poverty vanished. The small living room was elegantly furnished with Oriental rugs and Victorian antiques from some of the most exclusive shops on Royal Street.

Gilbert turned the woman's statement aside. "But you seem to be doing very well."

His hostess shrugged delicately. "People ask me to help solve their problems. An impotent husband with a young wife. A pregnant girl whose lover is hesitant about marrying her. They are always satisfied with my services, so they come back again."

"I have a problem too," he ventured.

The fingers on his arm squeezed sympathetically. "I wouldn't need to read tea leaves to know that. But I am glad that you came to me. Sit down and tell me your troubles."

He sank heavily onto a green velvet high-back couch, and she drew up a matching chair. How much could he trust her, he wondered.

She read the hesitation in his eyes. "Gilbert, I'm like a doctor or a lawyer. Your secrets are confidential here."

"There are men who want to find me so that they can control me," he blurted. "And there's danger to you if I say too much."

She waved her hand dismissively. "I have ways to protect myself from danger."

"Maybe not from these men."

"But you believe in the power of my magic, or you wouldn't be here."

Did he believe? Though he was well educated—with a Ph.D. in chemistry, no less—he'd seen what this woman could do. She was part witch doctor, part folk healer, and part charlatan. Maybe he had come here because he was desperate enough to believe in her power.

"We will make a charm to throw your enemies off the scent."

She stood up and left the room. He could either follow or flee. He chose to follow, his eyes trained on the back of her flowing robes as she led him down a narrow hall, which ended at a doorway closed off by a thick beaded curtain. Beyond was a room that he remembered all too well. It was a twilight place with bamboo wall covering, pungent candles, and carved wooden figures with jeweled eyes that jumped out at you in the dark.

The woman must have sensed the tremor that rippled through his body. "You were eager for my help once. Are you afraid to accept it again?"

That had been in an entirely different context, a different life. He had been willing to take what he could from her, as long as he didn't have to acknowledge the magic.

"I'm not afraid," he lied.

The beaded curtain rustled as she pushed it aside and gestured for him to sit down on one of the flat cushions that were the floor's only covering. When he had complied, his companion gave him a satisfied smile before kneeling in front of a low altar at the far end of the room.

He had watched her do that before. Only then drums had beaten a frantic rhythm in the background, and the room had been full of dark, writhing bodies. Now it was just the two of them, and he was a participant, not an observer.

For a moment the priestess was completely silent, then she began a soft chant as she lit more candles, the graceful movements of her body beneath the flowing silk caftan strengthening his sense of foreboding. In a way, he could trace the root of all his problems back to his fascination with this woman and her dark secrets. No, that wasn't fair. He accepted the responsibility for the mess he'd gotten himself into.

The woman had finished her chant. When she turned back in his direction she was holding a carved wooden box, which she set on the floor in front of him. Then she went to a cabinet along the wall and began removing jars and vials. As she opened them, he caught whiffs of rosemary, violet, sassafras, and less pleasant scents that he couldn't identify. They all went into a stone mortar and were pulverized.

Returning to kneel in front of him, she held up the bowl and began to chant again. The syllables were soft and sibilant in a dialect he didn't understand. They seemed to swirl around him like a suffocating mist.

When she finished, she set the mortar down and raised the lid of the box. Inside was a tapered silver knife. The repoussé on the handle matched the silver serpent on her turban, except that the two snakes' mouths were open where they met the blade.

He drew in a sharp breath. Though his heart rate had accelerated, he was powerless to move.

With one hand, she reached out and picked up his sweaty palm. With the other, she raised the knife.

"We need some of your blood to bind the potion."

The knife came down and he felt the point pierce his skin.

Chapter Two

"Did your brother have a stable personality before this drug-induced psychosis?"

Jessica propped her elbow thoughtfully on the edge of the wooden chair in the hospital consultation room. Across the oak-grained desk, Dr. Thomas Frederickson sat with his ball-point pen poised above a sheet of paper.

Drug-induced psychosis—so someone had finally put a label on Aubrey's disturbing behavior. At first it had been a question of saving his life. Though he now seemed on the road to physical recovery, he wouldn't communicate with her at all, and his only words to the nurses and doctors were little more than sporadic bursts of rage.

Just how well did she really know her younger brother? Over the past few years they hadn't spent much time together. It was probably her guilt about neglecting him that had sent her rushing back to Louisiana.

Dr. Frederickson waited patiently, making a point of not pressing the young woman who sat across from him. They'd already talked briefly a few times. Though she'd been distressed about her brother's condition, she hadn't gone to pieces. Now she looked a bit more rested. Her face, he supposed, was conventionally pretty. But there was a very personal style about this woman that took her out of the ranks of the conventional. And there was a sense that when she met his direct gaze, she was probing into his psyche as much as he was delving into hers. For a psychiatrist used to controlling this sort of interview, the observation was a bit unsettling.

She was wearing a navy-and-canary Indian print dress set off at the neckline with a hand-worked brass necklace, he noted, and her curly auburn hair was freshly washed and brushed, but not tamed. Her complexion was creamy peach, her large eyes a dramatic hazel. Right now she didn't look as if she'd spent long hours in the psychiatric unit's grim waiting room. But Dr. Frederickson knew that she'd agreed to go home and get some sleep only after she'd been assured that Aubrey was going to pull through.

"Was my brother stable?" she repeated the question in a clear alto voice that was softened by a faint southern accent. "I'm not sure what that means, exactly. He didn't have any serious problems like delinquency or drinking, but he and my parents used to fight a lot."

"About what?"

"The usual things. Not wanting to eat the dinner my mother had prepared or refusing to clean his room."

Frederickson smiled. "That's not out of the ordinary. How did he handle the conflict? Was there any violence?"

"Oh, no! Aubrey was famous for stomping off to his room to sulk—or disappearing for long bike rides."

"And what would you say about your parents? How would you describe them?"

"They were very rigid."

The psychiatrist looked up, wondering why she had singled out that adjective.

"You mean they were particularly strict about issues like dating and smoking?"

She nodded tightly. Yes, and going to church every week, and minding your elders. That had been part of her southern upbringing. But her mother and father had also had a way of snapping their minds shut to what they couldn't understand. Their lack of insight and support had caused a crisis in her own adolescent years. Could that be relevant to Aubrey's case?

"Was taking drugs a way for Aubrey to rebel against their authority?" Dr. Frederickson asked.

She raised a hand to her temple and stroked for a moment, the gesture partially hiding her eyes. "My parents were pretty old when they had us." She paused for a moment, suddenly immersed in all the old pain. "They died when Aubrey was twelve and I was seventeen. He went to live with our aunt, Edna Ballin, who ended up adopting him. I was already in college in the East and decided to stay there. But I've always felt guilty about not coming back here to take care of my brother." She didn't want to tell him the whole story of why she'd been compelled to put so much distance between herself and New Orleans.

Dr. Frederickson heard the distress in her voice. "It must have been a pretty rough time for both of you."

"It was." Let him make his own assumptions about why.

"But you were only a kid yourself," the psychiatrist reminded her gently. "You were hardly capable of shouldering the responsibility for a twelve-year-old. If your aunt adopted him, she must have cared strongly about him. Did he have a good home with her?"

"Yes. She was a wonderful person. She doted on him, and she wanted a relative to carry on the Ballin name. Except for a small legacy to me, Aubrey was her only heir. Most of the money is still in trust until he's twenty-five."

"So he was in good hands, and you don't have to feel guilty."

They talked for a while longer about Aubrey's background. Though a measure of Jessica's equanimity returned, there was still no way to come up with an explanation for what had happened to her brother.

"It just doesn't make sense," she concluded.

"Maybe he got in with the wrong crowd," Dr. Frederickson suggested. "Did you know any of his friends?"

"No. I haven't been back here in a long time."

"Are you planning to stay on for a while?"

"I want to be here for Aubrey now that he needs me."

The doctor cleared his throat. "Miss Duval, you may find this upsetting, but I think it would be better if you didn't visit your brother—at least for a while."

"Why not?"

"In his present state, seeing you seems to disturb him."

Jessica knitted her fingers together. "I see."

"Again, don't put the blame on yourself. Apparently, he just can't cope with you right now." The doctor looked down at his notes for a moment. "I wish I could be more encouraging about your brother. If I only knew what psychotoxin he'd been taking, that might help us proceed with treatment." He paused and shrugged. "But we haven't a clue."

"Maybe I can find out for you."

"Probing into the New Orleans drug culture could be dangerous. I wouldn't advise it."

"I'll keep that in mind."

MICHAEL ROME FLOPPED onto the grass under a century-old live oak tree and tossed his used chemistry book and red knapsack down beside him. They were part of his new cover. Before heading for the university, he'd reluctantly exchanged his snakeskin boots for a pair of scuffed Adidas, well-worn jeans, and a blue Jackson Square T-shirt that showed off the corded muscles of his upper arms. He wasn't about to submit to a Mohawk, but he'd used mousse to give his hair a chic, messy look. Though he was a bit old for an undergraduate, there was nothing much he could do about that except play it cool.

Leaning back against a gnarled root, he looked out over the well-groomed Chartres University grounds. From his vantage point, he could see groups of students enjoying the fine September weather.

Over the past few days, he'd spent hours getting to know the school—much of the time hanging around in the student union, the bars on the fringe of the campus, or out here.

It hadn't been difficult to get acquainted with the kids who had a buzz on. The proof was in the knapsack that rested within easy reach of his strong hand. Almost any kind of high or low you wanted was readily available. If he'd had the time, he probably could have arrested at least five per-cent of the student body for dealing. While that wasn't par-ticularly unusual these days, it was still depressing.

Though dope might be easy to come by, information was a more guarded commodity. His DEA badge had gotten him in to see the assistant chancellor. But the man had vehe-mently denied any university drug problem. When Michael had wondered out loud whether campus labs might be the actual source of illegal substances, the official had brought the interview to an abrupt end.

Next Michael had cruised the corridors of Sumner Hall, the chemistry building, representing himself as a student from out of state considering a transfer. He started with questions about which courses to take and professors to avoid and eased slowly into the real topic of interest.

His best line to the inside story had been a grad student who had joined him for a few beers in the Alligator Den, a dimly lit bar two blocks from campus.

The fellow had started with some nervous jokes about telling tales out of school. He'd lost some of his inhibitions after polishing off most of a pitcher of Jax. He remem-bered Daniella La Reine, although that wasn't the last name she'd been using at the time. She'd been in one of his lab sections, and he recalled she'd been a fair student—with a sexy body. But she'd dropped out before he'd had a chance to get her into bed.

On the second pitcher, he started talking about one of his fellow teaching assistants. The guy, whose name was Au-brey Ballin, had been a real straight arrow until a few weeks ago. The grapevine had it that he'd OD'ed on something or other. Whether that was true or not, he was gone from the scene.

Michael had taken judicious sips of his own beer and fished for more details. But a casual question about whether

Ballin's problems were connected to something new on the street made the guy suddenly clam up. Right after that he'd remembered that he was supposed to be in his office grading lab reports.

Leaning back now against the tree root, Michael considered his next move. He could smell something rotten in the chemistry department, and it wasn't sulphur dioxide.

A carillon chimed. Minutes later, a rush of students changing classes filled the campus. As Michael's appraising gaze scanned the crowd, his attention was caught by a woman he'd seen a number of times over the past few days. She didn't look quite young enough to be a coed and wasn't carrying any books. Now, in addition to the soft leather bag slung over one shoulder, she was clutching a large manila envelope.

The fast-moving river of humanity carried her down to the sidewalk. When the tide ebbed, she turned for a long look at Sumner Hall and sighed heavily before walking slowly in his direction.

He remembered seeing her come out of the department chairman's office the day before with a stormy expression on her face. He had wondered if she were an instructor who'd just been reprimanded. But the tag hadn't fit then, and it still didn't. At the time she'd been wearing a yellow-and-navy Indian print dress that might have passed for campus exotic. Now she sported a calf-length silk skirt and tunic that were much too sophisticated for the surroundings. They looked damn good on her, though.

However, he could tell from the way she carried herself that she didn't care what the students thought of her appearance. He'd always admired women who did their own thing, as long as it wasn't illegal.

He continued to study her. Her body was small-boned and her face almost elfin, with a short upturned nose and dainty mouth. Probably her most striking features were her large eyes and short, untamable hair, a riot of curls that captured the rays of the afternoon sun and reflected them in an auburn halo above her rounded face.

As she drew near, Jessica looked up and caught him staring. Pausing for a moment, she hesitated and then started across the grass toward the oak tree. She remembered seeing this guy several times in the chemistry department, joking with some of the graduate students. He'd had an easy, open manner and seemed to know his way around. Maybe he'd known Aubrey. She had been about to give up and go home anyway. One more shot wouldn't hurt.

God knows, the university administration hadn't been much help. The head of the chemistry department had commiserated briefly over her brother's hospitalization, but it was clear that he had his own concerns. He'd ended the short interview by handing her a manila envelope containing the contents of Aubrey's desk. It seemed the cubicle had already been assigned to another graduate teaching assistant who'd been without an office at the beginning of the semester.

Jessica had turned to the students next. She'd found people who'd been willing to talk about Aubrey up to a certain point. When she'd brought up the subject of drugs, they'd expressed their sympathy at his mishap and hastily departed for remembered classes and appointments.

Something about this guy made her think he was different from the rest. She watched him shift his position so that he was leaning back comfortably. Then he crossed his long, jeans-clad legs at the ankle.

She guessed his age at something over thirty. Despite the casual pose, the man radiated an aura of leashed power. It was there in the well-developed muscles of his arms, the street-wise look in his light eyes, and the hard planes of his face. If anything he reminded her of the hardened, world-weary Viet Nam vets who had attended the University of Maryland with her. Even if he wasn't a veteran of that particular conflict, she sensed that he'd seen action somewhere.

Suddenly she remembered Dr. Frederickson's speculations about Aubrey getting into the wrong crowd. This guy was certainly tough. Yet she was picking up conflicting vibrations from him, as if he were both more and also less than what he seemed to be on the surface. She didn't like the inner confusion that generated, and a small voice in her head warned her he might be someone to fear.

It was more than just an instinctive reaction. As a teenager, she'd begun to realize she was developing a surprisingly accurate sixth sense about people. Along with that had come knowledge of events she couldn't possibly have experienced through her own senses. For a little while she'd felt heady from the power—until it had almost wrecked her life. That was why she'd fled New Orleans in the first place. In Maryland, far from the scenes of her childhood, she'd worked hard to damp down the unwanted ability so she could lead a normal life. But since she'd returned, she'd felt the stirrings of that old gift. Even as she'd struggled to come to terms with it, the capability had begun to blossom again. Perhaps it was catalyzed by her frustration at not being able to get any hard information about Aubrey.

Stopping a few feet from the scuffed Adidas, Jessica watched as their owner looked up questioningly. She noticed that his eyes were the color of polished pewter and couldn't help being intrigued by their unusual color and the keen intelligence they projected. She should have felt at an advantage standing over him. Instead, it was just the opposite. Catching her skirt gracefully in back of her knees, she sat down a few feet from him and pulled the fabric protectively around her legs as she tucked them under her body.

"Do you have a minute?" she asked softly, her nervousness making her accent just a bit more pronounced. She was aware that until she'd intruded, he'd seemed to have nothing but time on his hands.

"I can make one." The voice was carefully neutral, yet she caught the undercurrent of his interest. Of a man for a woman? she wondered. Or was there something else as well?

"I've seen you around the chemistry department. Do you know many of the people here?"

"Some."

"Are you a student?" Her eyes flicked to the chemistry book on the grass beside his knee.

"No, are you?"

The question caught her by surprise. "No, no, I'm not either."

"I noticed you around the department too. Are you thinking of taking some courses?" His look told her that he doubted she was.

The query was innocent enough, but with her sixth sense working double time, she felt the tension inside him. Something about all this was very important to him. The realization made her more wary. Still, she sensed he might be able to help her, if she could probe cautiously enough to find out whether he was friend or foe. "I'm trying to get some information about a graduate student. Aubrey Ballin."

The gray eyes took on a speculative gleam. "Ballin."

"You know him?"

"He's the one who's in the hospital."

"That's right."

"Nobody wants to talk about it much."

"No, they don't," Jessica agreed.

"So what are you looking for?"

Drugs, Jessica thought, suddenly aware that this man was waiting to pounce like a tiger stalking a gazelle. Starting up a conversation with him had been a mistake. Yet her gaze was suddenly drawn to his eyes. Unaccountably, she felt herself drowning in their gray depths. For a moment she was completely disoriented, and then an image formed in her mind. First there was simply a flash of white. Then it resolved itself into wings flapping and a white bird soaring against an expanse of cold gray sky. Was it a gull? No.

She felt her heart rate speed up as if she were running headlong toward something that kept moving just out of her reach. A bead of perspiration formed at her temple, and she reached up to swipe it away. "Dove," she whispered.

The man on the grass sat up, suddenly alert. "What did you say?"

"I'm looking for a dove." Jessica stared at him, confused and almost overwhelmed by a sense of dread. "No, that's crazy," she denied. Scrambling to her feet, she backed away.

"Wait. Tell me who you are."

But she was already halfway to the sidewalk, and she didn't look back.

A THOUSAND MILES AWAY in the Virginia country inn called the Aviary, Amherst Gordon, head of the Peregrine Connection, paused beside a large gardenia plant. Inhaling deeply, he concentrated for a moment on the delicate perfume. To his right, a red-and-green parrot squawked and then made a noise that sounded like a man clearing his throat.

"Ah, Cicero, are you a bit anxious too?" the spymaster asked. From the corner of his eye he saw his long-time assistant Constance McGuire enter the solarium and sit down at the wrought-iron table.

He turned, his gray head cocked slightly to the side as he watched her discover the small gold box in the center of her luncheon plate.

"What's this?" she inquired, looking up at him over the rims of tortoise-shell half glasses. "I expected to find your illegible notes telling me what needs to be done today."

The Falcon shrugged almost imperceptibly. He and Connie went back a long way—more than forty years. They'd met when they were both in the old Office of Strategic Services where he'd been a covert operative and she'd been a desk officer. When that organization had been replaced by the modern intelligence agencies, they'd both signed on with the CIA. She'd retired at fifty-five vowing that she was done with keeping the world safe for democracy. But when he'd formed the Peregrine Connection, it hadn't taken all that much arm-twisting to convince her to come back.

She was the best there was, and he was damn lucky to have her. Although he would never admit it to her, he knew there were too many times lately when he had pushed her awfully hard. It was because he worried about his agents, and she was the only one here at the Aviary who had the same two dozen top-secret clearances as he did. That meant she took the brunt of his frustration when things went badly in the field.

He'd gotten to musing lately on Carl Jung's observations about marriage. The psychologist had argued that some pain helped cement that relationship. The comment applied as well to Connie and himself as it did to any couple who were actually married. The two of them had lived through a lot together and were the stronger for it. Today he wanted her to know she was appreciated.

Fingers that were wrinkled but still graceful lifted the lid of the box. Inside, nestled against black velvet, was an exquisite diamond-and-emerald parrot. When she looked up and saw the not-quite-concealed anxiety on Gordon's lined face, she forgave him all his harsh words.

"Do you like it?" he questioned gruffly.

"It's remarkable. Where did you ever find it?"

"Designed it myself and had it made up in New York. You deserve only the best."

"Amherst, you shouldn't have."

So the Falcon was coming as close as he ever would to acknowledging that he'd been rather difficult to work with lately. How like him, she thought, to give her a jeweled parrot instead of kind words. But if she were wise, she'd accept the apology graciously.

She saw him visibly relax and was unable to keep a slight smile from flickering at the corners of her aristocratic mouth.

Before moving toward the table, the Falcon paused and picked up the two folders he'd set discreetly on the sideboard.

"Back to business, I see," Connie observed with a measure of relief as he set down his cane and pulled out the chair opposite her.

"Yes, Michael Rome hasn't come up with anything definite in New Orleans, but Jed Prentiss reported in last night from Royale Verde in the Caribbean."

Slipping the jewelry box into the pocket of her skirt, she asked, "Has he uncovered something on that end?"

"He wants us to dig up any information we can on a place down there called the Blackstone Clinic. It's a private psychiatric sanitarium run by a physician named Jackson Talifero."

Connie looked puzzled. "What does a place like that have to do with his assignment?"

"He's not sure. But it's been whispered around the island that something unsavory is going on there."

"Like what?"

Gordon shrugged. "Well, for one thing, the upstanding local people won't go near the clinic. It seems there's some sort of voodoo taboo associated with the place."

"Voodoo. Now really!"

"It's a good way to ensure their privacy."

"That won't keep Jed away."

"No, it won't."

Chapter Three

"What are you doing down there on the floor, girl, scrubbing like a slave?"

Jessica's head snapped around to confront a pair of slender burgundy-hose-clad legs below the hem of a flowing designer dress. Her gaze quickly traveled upward to collide with a smiling fawn-colored face and a pair of familiar mahogany eyes.

"Simone? Is it really you?" As she spoke she scrambled to her feet.

"No, Memorex."

Jessica laughed. "You always were a smart-ass."

The two young women embraced warmly.

"Let me look at you," Jessica finally said, inspecting her old friend's chic clothing, neat chignon, and subtle makeup that brought out her striking looks. Simone was a good six inches taller than Jessica, but her lean figure had filled out in the right places since her adolescent years. "Well, you don't remind me much of the scrawny little scarecrow who used to chase snapping turtles with me down at the bayou."

Simone chuckled. "You do."

Jessica glanced down quickly at her smudged white T-shirt and faded jeans.

"I don't mean the charwoman costume. Jessica, I'd know you anywhere. But, honey, it sure has been too long."

"Aunt Edna's funeral."

Jessica's arms dropped to her sides. Both women were silent for a moment.

"You don't come back here unless there's trouble," the black woman observed.

"Then you heard about Aubrey?"

"Uh-huh. New Orleans may be a big city, but bad news travels like it's still a small town."

Jessica wiped her soapy hands on jeans-clad thighs. Over the past few days, she'd been putting her brother's apartment in order. Heaven knows, the place had needed it. Even though she hated house cleaning, she'd been glad to have something to do in the evenings after she'd come back from nosing around the Chartres campus. "Could I get you a cup of tea?" she asked her old friend.

"If you're going to have one."

"I was about to take a break." She stopped and moved the scrub bucket into the corner. "Make yourself comfortable. I hope lemon spice is okay. That's all I've bought."

"Lemon spice is fine." Simone pulled out a chair at the kitchen table and sat down. "So how is Aubrey doing?" she asked.

"They're still pretty guarded in their prognosis. I guess I just have to wait and see." Jessica put the kettle on the burner. "You know, I can't figure this whole thing out. Aubrey is the last person I'd think would get mixed up with drugs. And almost everybody I've tried to talk to at the university is acting as if they're afraid of something."

"Maybe with good reason."

Jessica's brows lifted. "What do you mean?"

"Honey, organized crime controls the drug market down here. Poking into their territory isn't good for your life expectancy."

Jessica could sense undercurrents of fear in her words. There was something here that she couldn't quite get a handle on, and she didn't like the feeling. "That sounds like a warning."

"It's just a piece of friendly advice."

"Well, what would you do if it were your brother?"

Simone's mahogany eyes clouded for a moment. "Nurse him back to health and stay clear of more trouble."

"The doctor says my coming to see him is making him worse."

"His own kin?"

The teakettle whistled and Jessica was glad of the excuse to turn away to get mugs and teabags from the cabinet. "Sugar?"

"No, this is fine." Simone accepted the mug of hot fragrant liquid. Leaning over it, she inhaled the citrus scent. "This reminds me of the time we decided to give our legs a hot-wax beauty treatment and melted down my mom's favorite lemon-scented candles."

Jessica laughed. "That stuff sure did burn! To this day I won't let a beautician come near me with hot wax."

"Uh-huh."

Jessica took a meditative sip of her tea. She and Simone had met and become fast friends the first summer her parents had let her go alone to Aunt Edna's summer place in the country. Simone was a full-time resident of the rural area. Every year the two girls had renewed the relationship right up until Jessica had gone away to college. "Those were good times."

"The best."

"Honey, we go back a long way. Tha.'s why I stopped by when I heard you were in town. If there's anything you need, and I mean anything, I want you to give me a holler. Let me give you my phone numbers." She took a small lilac-colored card out of her purse and handed it across the table.

"I don't suppose that means you're going to tell me where to ask some questions about Aubrey's drug problem now that I've drawn a blank at the university?"

"No way. Take my advice, girl, and stay away from that part of town."

Jessica nodded. There was no point in getting into an argument with her old friend. Instead she scanned the ornate script on the front of Simone's card. It advertised a boutique on Royal Street called This Is the Place. "Are you in business for yourself now?" she asked.

"Sure am. Selling cosmetics, soaps—" Simone paused "—and uh, charms. You know, things tourists want to buy and bring home as gifts."

"Charms? Not as in charm bracelets?"

"No."

"You mean love potions, herbal medicines, hexes?"

"Well, love potions and herbal medicines, anyway."

Jessica nodded. "I guess you always were interested in stuff like that."

"You used to be, too. It's in your Cajun blood. Remember the time we got the neighborhood kids together for a seance at midnight out in back of the corn crib—and you dressed up as a ghost?"

"I'm through playing around with ghosts!"

"Honey, I'm sorry. I shouldn't have brought it up. You're thinking about what happened later, aren't you?"

Jessica nodded tightly, feeling Simone's speculative gaze on her face. "Let's just forget about all that," she whispered.

"All right."

Silence hung in the air between the two women. Jessica took several sips of her tea, grateful for the feel of the hot liquid sliding down her throat. For a long time she'd told herself that she'd deal with the remembered pain in her life "some day." Since coming back to New Orleans she'd felt "some day" licking at her heels like a cold, black fog.

JACKSON TALIFERO put down his engraved silver fountain pen and adjusted the wooden blinds that kept the afternoon sun out of his spacious office. The view out the window of his psychiatric clinic reminded him of a very exclusive hotel complex. The two-story white stucco buildings with their Spanish-style roofs and wide verandas commanded a hill that swept dramatically down through the jungle to the ocean.

On the wide green lawn he could see old Mrs. Wallace waving her arms wildly at Perry Davenport as two attendants rushed to intervene. It wasn't hard to imagine the stream of four-letter words pouring from the old woman's mouth.

Mrs. Wallace suffered from Alzheimer's disease and had become rather an embarrassment to her high-society daughter after biting the finger of an important dinner guest. That was why the woman was willing to pay $5,000 a month to keep her mother out of sight down here on Royale Verde.

Perry Davenport, on the other hand, was quite another matter. His problem was paranoid schizophrenia and, until coming to Blackstone nine months ago, there hadn't been much hope of curing him. But he'd been responding remarkably well to the clinic's exclusive new drug therapy. The last time his parents had visited, they'd been astounded by his progress and more than willing to up their monthly payment to $7,000.

The tall, white-haired physician pursed his rather full lips and looked around the office, pausing to admire the Louis XIV sideboard that graced the center of one wall and the small Renoir that hung over it. Once fees like those from Wallace and Davenport had been adequate to support his style of living. But that was no longer true, and his expensive tastes weren't the only reason he needed a great deal of money. He had other aspirations as well.

At Blackstone he was a ruler with absolute power. He'd come to like the knowledge that when he gave an order, it was obeyed without question. But the clinic was such a limited environment for a man of his leadership abilities. He'd made plans to extend his autocracy, and they'd been proceeding well until the squeamish Dr. Xavier had decided to bow out without even saying goodbye.

Of course, under the circumstances, sneaking off without asking permission had been a prudent move. The wayward chemist had sense enough to understand that had he made his intentions known, he would have ended up in one of the clinic's padded cells for a bit of behavior modification. Xavier hadn't waited around for the padlock to snap closed. Instead, he'd bribed a native houseboy to hide him in the van that made twice-weekly runs to Queenstown for fresh produce and meat. Naturally, the man had paid dearly for helping the doctor escape. But his punishment had served its purpose. The staff now understood that the front gate would remain locked and *nobody* would come in or out without the director's personal knowledge.

Talifero glanced at his Rolex. Almost time to make afternoon rounds, he thought, standing up and taking a light-gray linen jacket from the coat tree in the corner. After slipping into the jacket and straightening his black tie, he gazed with satisfaction at his reflection in the mirror by the door. At fifty-five, he was still quite trim and athletic. Far from making him look older, the prematurely white hair and mustache gave his tanned face a properly distinguished look.

He had just crossed to the door when the phone rang. The Queenstown chief of police, Louis Barahona, was on the line.

"I wanted to let you know that we're finished with the investigation of that unfortunate boating incident," the police chief related, the lilting island cadence of his voice somewhat tamed as it always was when he spoke to Talifero.

"Yes?" The physician sat down in his comfortable leather chair again and crossed one linen-clad leg over the other.

"The coroner has found the death to be accidental. Your houseboy was obviously drinking when he took the sailboat out."

"Thank you for taking care of it so expeditiously for me."

"It's an honor to serve you, Dr. Talifero. And I have another piece of information you will be interested in."

"Go on."

"There's a man in Queenstown who's been asking questions about the clinic. He's an American named Jed Prentiss. Do you know him?"

"No. But I assume you'll keep me informed of his movements," the physician asserted.

"Certainly. I've already assigned two of our best men to keep him under observation."

"Well, Captain, some day soon your diligence will be rewarded."

"Thank you, sir."

SIMONE HAD OFFERED her help, Jessica thought as she looked out the window, watching the tall black woman walk gracefully down to the corner and disappear from view. But she'd drawn the line at getting involved with Aubrey's drug problem.

Turning away, Jessica walked to the living-room couch and sat down heavily. There'd been a time when either she or Simone would have walked through fire to come to the other's rescue. But that was in the past, and the breach was almost entirely her fault.

When she'd gone away, Simone had written regularly at first. Jessica had let the intervals between her answers stretch longer and longer until the other young woman finally let the correspondence dwindle to a card at Christmas. Doubtless the withdrawal hurt Simone. But Jessica hadn't been able to help herself. Her friend from the bayou country was too much a part of the past she wanted to forget.

She closed her eyes for a moment, remembering the séance Simone had mentioned. It hadn't been an isolated incident. As teenagers they'd both devoured books on psychic phenomena and listened for hours to the country folks talking about strange goings-on in the swamps. They'd tried communicating with the spirit world, predicting the future, and visualizing faraway scenes with their mental powers.

To their surprise and delight, some of it seemed to work, and Jessica had felt as if she were standing at the doorway to a rich new world. But when her parents, with their strong fundamentalist beliefs, had found out about the girls' occult studies, their disapproval had been immediate and severe. Jessica's mother had been furious at Aunt Edna for countenancing such behavior. They'd dragged Jessica to their new minister, the Reverend Peter Ashford, for several stern lectures and warnings. She'd taken an instant dislike to the man, and it had been many months later before she'd known the reason why.

His warnings that she was being controlled by the devil were so terrifying that she'd tried to draw back from what was happening. But she was no longer in control. She'd felt her mind opening up like a radio receiver scanning the airwaves and pulling in heretofore unimagined signals. She still remembered the day she'd chanced on a frightening channel that had riveted her attention. She'd wanted to turn it off, but the horrible images wouldn't be banished. The nightmare hadn't ended until one person was dead and the whole parish had turned against her, as if it had been her fault.

She'd always sensed that if she came back to live in New Orleans, her psychic ability would push its way out of the spongy loam of her mind like a stubborn weed that had been chopped off but refused to die. That's why she'd stayed away.

But now with Aubrey in such a precarious condition, the talent that had been her undoing might be the only way to find out what had happened to him.

Suddenly the scene two days ago under the live oak tree at the university flooded back into her mind. She remembered the man she'd been talking to, the one with the corded muscles and hard-edged face who'd evoked such a strong response from her. Something had happened with him that had never happened before, even at the height of her fascination with psychic phenomena. For just a moment she'd felt her mind merge with his.

Jessica shivered. She didn't even know his name. Yet for a few seconds she'd picked up a confusing image of a white dove from him.

The vision had taken her completely by surprise. Because she'd been alarmed, she'd tried to deny what had happened and fled. Now she could look at the experience more calmly and understand that the apprehension was simply a holdover from her past. What had happened at sixteen had been devastating. But she'd come through it a stronger person. She was no longer a frightened girl. She was a woman with the maturity to control the hidden forces that had once controlled her. And perhaps with maturity had come powers she hadn't even dreamed of before.

She sat for a long time with her head cupped in her hands, weighing the risks versus the benefits and wondering if she were kidding herself. But in the end, there was no alternative. She had to explore the old abilities that she'd tried to deny for so long if she had any hope of helping her brother. The choice made, she felt a new sense of potency seeping into her body. It was as if she were absorbing energy from some hidden source.

The mood swing was almost giddy. Suddenly she felt her heart race with excitement. She'd been hitting dead ends for days. Now she could *do* something.

Watch it, she told herself. *Don't let this run away with you.* Yet she knew she was experiencing a heightened state of psychic awareness in which almost anything could happen.

With a fresh sense of purpose, she squared her shoulders and looked around her brother's apartment. The place to start was where she'd had success before. One thing she'd been able to do all those years ago was get impressions of people and places from holding their possessions. She'd been straightening and cleaning for days and hadn't even felt a twinge of insight into which things of Aubrey's might help her. But her mind had been numb with shock and pain, and she hadn't let herself open to any psychic possibilities.

Perhaps the thing to do was start with something that wouldn't be too threatening. Standing up, she crossed to the tall pine bookcase pushed against one wall and looked at the contents. Along with the hardback texts was an assortment of paperback novels. Aubrey's taste ran to science fiction, she noticed, stroking her hand along the spines. One in particular drew her attention and she pulled the volume from the shelf. It was an old Robert Heinlein novel called *The Puppet Masters*.

Holding it in her hand, Jessica closed her eyes and tried to make her mind blank. At first, nothing happened, and she realized that the vulnerable part of her was secretly relieved. Perhaps that was the reason she didn't allow herself to give up. Her fingers pressed into the cover of the book. Her heart began to beat faster.

She wasn't sure how long she waited before she realized something was happening. As if emerging from a pool of shimmering water, a picture began to solidify. At first there were ripples and waves in the image. But soon she was surprised and delighted to find herself looking at a cluttered but brightly lit room. Along three walls were ornate bookshelves reaching all the way to the high ceiling. Several sliding ladders gave access to the books on the top shelves.

The smell of old leather and mildewed paper made her nose wrinkle. As if she were standing in the center of the room, Jessica mentally turned to face a wide window that looked out on to a wrought-iron balcony. It was partially blocked by a counter and a cash register. To her right she could see a flight of narrow iron steps leading down to the sidewalk.

The image tapped a buried memory cell. She knew this place! It was a used bookstore called the Book Attic down in the French Quarter. She'd spent many Saturday afternoons there in the parapsychology section. Had Aubrey also gone there?

As she stopped concentrating on the image, it wavered. Too late, she tried to bring it back into focus, but it was gone.

Feeling disoriented, Jessica sank into a chair and sat with her eyes closed. The image of the bookstore had been very real, but it proved nothing since she'd been to the place herself and could have summoned it from her own mind.

There was a way, however, to find out whether she was fooling herself. Setting the book on the floor, she crossed to Aubrey's desk and began to investigate the cubbyholes at the back. She doubted she'd get any vibrations from the assortment of pens, rubber bands and paper clips she found. But stuffed into the compartment on the extreme left was a crumpled paper napkin. The minute Jessica's fingers came in contact with the crinkly paper, they began to tingle.

The old fear leaped in her breast, and she snatched her hand back. For several seconds she sat staring at the napkin. This was it. Either she went on with the experiment or she backed off.

Teeth clamped together, she drew the napkin out of the cubbyhole. In the center was an inch-high letter "H." In the upper left corner Aubrey had scribbled four digits—3489. Part of a phone number? She looked for more clues. At the bottom he'd doodled a series of straight lines and filled them with circles and triangles. Her eyes were drawn to the patterns. They seemed to have some sort of pull on her, and she had the strange sensation that she was being physically tugged forward. Alarmed, she tried to look away. But she had lost the power to make a choice.

The pool she'd seen before began to shimmer again. Only this time, she was in the middle of it. Drowning.

"No." The syllable was a gasp on her lips.

Her senses spun, and vague shapes wavered around her. She grabbed for something solid, and felt as if her fingers were closing around wood. A doorframe.

She seemed to be standing in a doorway looking into a room. She gasped again when she saw her brother lounging in a scarred wooden booth in a dimly lit bar. The image was so real, that she expected him to look up at her, but he went on sipping his beer. Putting down the glass he began to doodle on the napkin in front of him. The very napkin she now held in her hand!

Another man was sitting across from him in the booth, bare elbows resting on the wood table. His T-shirt was torn at the neck. His dark eyes were red-rimmed; his thin, almost colorless lips slack; his long hair uncombed across his high forehead. On his cheek was a wicked, star-shaped scar. The beer glass in front of him was almost empty.

Jessica shivered. She could smell alcohol and cigarette smoke and sweaty bodies. The air around her felt hot and oppressive. In her ears she heard a dozen low, jumbled conversations pitched above an acid rock tune blaring from the lighted jukebox in the corner.

This wasn't like the bookstore. She had never been to that place before, of that she was absolutely certain. But she felt as if she were there now. And she was totally caught up in the experience. Her fingers tightened around the napkin as if trying to squeeze its secrets from it.

In her mental picture, her eyes scanned around the room and its rather unkempt patrons, looking for some clue to the bar's location. The glass window at the front was grimy, but she could make out red letters painted on the outside of the panes. From her vantage point inside the bar, Jessica could read four letters: H-A-R-L. The rest were blocked by the wooden booths.

For a moment longer she strained to complete the name. But as she did, the image began to waver. Though she tried to hold it together, it was like trying to put substance to mist. The picture disintegrated, and she was left blinking and a bit disoriented.

Her first feeling was of relief that she was back in control. It was replaced by disappointment at not being able to complete the task.

Then she reflected with a sense of wonder on what she'd done. She'd actually taken herself mentally to a place where Aubrey had been by holding an object that had been there with him.

The realization brought a mixture of emotions. She had used the powers she'd repressed for so long. Or had they used her?

She shivered. Once she'd taken the napkin in her hand, she'd been helpless to control her reaction. It was almost as if some power outside herself was exerting an influence she couldn't block. But it had stopped short of letting her find out exactly where Aubrey had been. Well, there were no rules that said she had to solve this problem completely with psychic powers. Maybe if she got out the phone book and went down the list of bars, she could fill in the rest of the name.

As it turned out, there were only two establishments whose names began with that letter combination. One was an uptown watering place called Harlow's. The other was a bar called Harley's Pub. Near the docks, it was far and away the more likely choice.

After writing down the address, Jessica was about to grab her purse and open the front door when she happened to glance down at her streaked shirt. She was still wearing the "charwoman" outfit Simone had remarked upon. While she suspected that the clientele at Harley's wouldn't notice, she'd feel more confident if she were cleaned up a bit.

Half an hour later, wearing a blue denim skirt and a yellow camp shirt, she glanced at her watch. Lunch had been a carton of blueberry yogurt and it was now almost dinnertime. Getting a bite to eat at the pub would give her an excuse for hanging around.

Down on Jefferson Boulevard she hailed a taxi.

"Lady, it'll be dark soon. You sure you want to go to that part of town alone?" the cabbie questioned.

"Well, at least drive me by this address, and I'll let you know if I want to get out."

The man gave her a strange look and shrugged. "It's your nickel, lady."

Fifteen minutes later they pulled up across the street from Harley's Pub. Jessica peered out the window of the cab. There weren't a lot of people on the streets, but up the block she could see several men gathered beside a lamppost drinking from paper bags. Not the best neighborhood, she thought.

"Want me to wait for you?" the cabbie asked as she fumbled in her purse for money.

The offer made her feel more confident. "Please. But I may not be right back."

"Take your time. The meter's running. Just give me ten dollars on account."

After paying the man, Jessica stepped out on the paper-littered street. Was this really a good idea? But the more steps she took toward the bar, the more certain she was that this was where she had seen Aubrey in her vision.

Glancing back over her shoulder, she was reassured to see that the cab driver had slumped down in the seat and leaned his head back as if he were prepared to wait indefinitely.

Once inside the bar, Jessica stood for a few moments allowing her eyes to adjust to the dim lighting. It was a shock to see that the interior matched her mental picture almost exactly—right down to the scarred wood furniture. She could even locate the booth where Aubrey had been sitting.

At this hour there were only about a dozen patrons. Most were rough-looking men garbed in jeans and T-shirts gathered around the far end of the bar. They might well have been dock workers.

Several gave her appraising glances as she crossed quickly to the booth her brother had occupied and sat down. She was careful not to make eye contact with anybody, lest they think she wanted company. Instead she reached for the plastic-encased menu stuck between a half-full catsup bottle and a heavy glass sugar dispenser.

After a few minutes a stoop-shouldered, apron-clad man appeared and swiped a gray cloth over the Formica table-top.

"You want to order something, sweetheart, for here or to go?" he asked, glancing out the window at the waiting cab.

"A burger and fries." That was probably safest. At least they'd be cooked fresh.

"We have Jax and Miller Light on draft."

"I'll have a Coke."

The man grunted and shuffled away.

While she waited for the food, several customers left. Maybe this would be a good time to approach the bartender. Sliding out of her seat, she moved into his line of vision, not speaking until she caught his eye.

"What can I get you?" he finally asked.

"I'm looking for a friend who used to come here." Quickly she described her brother.

The balding man shook his head. "Don't remember him. But we get a lot of kids down here looking for excitement or trouble on Saturday nights."

"Thanks anyway."

Jessica found she was drawing attention from the few patrons who remained. For a moment she considered trying her question on them. Instead she returned to the booth to find that her Coke but not the food had arrived. It was sitting on a napkin identical to the one she'd found in the apartment, except that the doodling and numbers were missing. Picking up the napkin, she smoothed it with her fingers, feeling nothing in particular.

It was funny, she thought. Now that she was physically at Harley's, she had less sense of the place than when she'd seen it in her mind.

When the waiter brought the food, she cleared her throat. "Say, I was looking for someone I know down here," she began, getting ready to describe Aubrey again. But to her own surprise, the words that tumbled out of her mouth were not a description of her brother but of the man with the scar who had been sitting across from him in the booth.

The thin waiter shook his head, but she caught a flicker of recognition in his muddy green eyes.

"You know who I mean, don't you?" she challenged, giving him an unflinching look. Just for a second she caught an image from his mind. It was of flapping white wings and a bird soaring against a leaden sky.

"Dove," she whispered. "He's involved with the dove."

A look of incredulity flashed across his pasty features to be replaced by fear. He turned and quickly glanced over his shoulders. "If Lonnie knows you're talking about Dove in here—" Instead of finishing the sentence, he drew his finger graphically across his throat.

Jessica shuddered. She didn't even know what the dove image meant.

"Here, let me write up your bill." He changed the subject abruptly, taking a pencil stub from his pocket and licking the end before scribbling on the pad.

He wasn't going to talk, Jessica thought. There was nothing to do but eat her hamburger and go home. When she took a bite, it tasted like greasy sawdust in her mouth.

The waiter left the check facedown on the table. Picking it up, she saw that her meal had cost her five dollars and change. Then her eyes widened. Scribbled at the bottom was an address on the cross street a block away from the bar. The number was 3489—the same as the one she'd seen on the napkin in Aubrey's apartment.

Chapter Four

The streetlight winked on overhead, and Michael Rome took another swig from his paper bag-wrapped Ripple bottle. Of course, his "wine" was more than half grape juice, but his new drinking buddies on the corner didn't have to know that.

"So what about Harley's?" he questioned, wiping his mouth on his forearm and gesturing toward the pub near the corner. "I hear there's some action around there."

"Yeah. That's right, man." There was a chorus of agreement around the little group.

To his disappointment, nobody volunteered any more information. The lead that had brought him there had come from a helpful police officer named Lieutenant Devine who suspected the rundown pub was the center of drug traffic.

So he'd been hanging around the neighborhood asking discreet questions. He was looking in the direction of the bar when a cab pulled up across the street. The passenger who emerged was a petite female with an unruly mop of auburn curls. Even halfway down the block, he recognized the woman he'd talked to two days ago at the university. He'd checked around and found out that her name was Jessica Duval and that she claimed to be the sister of the guy from the chemistry department who'd almost barbecued himself last week. But nobody could confirm that piece of information or come up with her address.

She'd been invading his thoughts at odd moments ever since that strange interview they'd had out on the university lawn. In another context he might have admitted to himself that he found her damn attractive in an offbeat sort of way. But that was entirely beside the point. She knew something about Dove, and he wanted to find out what it was.

Automatically he faded into the shadow of a brick wall and raised his Ripple bottle to hide his face. As he watched, she handed the cab driver some money and then crossed the street to the bar. Today, he noted, her steps were a lot more hesitant than at the university. What's more, she'd asked the cab to wait for her. He'd bet she didn't venture into this part of town too often. But what was she doing at Harley's, of all places?

His first impulse was to follow her down the block and into the bar. But she'd run away from him last time, and he didn't want to force a confrontation. Maybe he'd just stroll past and have an unobtrusive peek inside.

After waiting ten minutes, he did just that. She was sitting in a booth alone, her back to the window. Then she got up to ask the bartender a question. When she returned to her seat, she looked dejected. Maybe she really was trying to get some information about her brother—or a boyfriend who was in trouble. But that still didn't explain how she'd found this place.

Fifteen minutes later Michael was surprised to see the waiter who had taken Jessica's order slip out the side door and head across the street to the waiting cab. After he handed the driver a bill, the man started his engine and pulled away. The waiter nodded in satisfaction and then took off down the block at a trot.

A few minutes later Jessica herself emerged and was apparently puzzled not to see the cab. After looking at something in the palm of her hand, she started hesitantly off in the direction the waiter had taken. Michael guessed that she was heading for trouble. He'd better follow. Maybe she was finally going to lead him to someone connected with Dove.

JESSICA CURLED her fingers around the paper in her hand. She hadn't liked this neighborhood when she'd arrived. With the last light of evening fading, she liked it even less. Probably the wise thing would be to give up for now and come back tomorrow.

Her heels clicked on the empty sidewalk as she turned the corner and hurried up the block toward the avenue where she might be able to get another cab.

Taking a deep breath of the humid night air, she tried to calm her growing sense of misgiving. The skin at the back of her neck was beginning to crawl. Was she being watched? she wondered, glancing quickly back over her shoulder. Though nothing moved in the shadows, she knew that coming here alone had been a very bad idea.

She was walking rapidly in the direction of the avenue when she heard footsteps behind her. Instinctively she began to run. Before she had gotten more than a dozen paces, someone grabbed her arm. It was the stoop-shouldered man who had served her at Harley's.

She tried to wrench away, but his grip was surprisingly firm for someone who looked so anemic.

"Thought I'd better tell Lonnie you were here. He's expecting you." He urged her toward one of the houses on the street.

"Let me go." Though she tried to hold her voice steady, she could hear it rising half an octave.

"Come inside."

His grip tightened on her arm. When she flailed out at him, he gave her the back of his hand across the face. Suddenly another man—one with a star-shaped scar etched on his cheek—was at his side. Lonnie, she thought, even as she began to struggle in real panic. But she was no match for the two men. Together they half dragged, half escorted her to the gaping doorway. When they reached the front door, Lonnie shoved her inside and slammed it closed with his foot.

"All right, what gives with you, bitch? Are you a cop, a reporter, what?"

It was hard to make her voice work now. "I came down here to find out what happened to Aubrey Ballin."

The name triggered a violent reaction. The man had his hands on her shoulders again before she could take a breath. "That meddler Ballin stuck his nose where it didn't belong and got what he deserved." He shook her roughly. "Why are you stirring up more trouble?"

Before she could even begin to frame an answer, a nasty gleam took over his dark eyes. "Not just Ballin. You want to know about Dove?" he baited her.

Despite herself, she nodded slightly.

"Then we'll give you some firsthand experience."

The other man laughed. It wasn't a pleasant sound. "We had to sit on your friend Ballin the first few times too. But then he grew to appreciate the stuff."

"Go get some," Lonnie ordered, shoving Jessica down to the dirty couch as he spoke.

Terror ripped through her. All at once she realized that Dove was a drug. The drug that had turned Aubrey into a maniac. These men had given it to him, and they were going to give it to her.

"No!" Jessica struck out blindly at the man's face. She had to get away. She couldn't let him do this to her.

Lonnie grunted and hit her back, momentarily knocking the breath out of her lungs. When she continued to pummel and kick at him, he threw his weight on top of her struggling body.

"Hurry," he said with a snarl.

The other man was back almost at once. To her horror, Jessica could see he was holding a hypodermic. Her frantic struggles redoubled. It took both of them to hold her down and stretch her arm out now. But inevitably she felt the sharp prick of the needle invading her flesh. Almost at once a warm lassitude seemed to spread through her bloodstream and her head felt as if it had filled with cotton candy. A wave of warm, syrupy heat seemed to wash over her.

"That's better now, isn't it?" Lonnie asked, his voice silky.

His face swam in and out of her vision; it was as if she were inside a fish tank viewing him through the glass.

"What have you done to me?" she croaked. Her body felt very heavy and at the same time almost buoyant.

"Given you a hint of Dove, honey. It makes you horny the first few times. That's why people get hooked," he said in a conversational voice. Pausing, he pulled his shirt off and tossed it on the floor.

Then he started to unbutton her camp shirt. His fingers seemed to burn her flesh.

"No." God, she wanted to get out of there, but she felt weighed down with sandbags.

She was trying to muster a scream when a loud crash split the air. From the corner of her vision, she saw the door cave in on its hinges.

"What the hell?" one of her tormenters exclaimed.

Michael Rome didn't dignify the question with an answer. He spared a brief glance at the woman on the couch. She looked unharmed but dazed. Drugged. The observation registered in a corner of his mind. But there was no time to worry about her now. Both men in the room were already converging on him.

He met the taller one's lunge with a well-placed kick that sent the man backward onto the floor. At the same time he ducked a blow from the other aimed at his jaw. In the next second Michael's hardened hand came up with a quick chop to the man's shoulder.

The one on the floor groaned and staggered to his feet. As if he'd made a quick decision to cut his losses, he stumbled out of the room while Michael was otherwise engaged with his partner. The other man kept fighting but was no match for the Peregrine agent. In a few moments he was on his knees.

"All right, what did you give her?" Michael demanded.

"Dove. We were just going to show her a good time."

"Sure. Where did you get it?"

"Lonnie. I don't know anything else."

"Lonnie's the guy who ran out on you?"

The man nodded.

Michael pulled a pair of handcuffs from inside his shirt and snapped the man's wrists to an exposed water pipe. "Maybe you're just a mule, but you can tell the police all about it when they get here."

Striding to the back of the house, he found a phone in the kitchen and quickly called the local stationhouse, telling them he'd check in after they'd picked up the suspect. Then he went back and knelt beside Jessica. He tried to be matter-of-fact as he drew the yellow fabric of her camp shirt across the lace-covered swell of her breasts. She didn't protest, and he redid the buttons as quickly as possible.

She stared at him, her lips moving, trying to form words. "They...wanted...hurt...me," she finally managed.

"I know." He hesitated, then made a decision. He had waited outside long enough for the two men to reveal whether they knew her. Now he cursed himself for not bursting in immediately. "I want to get you out of here before the police come. Can you walk?"

She stared at him blankly.

"Jessica, can you walk?" he said more loudly.

"Um." But when he pulled her to her feet, she sagged heavily against him. Muttering an imprecation, he scooped up her purse, picked her up in his arms, and strode out of the house. She was light, and he could carry her around the corner to where he'd left his car.

Once he'd deposited her on the front seat, he fastened the seatbelt shoulder strap to keep her upright and closed the door. When he'd slid in behind the wheel, he looked at her with concern. Her face was flushed, her breathing ragged, but the only life-threatening problems he'd heard of with regard to Dove were from continued use.

"Have you ever taken Dove before?"

After a long moment she shook her head almost imperceptibly.

To be on the safe side, he took her arms and turned them over, looking for needle marks. The only one was the recent present from that bastard Lonnie. There was no sense in taking her to the hospital. There was nothing they could do for her. And he wanted to get some information.

She shivered slightly as his finger moved up and down her arm. "Feels good," she murmured, her southern accent more pronounced than he remembered it.

He looked at her questioningly, but she didn't volunteer anything else. "Can you tell me where you live?" he probed.

In a halting voice, she gave him an address that didn't sound like it belonged in the city.

"Where's that."

"Annapolis."

"Maryland?"

"Uh-huh."

Oh, great, he thought, running exasperated fingers through his already ruffled hair.

"Where are you staying here?" he tried again.

"Brother's apartment." Her eyes fluttered open and she stared across the front seat, seeing him for the first time. "The man with the chemistry book—and the muscles—under the oak tree." Her speech was less thick now. Was she going into another phase of the intoxication? He'd never had an opportunity to observe someone who'd been hit by Dove before.

"My name is Michael Rome. I'm going to take care of you."

"I like your name. It fits." She paused for a moment, studying the strong lines of his face. "You won't hurt me." The words were spoken with quiet conviction.

"I want to help you."

"Michael, I feel . . . strange."

"Are you going to be sick?"

"I don't think so."

"Dizzy?"

"Floating. No, flying. Feels nice." She reached over and put her hand on the back of his arm, trailing her fingers through the thick covering of sun-bleached hairs. "You feel nice too."

He gave her an assessing look before putting her hand back in her own lap. Sighing, he took her purse, dug through the contents, and found a letter from her brother. The return address was near Chartres University. Looking over at the woman beside him in the car, he saw that her breathing was a bit more regular and her color was less bright. It was probably safe to take her home.

It wasn't a long drive. When he pulled up in front, he could see that it was a two-story house that had been converted to apartments.

"Upstairs or down?" he prompted.

"Up."

Even though she was light, it was an effort to get her boneless body up to the second floor. The way her arms were now clutching him desperately around the neck didn't help.

It was as if she were trying to provoke him by pressing her breasts against his chest, he thought. And despite the circumstances, he wasn't immune to having a desirable woman come on to him.

With a key he'd also found in her bag, he opened the door and stood looking around. It was a pleasant room with old but durable furniture. Everything was extremely clean and tidy, as if it had been set to rights very recently.

Striding down the hall, he found the bedroom and set her gently down on the double bed. After slipping off her shoes, he turned to leave so she could sleep off the drug's effects and he could call the stationhouse back. But her fingers grasped his arm.

"Don't leave me." Her voice was a whispery plea.

He let her pull him to a sitting position on the bed. "Do you need anything?"

"Yes . . . no."

"What is it?"

"I feel as though I'm out of control." Her voice was edged with fear now. "I don't like it."

Since Michael Rome had put her in the car, she'd felt powerful needs beginning to coalesce inside her. Now they were stronger than her ability to contain them. She shifted restlessly and felt his fingers smooth the damp hair back from her brow. In her oversensitized state, she could feel strength flowing from his calloused hands.

"Is it bad?" His voice was husky. He could see awakening desire in her eyes mixed with panic.

The question focused her attention more tightly on him. She had always shied away from any sort of casual intimacy. The man beside her on the bed was a virtual stranger. Yet under the potent influence of the drug she felt herself opening to him. She could sense his perplexity and his concern. But more than that, everything about him drew her toward him. She felt her senses extend beyond their normal bounds and merge into each other. Through half-closed eyes she studied him. It was as if her body *felt* the impact of the appealingly hard planes of his face, his broad shoulders and lean hips. She inhaled his masculine scent and *tasted* deep forest on her tongue.

At the same time a magnetic tide of arousal swept through her body. She tried to resist it, but the intense pleasure-need bordered on pain. If this man didn't save her, she would drown in it.

"Michael, I can't—"

"It's all right."

Simple reassurance or invitation? She was beyond caring. Turning, she moved against his jeans-clad thigh. Immediately a frisson of pure delight traveled along her nerve endings.

Michael tensed. There was no way to misinterpret what the drug had done to her. Dove was rumored to be a powerful aphrodisiac. Apparently the rumors were correct.

She moaned, and he realized she'd reached the point of desperation. Pushing up her shirt, she seized his hand and cupped it against her breast. Through the stretchy fabric of her bra he could feel that her nipple was already hard. As she pressed his hand against herself, it beaded to an even tighter point.

He heard her gasp and her hips began to rock urgently against his. Her skirt had ridden up her thighs. Without thinking about what he was doing, he wrapped his free arm around her. Bending his leg, he wedged it high up between hers, giving her something solid to press against. She moaned and rocked more urgently, her whole body trembling now. In the next second he felt her tense and then shudder.

"Jessica?" he questioned.

"That was so nice. Thank you."

"I didn't do much."

Realizing that his hand was still against her breast, he drew it out from under her shirt. With a gentle finger under her chin, he tipped her face up so that he could look down into her hazel eyes. They were dilated—and very beautiful.

"You're a very sexy man." The words came out unfiltered through the brain's usual censoring mechanism.

Would she remember this conversation? he wondered. And how would she feel about it and her uninhibited behavior?

"Jessica, perhaps it's that Dove is a very sexy drug," he tried.

"Mmmm...maybe..." She snuggled against him and pressed her hands to his hard chest. He suspected her arousal was beginning to build again.

His fingers moved along the line of her jaw and tangled in her curly hair. It felt bouncy and alive and very appealing—like the woman herself. He had no right to be sharing this kind of intimacy with her. To be *enjoying* this kind of intimacy, he corrected himself. Because, despite any noble intentions he might have, he was enjoying it, very much. It was impossible not to respond to her and her unleashed sensuality. Even if she were held enthralled by a powerful drug, he recognized that he was reacting to something much deeper than its influence.

"Baby, you're so damn vulnerable right now," he muttered.

She gazed up at him trustingly, and he had the odd feeling that she read him very accurately. "On the outside you're tough. Inside you're"—she searched for the right word—"good."

Sure. Saint Michael, he thought. "You hardly know me."

"I know you. Those men who gave me the injection wanted to hurt me. You never would."

He stared down at her. My God, he'd almost forgotten how she'd gotten this way in the first place. The thought of what those bastards had been going to do to her made his stomach suddenly churn.

She pressed her cheek against his, enjoying the bristly scrape of his beard. His fingers stroked her arm, and she *heard* the touch as the sound of sea grass whipping in the wind. With a little whimper, she fumbled for his hand. He knew the drug-induced passion was overwhelming her.

"Please—" She was burning up with need, and there was no way to hold back the fire.

"Easy, baby. I'm here."

Sitting up, she unbuttoned her yellow shirt and slipped it from her shoulders. Then she unfastened the skirt and drew it up over her head. In her wisp of a bra and lacy panties she looked like an erotic fantasy.

When she unhooked her bra and tossed it to the end of the bed with her other clothing, his breath caught in his throat. Her breasts were high and firm and very tantalizing. He was unable to suppress a groan as she pulled him back into her arms.

Saint Michael, he thought again as she began to writhe against him. No man should have to endure a night like this. Heaven and hell mixed together. Yet if he let himself make love to her, he would be no better than the men who had drugged her.

One hand caressed her breasts, the other slipped inside the waistband of her panties and slid downward. When he began to stroke her, she cried out in pleasure and arched into his caress. She was so close to the edge that she slipped over with very little help from him.

His own breathing was ragged, his body taut as he lowered her gently back to the bed.

"Better?"

"Much."

For a few minutes she nestled comfortably against him. Then she reached up, her fingers stroking his perspiration-damp brow. "This is driving you crazy."

He laughed. "Yeah."

"Michael, why don't you want to...to make love to me?"

"I'm afraid you won't respect me in the morning."

"Saint Michael."

"What?" His voice was hoarse.

"Saint Michael slew the dragon—with his sword."

"You meant Saint George."

She giggled. "Oh, yeah." Then she sobered. "You don't want to take advantage of me." But her breath was already accelerating again, her body tensing.

"Jessica, can't you understand? It's the drug that's making you this way."

"Not just the drug, Michael Rome."

"You're not thinking straight."

"It's coming back. I need to feel you inside me."

"Don't say that!"

"Maybe it's the only way to slay the dragon."

She pressed her face against his chest. When she spoke, her voice was barely above a whisper. "Michael, I'm not usually like this."

"I know, baby, I know."

"I—I can't help it. My body aches."

So did his.

She looked up again. "Michael, I promise you—it's more than just Dove." Then with shaky hands she reached up and captured his head, dragging his mouth down to hers. Suddenly he realized that in all the intimacy they had just shared, they hadn't yet kissed.

Her mouth was sweet and warm. He brushed his lips back and forth, then settled with a steady pressure. He felt her tongue test the serrated edges of his teeth and then dart beyond. He accepted the invitation, meeting her thrust with one of his own. She had pushed him almost beyond the limits of endurance, and now his control was just about shredded.

When he lifted his head, it was to gently kiss her cheek, her forehead, the line of her jaw. His lips slid downward to the throbbing pulse at the base of her neck.

He had wanted to taste her breasts too. Now he could no longer resist. Taking one hardened nipple in his mouth, he sucked, feeling her quicken with pleasure in response.

Her body was on fire, but not just from the drug pumping through her veins. In her heightened state of sensitivity, Michael's fingertips were like fine tracery on silver, scoring her body. His mouth was a moist balm, polishing her skin to a high sheen. She wanted this man, wanted all of him, and very urgently. Her fingers slid down his body, finding him through the fabric of his pants.

He groaned in response. "Jessica, don't."

But she didn't listen. The provocation had the desired effect. With a curse he stripped off his clothes and then her panties. No woman had ever driven him to the brink of insanity like this. He was beyond thought, beyond reason, beyond even gentleness.

She felt him pierce her most sensitive flesh. But she welcomed the invasion, arching her hips to meet it. Her movements were frantic as she twisted against him. It was impossible to slow down, to savor the experience. Her body drove for release and found it in a quick, shattering climax. A few moments later she felt his body shudder.

Then he started to ease away from her, and her arms tightened around his shoulders. "Don't."

He buried his face against her hair. "Are you all right?"

"Yes."

Her fingers stroked across the broad expanse of his back, feeling the tense muscles relax. "I think this time I really may be all right," she whispered.

"Good."

"You won't leave me?"

"No."

"Tomorrow we have to talk."

"Tomorrow."

Chapter Five

Lieutenant Hugh Devine had been going off duty as the call came into the precinct. But when he glanced at the dispatcher's sheet and saw the address and the informer's name, he promptly forgot all thoughts of the midweek ball game and six-pack of beer he'd planned for the evening's entertainment.

"I want to be in on this one," he told Pendowski at the desk.

"Up your alley, huh?"

"Yeah."

"I'll tell car twenty-three to expect you."

"Thanks."

He was out the door in a hurry, thinking it was a lucky day when Michael Rome had gone through the rap sheets looking for unusual drug activity. He'd liked the tough DEA agent, and he'd suspected he could learn a thing or two from the man.

When he arrived at the address Rome had given, he was surprised to see an ambulance as well as Patrol Car 23.

With only a brief glance at the crowd of curious neighbors, he hurried up the cracked front walk.

Inside, attendants were just lifting a sheet-covered body onto a stretcher. A white chalk outline on the floor indicated where the body had been found.

"What happened?"

"We're not sure yet," the patrolman answered. "The guy was handcuffed to the water pipe. But he wasn't going anywhere. He was dead when we arrived."

Devine cursed.

"There was some evidence of a fight. But unless he died from internal injuries, I don't think that's what killed him. There was a fresh needle mark on his arm. Maybe it was a drug overdose, but with both his hands cuffed, I don't think he gave it to himself. We're going to have to wait for an autopsy report."

Devine looked around the scene of the homicide. Michael Rome had been sure this guy would have some information. He was going to be disappointed when he called in.

JESSICA COULD FEEL the warmth of the sun caressing her face, and for a few seconds she simply enjoyed the drowsy lethargy between sleep and alertness. She didn't want to wake up. As consciousness seeped back into her mind, she knew why.

Turning her head, she looked at the white pillow beside her own. It still bore the indentation of a head. So last night hadn't been a wild dream as she'd been hoping.

Images and sensations came rushing back to her, bringing a red tint to her cheeks. God, what a fool she'd made of herself.

Sitting up, she covered her face with her hands as if that would block out the graphic pictures in her mind. Her body ached from the night's activities.

After she'd begged Michael Rome to make love to her, she'd thought she was going to be all right. But she'd awakened one more time before dawn, caught by the demon that was possessing her body. Michael had been there again for her. Though she'd felt his arousal, he'd done no more than given her release with his hands and lips. Afterward, when she'd finally broken down and cried, he'd rocked her and whispered reassurances until she'd fallen back to sleep.

Now she could hear water running in the bathroom and could smell the aroma of strong New Orleans chicory-laced coffee. So he was still here—apparently waiting for her to reappear. How was she going to face him? she wondered, pressing her palms against her eyelids.

When she heard him move down the hall again, she grabbed a robe and scurried into the bathroom. A long hot shower washed away some of her body's aches and postponed the moment of truth. But finally there was nothing she could do besides slip into a cotton shift and march forth to meet her own dragon.

As she entered the kitchen, he was sitting at the table, his large hands wrapped around a steaming mug of coffee. He was dressed in his jeans but had borrowed a clean T-shirt from Aubrey's dresser. It was a size too small and emphasized the strength of his chest and arms. There was something about his posture that suggested brooding frustration. Sensing her presence, he looked up, his gray eyes unfathomable.

Michael's gaze swept over the woman he'd held in his arms last night. He'd told himself that there hadn't been any emotional involvement on his part. But the sight of her made something inside his chest contract. She was wearing a simple amber cotton shift and sandals. With her curly hair still wet from the shower and no makeup, she looked like a teenager. He could see that she was struggling to keep her features neutral, yet it was impossible to completely hide the embarrassment she felt.

"How are you doing this morning?" he finally asked, his voice very gentle.

"I feel as if I've been run over by a Mack truck."

He laughed, grateful for the touch of humor. Then he sobered again. "How much do you remember about what happened last night?"

Her cheeks flamed and she looked away. "Too much."

"You don't take drugs, do you?"

"Never."

"That's one reason it hit you so hard. And they must have given you a huge dose."

She shuddered.

"How about some café au lait?"

"Thanks." She watched as he got up and made the half milk-half coffee concoction with the practiced ease of a man who was used to taking care of himself. When he returned to the table, she had pulled out the chair opposite his.

"What can you tell me about the drug's effects, besides . . . ?" He didn't have to finish the sentence.

"At first I couldn't move. Then I felt as if I was flying."

"You said that in the car."

She nodded.

"Did it affect your senses?"

Her eyes widened. "Yes! They were mixed up and very intense. I could feel things that I usually only see, taste things that should have been aromas."

"Like what?"

She looked down into her coffee. "The scent of your body is like a deep pine forest. I could taste it," she mumbled and then paused. "Please don't make me talk about it anymore."

He took a sip from his mug. Her words brought back memories of the way her skin had felt under his fingers— like warm silk. And the way her body had moved restlessly against his. Damn! This was a hell of a morning after. He wanted to reach across the table and cover her hand with his. Not knowing whether she'd welcome the contact, he decided not to take the chance. Besides, he reminded himself, he had no intention of getting emotionally entangled with this woman. They both needed to distance themselves from the intimacy that had been thrust upon them. He had better stick to business.

"Jessica, this is difficult for me too, believe it or not. But I need information."

"Who are you, Michael Rome?"

"I'm a drug enforcement agent." There was no need to tell her what else he was.

"So you were just doing your job last night?"

"It was more than that." Suddenly, despite his recent resolve to be strictly objective, he needed to bridge the gap between them. He pressed his fingers over hers. She flinched but didn't pull away.

"Michael." Her voice was very low. "I have to ask you a question."

He waited.

"Am I addicted to Dove? Am I going to go crazy the way my brother did?"

He squeezed her hand reassuringly. "You're going to be all right. It takes more than one dose to cause addiction."

She let out the breath she'd been holding. "Are you sure?"

"Yes. Listen, Jessica, how did you get mixed up with those guys?"

"I was trying to help Aubrey. You heard about what happened to him. The doctor told me it might help if he knew what he'd taken."

"But you knew it was Dove. You said so on the campus."

"I didn't know Dove was a drug. I didn't know what it was."

"Where did you hear the name? From him?"

She looked down again. "From you."

"Come on, I didn't let that slip."

"You didn't need to. I got the image from your mind."

"Do you expect me to believe that?"

"It's the truth. Sometimes I can do that."

He let out a curse. "After last night, I thought you might be willing to level with me this morning."

"Is that why you were so accommodating?"

He ran an exasperated hand through his thick hair. "Damn it, no. You were a fellow human being in need."

"Spare me the pop philosophy."

They glared across the table at each other. Jessica broke the eye contact first. "I'll show you what led me to Harley's."

"That ought to be interesting."

She got up and moved to the living room. In a few moments she reappeared with the napkin, which she flung onto the table.

He picked it up, noting the cheap recycled paper as well as the printed "H," doodles, and number. "So, what's that supposed to prove?"

"I'd never been there. But when I held it in my hand, I could see my brother sitting in one of the booths with another man—who turned out to be Lonnie."

He raised a sardonic eyebrow. "Do you tell fortunes too?"

"I'm not surprised at your attitude. After all, you *are* a policeman."

"What's that supposed to mean?"

"Forget it. Don't you have to go question that guy you handcuffed to the water pipe?"

"I checked in with the police this morning. That guy's not going to tell me anything. After we left, Lonnie apparently came back and killed him."

Her face whitened. Lonnie had killed his friend to keep him from talking. What had he planned for her?

"These guys are playing for keeps." He pushed back his chair and stood up. "So listen, baby, stay out of this from now on."

The offhand endearment was the same one he had used so tenderly the night before. The way he said it now made her feel patronized. Despite his frightening words, she bristled. "Don't think that last night gives you any right to tell me what to do."

"Well, my official capacity does. Keep your nose out of my investigation."

Without waiting for an answer, he turned on his heels and left the apartment.

THE VOODOO PRIESTESS had also had a close encounter with Dove during the night. Unlike Jessica Duval, she had administered the dosage herself and knew exactly how much to take to get the desired effect. After all, the drug had started out as a chemical distillation of rare swamp plants that had been used in voodoo rituals for generations.

She wasn't addicted, but when the silver disk of the moon hung round in the sky, she allowed herself to fly on the white wings of the Dove. For those who took the drug intravenously, the aphrodisiac effects wore off with overuse, and the next phase of addiction was a lot more violent. She knew how to avoid the danger by making it into a perfumed cream that was absorbed slowly by the skin. Even in this relatively safe fashion, she never overindulged.

Each man who was invited to share the ceremony of the full moon with her counted it as an honor. Into the small hours of the morning under the stimulation of the drug, she and her chosen partner paid tribute to the goddess of love again and again with their writhing bodies. The pleasure was beyond compare. But, as the ritual demanded, each man was required to leave her bed before the first rays of the sun tinged the sky with pink.

She was feeling thoroughly replete when the phone rang around nine. But she wondered who in the Crescent City had dared to disturb her on a day she was known to be fasting after the moon ceremony.

Her tone was imperious as she answered. When she heard the voice on the other end of the line, the haughty words she had intended froze in her throat.

"Moonshadow."

Jackson Talifero from the island of Royale Verde was the only white man who knew that secret voodoo name, or who would dare to use it.

She sat up in bed, pulling white satin sheets up around her breasts. The contrast against her richly colored skin was striking. "What do you want?"

"You know what I want. Gilbert Xavier."

"He isn't here."

"But you know where he is."

"He's in the city. He wouldn't tell me where he's hiding. But I've made sure he won't leave."

"How did you do that?"

"He came to me for help. I gave him a potion 'to ward off his enemies.' It was really a charm to bind him to this place."

A string of imprecations sizzled across the phone wires. "You're using that voodoo garbage for something this important!"

The priestess's voice dripped with venom. "It suits your purposes well enough when you want it to."

"That's just for show."

"Don't be so sure. If I wanted to I could cover your body with boils—or something a lot worse."

His voice took on a steely edge. "But you know very well that if anything happens to me, a very thick folder on your activities will be delivered straight to the New Orleans police commissioner. It would make very interesting reading—particularly the times your sacrificial ceremonies have gotten out of hand."

"You wouldn't dare."

"Push me and find out."

They were both silent. It was a stalemate that had spanned almost a decade. Each had a grip on the other's throat. The one whose hold loosened first was the one who would strangle to death.

Talifero finally broke the silence. "Xavier on the loose is a threat to both of us. You're a lot safer if you deliver him to me."

"The man is about to crack. If you take him by force, he's liable to do something crazy, and you're not going to get what you're after anyway."

Unfortunately, the woman was probably right. "Can you help him make the right decision?"

"Perhaps."

"You'd better." He didn't say what would happen, but the threat was there nevertheless.

Despite her bold manner, Moonshadow shuddered. She could sense the long arm of Jackson Talifero stretching toward her from the Caribbean island of Royale Verde. She suspected that it had the power to reach all the way to New Orleans.

CONSTANCE MCGUIRE laid down the black sheets of paper covered with tiny white letters and glanced at her watch. It was already close to 3:00 p.m., and Amherst would be waiting for her in the solarium—probably rattling the teacups.

After taking off her half glasses, she rubbed her aching eyes. Whoever had come up with the idea of photostating microfiche should be roasted in hell—preferably while reading a continuous ream of the stuff. Perusing the blurry white letters produced an almost instantaneous headache. Long association probably led to blindness.

Thank goodness the newer material was being archived to optical disks and could be accessed from the terminal in the Aviary. But when the information needed had to be dug out of the old newspaper articles, there was really no alternative to the microfiche.

The photostats had been sent by special messenger from the Library of Congress this morning. A rapid scan of the material had verified the startling contents. Knowing that the Falcon would want a summary, she'd set to work at once.

Within minutes she printed out a report, slipped it into a folder, and was on her way to the solarium.

Gordon was indeed almost at the edge of his control. Glancing up as she entered, he bit back a sharp comment about punctuality. He knew his assistant had spent the better part of the day getting ready for this briefing. If she'd been able to finish any sooner, she would have. Besides, judging from the glint in her usually calm blue eyes, he surmised that she had found something very interesting indeed.

However, he wasn't going to give her the satisfaction of asking what it was. The folder lay between them on the table while she poured herself a cup of tea and cut a piece of the chef's excellent chocolate butter cake. The rich concoction was almost an adequate compensation for her labor with the photostats, she thought.

"I'm sure you're eager to hear what I've found out," she told the Falcon after she'd enjoyed several bites of cake.

Her employer grunted.

"Jessica Duval is quite an unusual woman."

"Go on."

"Twelve years ago when she was a junior in high school in New Orleans, a seven-year-old girl in the neighborhood disappeared. When Jessica handled the girl's schoolbooks and scarf that were found in the woods, she had some sort of extrasensory experience in which she visualized the child being trapped in a dry well. She was able to lead the police to it and they found the child battered but still alive. The girl had been molested. She was so frightened by the whole experience that she wouldn't talk about it at all. Naturally the papers sensationalized Jessica's part in the rescue."

"Naturally."

"Jessica was quite upset by the publicity. And her parents, rather than giving her support, told her that her psychic ability meant she was possessed by the devil. However, the next time a child disappeared, the police came to her for help. She was afraid to have anything to do with the case. But when they insisted, she went behind her parents' back and provided the lead necessary to find the boy. He, too, had been molested, and as in the first case, he refused to talk about what had happened."

The Falcon reached for the folder on the table and quickly scanned the material. "Do you believe she accused the right man when she named the molester?" he finally asked.

"Why should she have made it up?"

He shrugged. "Hysteria, maybe. The need to find a convenient target. Like the Salem witch trials where young girls went around accusing old women of putting spells on them. Later, after several poor souls had been hanged, they confessed their little prank."

"In the Salem incident, as I recall, the girls were egging each other on. Jessica acted on her own. And she was certainly right about the location of the missing children. I'd say there's no parallel at all."

The Falcon pushed back his chair and stood up. Leaning heavily on his silver-headed cane, he walked to the perch in the corner where his favorite parrot, Cicero, sat watching the exchange. For a few moments he didn't speak as he affectionately rubbed the bird's large beak. Finally he turned back to Connie.

"When I asked you to check out Jessica Duval last night, I didn't want to bias your report or have you look for evidence that would support a particular conclusion, so I didn't give you a transcript of Michael Rome's phone report."

"But you're going to tell me something about it now, I take it."

"Yes. Michael was quite angry, really. He told me Jessica Duval had been interfering in his investigation, claiming that she was trying to find out what drug her brother had overdosed on. She contended that she had picked up several leads 'psychically.' "

"And Michael Rome, being the well-trained, no-nonsense, down-to-earth investigator that he is, didn't believe her explanation."

"Correct." The Falcon sighed. "When it comes to digging out facts and charming his way into someone's confidence, Michael's the best we've got. But he hasn't made very much headway by himself on this case." He paused. "I believe Jessica Duval can help him."

"So you're going to order him to work with her?"

"Yes."

"Even though you know Michael's hang-ups about working with women?"

"I'm well aware of Michael's hang-ups. I'd say it's time he got over them."

Chapter Six

As the dark-blue motorbike approached, Jed Prentiss uncurled his athlete's body and stood up. Under the shade of the fig tree, his wind-ruffled hair was fairly dark. But once he stepped out into the late-afternoon sun, it would pick up the golden highlights that, along with his broad shoulders and burnished tan, made him look more like an off-duty lifeguard than the experienced intelligence agent he was. Fluent in Spanish and Portuguese, he usually worked a Latin American beat.

But Amherst Gordon had pulled him out of El Salvador for a short-term assignment on the Caribbean island of Royale Verde. His initial instructions had been to play tourist and pick up what he could about local politics and power. But he'd known the Falcon had something more specific in mind.

He'd quickly discovered that all was not sweetness and light in this tropical paradise where tourists who appreciated a low key vacation lazed on the beaches, bartered at the native bazaars, and took advantage of the incomparable fishing and water sports. Jackson Talifero, the director of a ritzy sanitarium called the Blackstone Clinic on the far end of the island, apparently had serious and rather unsavory political ambitions.

That wasn't so unusual in itself, but Talifero had consolidated his power base so rapidly that it could only have been through highly illegal means. The man seemed to have a cozy relationship with every local government agency. Once Jed had started asking questions, the chief of police, Louis Barahona, had assigned two undercover men to keep tabs on him—presumably on Talifero's orders. At first he hadn't bothered to shake the surveillance since it would give Barahona a false sense of security to know what he was doing. But tonight, as on several occasions, it was necessary to move without a shadow. So he'd spent the late afternoon in Queenstown's favorite watering spot and waited for the happy-hour crowd to jam the place. Under cover of the boisterous confusion, he'd slipped out the back door.

The motorbike pulled to a stop, and Jed dusted the sand off his green cotton twill slacks. The equipment he was going to need was sealed in a waterproof knapsack that rested against the trunk of the tree. Slinging the thirty-pound kit over his shoulder as if it were a picnic lunch, he ambled over to the side of the road.

The dark-skinned boy from Royale Rental grinned, showing a mouth full of white teeth. "With a full tank of petrol like you asked for," he related in the ubiquitous island singsong.

"Thanks." Jed reached into his pocket and deposited a handful of coins into the outstretched palm. "Sorry to make you walk back to town."

"No problem, mon. I'm used to walking."

"I'll return the bike tomorrow."

"No problem. No problem."

After securing the pack to the luggage rack in back, Jed kicked the pedal and gave the small machine some gas. He headed down the road a half mile, then turned back and started for a dirt lane that led to a small bay where he'd hired a motorboat for some night fishing. The owner didn't seem to care what he was fishing for, and that suited Jed just fine.

A week and a half of inactivity was about all he could stand, Jed thought as he stowed his rented rod and tackle and checked the engine.

"You sure you don't want a guide?" The owner tried once more, his hand on the rope that moored the sturdy little craft to the dock. "Very cheap."

"Thanks for the offer, but I prefer to go out alone."

"You sure you know the area?"

"I've got a good map."

"Boss, you know where Devil's Point is?"

Jed unfolded the map and pointed to a jagged promontory.

"You stay away from it."

"Don't worry." The Blackstone Clinic was located just south of Devil's Point. But there was no reason to broadcast his destination.

"Take care of my boat, mon."

"You know it."

Jed steered slowly out of the harbor and then opened the throttle. As the little craft picked up speed, it began to bounce along the crests of the deep-blue waves, sending a shower of salty spray over the lone helmsman. Jed lifted his face into the sea breeze and grinned. If orders hadn't come through from the Falcon to check out the Blackstone Clinic, he would have put it on his "must see" list anyway.

But he hadn't needed to take the initiative. When Jed had been covering the airport several days ago, something very interesting had turned up in the person of Franco Garcia, who'd cleared customs with a Brazilian passport. He was allegedly there to invest in a sugar plantation and was staying in Jed's hotel. Jed's curiosity had been aroused by the man's European accent—even before he'd hired a cab to take him out to Blackstone. While Garcia was visiting the clinic, Jed had surreptitiously checked his room and found a fountain pen that did double duty as a stiletto and a cheap-looking pocket radio that was really a short-wave receiver. A concealed weapon and disguised communications equipment weren't absolute proof of covert activity. Garcia might be there inspecting the clinic with an eye to committing his crazy mother. But Jed didn't think so, particularly since he recognized the knife as a model that was hand-crafted in the Soviet Union.

A coded query to the Falcon along with a set of Garcia's smudged fingerprints taken from a glass in the bathroom had brought a surprisingly swift reply. There was an excellent possibility that Franco Garcia was a Soviet agent named Feliks Gorlov who'd had a recent run-in with another Peregrine agent in Madrid.

A KGB operative, Gorlov had been involved in some extracurricular drug dealing. So whether he was there in his official capacity or on his own time was anybody's guess. But the Falcon wanted to know why the man was on Royale Verde and why he was meeting with Jackson Talifero.

Now, as Jed approached the cape called Devil's Point that sheltered Blackstone's private bay, he cut the engine and got out his fishing equipment. He wasn't going to risk getting any closer until after dark.

JESSICA HUNG UP the phone, closed her eyes, and sagged back into the padded armchair. Though she still couldn't visit Aubrey in the hospital, she talked to Dr. Frederickson every day. Her terrifying encounter with Lonnie had at least produced the name of the drug Aubrey was probably on. But when she'd relayed it to the doctor, he'd reported back that the street name wasn't in his computer data base.

For a while it was almost as if she'd held the Dove in her hand. But it had fluttered away again, and she was left clutching air. To make matters worse, that afternoon Dr. Frederickson had gently introduced the idea that Aubrey might do better in a private clinic. She counted that as a very concrete indication that the staff at City Hospital wasn't expecting any miracles.

Her brother's lack of progress was depressing and made her want to take some action. Deep down she couldn't shake the belief that she might have the power to solve the puzzle of what had happened to Aubrey. On the other hand, she'd been badly frightened by the vicious way Lonnie and his friend had drugged her. If Michael Rome hadn't come along, she would almost certainly have ended up in worse shape than her brother.

It was equally disturbing to think about the cool DEA agent who had rescued her, yet her thoughts kept returning to him.

Her clearest visual image of Michael Rome was the way he'd looked sitting in the kitchen with his large hands wrapped around a coffee mug. It was inevitably replaced with more tactile memories of his hands wrapped around her body. She knew her frantic arousal had triggered a strong response from Michael. But he'd been very reluctant to turn the situation to his own advantage.

Clenching the arms of the chair, she wished for the hundredth time that none of it had happened. But she'd never been able to deny facts. One of them was that she'd reacted to Michael Rome not just as a convenient target for her sexual frustration but as an individual. Once she'd made the decision to trust herself to his safekeeping, her anxiety level had diminished considerably.

Though he was a man who needed to appear tough on the outside, in her heightened state of awareness she'd sensed the hidden warmth and sensitivity of his personality and responded to it. In fact, she realized that her very defenselessness had melted the hard shell that encased his real emotions.

That had pulled her to him. But she'd also felt an instinctive recognition that they had something important in common. While he'd held her in his arms, she'd been too caught up in her own frustration to analyze what that was. Since then she'd probed at the insight like someone with a chipped tooth who can't keep her tongue away from the jagged edge.

Finally it had come to her—as perceptions often did—that there was something in the past that had hurt and frightened him very deeply. It was a vulnerability that he kept well hidden, yet it was a strong component in his personality. What's more, he was afraid to take the chance of getting hurt again.

Jessica shook her head. From the way Michael Rome had stomped out of her apartment, it was unlikely that she was ever going to see the man again. Rather than continue to think about him, it would be more profitable to start going through Aubrey's apartment again looking for clues to his connection to Lonnie.

In the top of his closet was a shoe box with letters and notes. Bringing it to the kitchen table, she went through everything carefully, sometimes pausing to smile when she encountered her own letters and remembered some of the funny stories she'd relayed to Aubrey. But they certainly weren't relevant now. Nothing in the box was. Next she went through his briefcase. That netted her a folder full of test papers he'd never graded. When the obvious places yielded nothing, she began thinking more creatively.

She had just pulled up the edge of the mattress when there was a knock at the front door. She wasn't expecting anyone. Had Lonnie tracked her down to finish the job he'd started? Unconsciously she clutched the neck of her Indian cotton shift.

There was another loud rap at the door. Hesitantly she tiptoed down the hall and slipped the chain on the door, aware that whoever was on the other side could certainly hear the metal links rattling even if he couldn't see her trembling hands.

"Who is it?"

"Michael Rome."

A wave of relief washed over her. It was followed by anticipation that she shouldn't be feeling.

"Just a second." She threw open the door, and they stood looking at each other cautiously. From the expression on the DEA agent's face, she could tell he wasn't glad to be there.

She noticed that Aubrey's T-shirt was folded neatly over his arm. It appeared to be freshly laundered.

"Thanks for the loan," Michael said, extending the garment toward her. She'd only seen him in T-shirts and jeans. Today he was dressed quite differently, in a blue Oxford cloth shirt, dark slacks, and a pair of expensive-looking western boots. The effect was more civilized, but it didn't fool her. No matter what this man wore, she would always see the toughness under the clothing—and the compassion that was buried below the hard exterior.

"You're welcome. But you didn't come here just to return a shirt."

"No."

Stepping aside, she ushered him into the apartment. In the living room, she took a seat on the sofa. After hesitating for a second, he lowered his rangy frame into an easy chair opposite her.

"I didn't expect to see you again," she observed quietly.

He nodded. "My supervisor thinks you may be able to help me with the investigation." The tone of his voice suggested he didn't agree.

"So you're acting under orders."

His jaw tightened. "Frankly, I wasn't being very professional when I left. I should have given you a number where you could get in touch with me if you thought of anything important." He handed her a scrap of paper with his hotel name and extension. "And there were some more questions I should have asked you," Michael added.

Why was she disappointed that he was here just on business? Jessica wondered.

"And I did want to know whether you were all right."

"Did you?"

He looked down at the hard-edged hands clasped in his lap. "Yes."

The syllable was so low, she wondered if she'd imagined it.

"I'm all right, Michael." She shouldn't have used his first name. It had simply slipped out.

Their gazes collided then flicked away. They would have to go on pretending that they were nothing more than polite strangers. But the night they had spent together was burned into both their memories. Though it might have been drug induced, they had both reacted to a power stronger than the drug. Because of the circumstances that had brought them together, their mutual attraction was something neither of them dared bring out into the open. Nevertheless, it hung in the air between them like the musky scent of lovemaking the morning after.

He cleared his throat. "I'd like some more information about your brother."

"Like what?"

"Background, to start with."

The subject might be painful, but it was safer than dwelling on what had transpired between herself and Michael Rome in the dark hours of the night. Briefly she repeated some of the same facts she'd imparted to Dr. Frederickson.

"So getting involved with Dove was out of character for him, as far as you can determine?"

"Yes." She hesitated. "I have a theory about how it happened, if you want to hear it."

"Go on."

"Lonnie." Her voice stumbled over the name. "Lonnie said my brother had been sticking his nose in where it didn't belong."

"It could have meant he was trying to horn in on the guy's drug distribution territory."

"I can't believe Aubrey would do that! Besides, Lonnie also implied that he'd taken care of Aubrey to keep him from talking."

"Huh. That does add an interesting element, but it could just be wishful thinking on your part. I get the feeling that you didn't really know your brother very well."

Jessica knit her fingers together. "That's right."

"Why not?"

"I moved away when he was twelve."

His gray gaze seemed to pin her to the sofa.

"That was the summer you hit the papers?"

Her eyes registered shock and indignation. "You've been checking up on me, and you forgot to mention it."

"I want to hear your version of what happened."

"That's buried in the past. You have no right to ask me about it."

"Listen, my boss thinks your psychic ability or whatever it is may help crack this case. But to put it bluntly, I don't believe in phenomena that I can't explain scientifically. And I don't have time to waste. According to my best information, a ton of Dove is about to hit the streets. When it does, there are going to be a lot more whacked-out kids like your brother."

Jessica stood up and walked to the window. Her back was rigid. "I don't have to prove anything to you."

"Tell me about the Reverend Peter Ashford."

He saw her shoulders begin to tremble. Now was the time to press her as hard as he could.

"Tell me!"

She whirled to face him, her skin drained of color. God, what was this man doing to her? When she was in need of his aid, he had bought her trust with his care and understanding. Now she felt as if he had slipped a knife between her ribs. "Why do you want to hurt me?"

"I don't."

"Liar." She sucked in a steadying lungful of air. The old pain was as fresh in her mind as though it had been yesterday. "You want to know about the Reverend Peter Ashford? Well, he was going to kill me, and he would have if my parents hadn't come home early from choir practice that night. They thought he'd come over to save another soul from the devil."

"He tried to kill you? That wasn't in the papers."

Her voice was taut with emotion. "I've never told anyone about it."

Her knees buckled, and he was out of the chair and across the room before she sagged to the floor. "Easy, baby." The soothing note in his voice was the one he'd used the night he'd brought her home from Lonnie's.

Sitting her on the sofa, Michael turned her toward him and cupped her shoulders in his large hands. "Jessica, I shouldn't have—"

She reached up and removed the hands. "But you did." Squeezing her eyes shut, she tried to hold back the memories, but they came washing over her like a giant wave knocking her flat against hard sand. "How much do you know about that summer?" she whispered.

He could see that he was going to get exactly what he had asked for. "Just what was in the papers. You helped the police find two missing children by handling their possessions."

"The first one, Darlene Carpenter, was a child I baby-sat for occasionally. Her parents were frantic when she didn't come home from school one afternoon. Her books were discovered in the woods near her home."

Michael studied her drawn face. Her eyes were dark pools of emotion. He sensed they no longer focused on their surroundings.

"When I put my hand on the books," she whispered, "it was like watching a horror movie that I couldn't turn off. I could see everything that was happening, but I couldn't see her attacker's face."

"Lord! Jessica."

She didn't seem to hear his words. "It came back to me every time I closed my eyes. I kept seeing the look of terror on Darlene's face and hearing her plead and then scream. And then I'd start screaming myself. My parents thought I was possessed by a demon. They had the minister over that same evening and tried to calm me down. It was Ashford. Every time he came into the room, I started to shake, but I didn't know why until later."

She was trembling almost uncontrollably now.

"What happened?" Michael rasped. He had wanted to determine if this experience was real. Well, now there was no doubt about the verity of her gut-wrenching emotions. But were they the result of hysteria or a psychic experience? He still didn't know.

"My parents were very religious, and Ashford had a tremendous amount of influence with them. Together they kept me from going straight to the police, but the next day when a detective came around the neighborhood asking questions, I couldn't help myself. I started babbling about the visions and when he wouldn't believe me either, I dragged him to the place where they found her. Thank God she was still alive.''

Violent shudders racked her body. Michael could hear her teeth chattering.

"Before, when my friend Simone and I played around with magic and stuff, it was fun. But this thing was something I couldn't control. I was frightened and alone. All I wanted to do was be like everyone else again.''

"So how did you get involved when the second child disappeared a couple of months later?''

"That time the police came to me. I was terrified, and my parents were furious. But from the moment the detective put that poor boy's muddy sweater in my hand, I was seeing his ordeal too. God, it was horrible! The first time there might have been a chance that I'd stumbled on Darlene because the dry well was in the wooded area near our school. But I didn't even know this other kid or the neighborhood where he was accosted.''

She pressed her face into her hands.

"Jessica,'' he soothed.

When he took her shoulders and drew her trembling body against his, she didn't have the strength to object. She felt his fingers stroking her back, her hair.

"That time I saw the molester's face.'' She looked up at Michael, eyes pleading for his understanding. "It was Ashford. At first I told myself I was wrong or that I'd made it up somehow because I was already afraid of him. There was no evidence to support the revelation, and the children were too frightened to tell their parents what had really happened. But after I led the police to the second victim, Ashford took on my salvation as a personal crusade. Nobody else could tell. But I knew he was going to kill me if he could just get me alone.''

Michael swore under his breath. "And when you told the police, they didn't believe you.''

"They'd been so insistent on wanting my help. When I started saying things they didn't want to hear, they stopped taking me seriously. One of the officers on the case leaked my accusation to the papers. Suddenly the whole community was up in arms against me."

"Why did they think you'd lie?"

"You have to understand what kind of people they were. They held anyone who was a minister next to God. There was no way they could believe what I was saying about Ashford." Her voice took on the character of a bewildered child. "And when the man committed suicide the night after he'd been at our house, everybody blamed me because I'd accused him. They thought I'd driven him to it—that he couldn't take the shame and humiliation."

Michael could hear the remembered pain and frustration behind her words. "Wasn't there anything to support your side of the story?"

Jessica laughed harshly. "The victims were too traumatized to talk. I can understand why. Ashford had a very strong personality. He'd frightened me almost witless. He probably convinced those kids they were going to roast in hell if they told on him. But I finally became so hysterical that the police agreed to search his house. By that time it was too late. His sister had already cleared out his belongings. The detectives found nothing incriminating."

"I'm sorry you had to go through that."

The empathy in his voice was like a healing salve on wounded flesh. It also released the torment she'd been afraid to expose to the open air. During that whole time, she'd never been able to cry out her fears and desolation. Later she'd determinedly locked the experience away. Now in Michael's arms, she could weep for the girl who had suffered so unfairly.

He held her and rocked her gently. It was strange that though he had precipitated the pain, she could take such comfort from him. Gradually her tears tapered off.

When he sensed her control returning, he pulled a handkerchief from his pocket and handed it to her.

She blew her nose. "Why did you do that to me?"

His voice was gruff. "Because I had to know if it was real. Putting my trust in your information is like putting my life in your hands. If you were playing games, I'd be in a hell of a fix."

Drawing back, she studied his face, aware that he believed what he was saying but also certain that he was hiding something—maybe even from himself. "That may be true. But I think what you really wanted was for me to say I wouldn't work with you. Isn't that right?"

"Why would I do that?"

"So you could go back and report to your supervisor that you'd struck out."

His eyes had turned the color of gun metal. "I told you this could be dangerous. I wanted to keep you out of it."

"Thanks a bunch. Are you always so straightforward?"

"When I'm out on the street doing my job, I'm hardly ever straightforward."

"Well, you're not going to manipulate me again. I'm in this thing whether you like it or not."

Michael sighed. "I don't like it, but I guess I don't have a choice."

Chapter Seven

An hour after nightfall, the drums started. Despite his years of fieldwork, the hollow, primitive cadence made the hair on the back of Jed Prentiss's neck bristle as he maneuvered the boat close to shore. It was hard to believe that Jackson Talifero couldn't hear the same insistent rumblings so close to the sanitarium. The observation made him wonder even more strongly what the hell was going on at the Blackstone Clinic.

The only other sound was the lapping of water against the sides of the fishing craft. He looked up at the velvet canopy of the sky studded with brilliant points of light and an almost full moon. Though he'd traveled less than ten miles from the other side of the island, he had the eerie feeling that he was very far from civilization.

As he drew near shore, he could see a break in the thick vegetation that must be the outlet of a small creek. Cutting off the engine, he got out the oars and paddled several hundred feet up the waterway. The raised roots of a mangrove tree offered a convenient mooring. After securing the craft, he jumped out and gathered up his pack. Inside was a machete, a pair of high-powered infrared binoculars, and some tiny transmitters that he intended to plant in some of the clinic buildings—preferably in Talifero's office. Quickly he changed into the black fatigues and long-sleeve shirt he'd also brought along and fastened on his holster.

The jungle around him was teeming with animal life. Small feet scurried in the underbrush, and thousands of insects added a steady background hum. They made him feel like an intruder and reminded him to proceed carefully. The dense foliage hid patches of marshy ground and, for all he knew, quicksand and poisonous snakes.

It took him an hour to go a quarter of a mile, relying on the machete only when necessary so as not to leave an obvious trail. As he moved through the ferns and vine-covered trees, the drums grew louder and the tempo increased. Was Talifero holding a ritual for the psychotic inmates?

He would have given the party a wide berth, but it seemed to lie almost directly on his route to the sanitarium. Through the foliage he caught a flicker of firelight. Now that he was closer, he could distinguish the chanting of many voices accompanying the drums. It sounded as if there were more people than he had originally thought. Was anyone standing guard?

The thought crossed his mind that perhaps he'd picked a bad night to come visiting this end of Royale Verde. Despite his message to the Falcon, he hadn't given the voodoo angle much credence. But this sounded pretty serious. On the other hand, he wasn't sure he could give Barahona's gumshoes the slip two evenings in a row. The next time he had a few in a bar, they'd undoubtedly follow him to the men's room. Probably his best strategy was to reconnoiter and then make a decision.

Glancing around, he spotted a sturdy tree that looked as if it would be relatively easy to climb. Perhaps from the top he could get a better view of the clearing. After slinging the binoculars around his neck, he checked to make sure his gun was secure in its holster and set the pack and the machete down in the brush.

Silently he swung himself up onto the lowest branch and then began to climb. About twenty-five feet from the ground, he paused and peered out from between feathery leaves. To his right he had a good view of the clearing that had been drawing his attention.

From his vantage point he saw that flaming torches had been stuck into the ground at intervals of about eight feet, forming an almost perfect circle. Inside its boundaries perhaps thirty or forty dark-skinned men and women were chanting and swaying in time to the thudding beat of the drums. All were facing away from him in the direction of a stone altar topped by two thick wood posts about five or six feet apart.

As Jed watched, a tall figure wearing a mask and robe made of bright bird feathers ascended the steps and stood surveying the crowd. The man stretched his arms and the writhing bodies before him accelerated their pace and became more frantic in their movements. Arms and legs suddenly jutted out at odd angles. Necks bent as if they might snap off.

The man had strong power over the assemblage. Was he the priest? And for what sort of ceremony?

Even from this distance it was a breath-stopping scene. Though Jed had spent months in the jungles of South America, he had never witnessed anything quite so primeval. Wrapping one arm around the tree trunk, he adjusted the binoculars. They gave him a close-up view, but not of the panorama. He could see more details, but only in bits and pieces.

He was concentrating on the frenzied drummers who sat cross-legged at the far edge of the circle when a scream drew his attention to the altar. Swinging the binoculars back, he was just in time to see two large men dragging a struggling woman to the base of the low steps. The priest gave a sign and the men pulled the protesting captive forward. A white cloth was wrapped around her hips, but from the waist up she was naked except for the intricate painted design that covered her exposed brown flesh. In a moment her hands had been secured to metal rings in the wooden posts.

Focusing on her face, Jed caught the look of pure terror that washed over her features. In the next second the priest came forward with a small wooden bowl. One of the men grabbed the woman's hair and pulled her head up. Jed's view was blocked momentarily. When he trained the binoculars on the victim once more, her body had sagged forward. He could only guess that the priest had administered some sort of drug.

What in hell was going on here? he wondered, shifting uncomfortably against the tree trunk. Was there any chance of rescuing the woman? He did have a gun, he reminded himself, and the worshipers down there probably weren't armed. But they were so caught up in the primitive frenzy of the ceremony that they might well attack him anyway.

Jed was still debating what to do when a rustling in the underbrush made his head whip around. He could see nothing. But in the next second he heard a whooshing sound and felt a sharp pain in his shoulder. It was like the prick of a giant hypodermic needle.

Blowgun, he thought, as his vision began to swirl and a roaring noise in his ears all but shut out the sound of the drums. He grabbed frantically for the trunk of the tree, but his hands would no longer obey his clouding mind. His fingernails scraped uselessly against the soft bark. Then, in slow motion, he felt himself slipping toward the ground.

He wasn't even able to scream. His body bounced against a tree limb and then another, breaking his fall. Nevertheless, when he slammed into the ground, it was with bone-jarring force. Pain washed over him. But the drugged dart had done its work. Mercifully, in the next second he slipped from consciousness.

"IF I'M GOING TO WORK with you, perhaps we should lay down some ground rules," Jessica suggested. Her voice was calm, but it held an undercurrent of determination.

Michael stood up and jammed his fists into his pockets. Whatever else he thought about this woman, he had to admire her resilience. "You're the one who's dealt yourself in."

"Nevertheless, I want to know where I stand with you."

"If you can provide me with any information that might help, I won't refuse to use it."

"And you'll share with me what you know."

Michael grimaced. He wasn't willing to make that commitment. "Right now that's damned little. I've never come up against so many people who were afraid to talk. Whoever is controlling Dove has a lot of power in this city. But there is an angle we might try. Would you consent to my searching your brother's apartment?"

"That's what I'd started doing when you knocked on the door. I didn't find anything."

"You probably weren't very systematic. Do you mind if I have a look?"

"Be my guest."

Michael stood up and gazed around the living room. "Then I'll begin in here." To her surprise, he started with the baseboards and worked his way up the walls, checking behind every picture and curtain. Next he made a careful inspection of the furniture, removing cushions, checking seams and bottoms. After putting the sofa back together he handed Jessica a fistful of loose change and a ball-point pen before turning to the anniversary clock on the mantel.

"You really think you're going to find something in there?" she asked, looking at the glass-domed timepiece with its exposed mechanism.

He shrugged. "I've found dope hidden everywhere—tea bags, toilets, flashlights. You name it."

"I didn't know we were looking for dope."

"There may still be some of your brother's supply of Dove around here."

"I never thought of that."

"You're not a DEA agent. But whatever may be hidden in his apartment, there are rules for doing a thorough search, and they've served me well for years."

As Jessica watched him work, her respect for the man grew. She'd thought he spent most of his time on the street rapping with likely contacts. Now she realized that his job also involved hours of painstaking detail work.

His methodology paid off when he noticed the seal on the bottom of the bathroom scale had been broken. Prying up the metal plate, he removed the cover. Taped to the inside was a plastic bag with several sheets of paper inside.

"This sure isn't the warranty," Michael observed as he brought the booty back to the living room. Jessica could barely contain her excitement. Michael opened the plastic carefully before pulling out photocopies of two letters and a sheet torn from a directory. After reading them, he handed them across to Jessica. "What do you make of these?"

The first was a piece of correspondence from Henry Bergman, the head of the chemistry department at Chartres University, dated about a year ago. It informed a Dr. Gilbert Xavier that the federal government had reevaluated his grant proposal and rescinded their support of his research as of the end of the semester. Under it was another letter from Bergman, written several weeks earlier, that withdrew the university's request for an extension of the stipend in question. The last piece of paper was page 18 from the *International Directory of Private Psychiatric Clinics*.

Jessica's brow wrinkled. "I remember the name Xavier from some of Aubrey's letters. My brother worked for him one semester as a lab assistant. He was disappointed when the man left."

"Xavier left the university?"

"That's what I remember."

"It looks as though Bergman was playing games with him."

"Yes. What kind of research was Xavier doing, do you suppose?"

Michael didn't immediately answer the question. "You remember that we first saw each other at the university?"

"Yes."

"I wasn't there on a random fishing expedition. I was trying to find out if anyone knew about a former student, Daniella La Reine." Briefly he filled Jessica in on what he knew about the woman.

"And she was in the chemistry department, like Aubrey and Xavier."

"That's right." Michael looked thoughtful. "I saw you coming out of Bergman's office. What happened when you tried to talk to him about your brother?"

"He made it clear we didn't have anything further to discuss."

"Exactly the reaction I got in the chancellor's office. I assumed they were just nervous about publicizing a university drug problem. Now I'm wondering if the reason is a bit more sinister."

"What are you thinking?"

"That maybe Xavier was fooling around with psychoactive drugs. Maybe he even synthesized something new."

"Dove?"

Michael shrugged.

"Do you think he was trying to develop something with commercial value? Or was he in it for some other reason?"

"I can check the records tomorrow to try and find out what he was researching, but I have a hunch I won't find anything. Too bad your brother didn't write down what he suspected was going on."

"Maybe the university was worried by Xavier's research and wanted to get him out of there before it turned into a scandal."

"I'm not sure I buy that. And it doesn't explain what this listing is doing with the letters." Michael gestured toward the sheet torn from the directory.

Jessica picked up the page and scanned the entries. There was a brief description of each clinic's professional services and staff along with phone numbers and addresses. But she had no idea what she was looking for.

Then she reached out her index finger and began to run it slowly down the entries. Halfway down the page her finger began to tingle, just as it had when she'd picked up the paper napkin from Harley's.

"What is it?" Michael questioned.

"Something about this one."

He moved to her side and read the entry. It was for the Blackstone Clinic, a private sanitarium on Royale Verde, a former French protectorate in the Caribbean.

"What?"

"I don't know. I'm just getting . . ." She paused and gave Michael a direct look. "Getting a sensation from it."

He shook his head. "A sensation?"

"A tingling feeling in my finger."

He swore under his breath. "I'd feel damned silly making a report based on a tingling sensation in your finger."

"But you can have the Blackstone Clinic checked out."

He shrugged. "I suppose there's no harm in doing that."

AFTER DROPPING several coins into the collection box, Gilbert Xavier turned and made his way down the far-left aisle of the old cathedral. Slipping into a pew that was partly hidden by a gold-topped pillar, he clasped his thin fingers and bowed his slightly balding head as in prayer.

He hadn't been to church in years, and he'd told himself that he was there now because it was a very unlikely place for Talifero's men to look for him. But under the vaulted ceiling with its figures of angels and saints, he felt a sense of peace steal over him. He'd been on the run for weeks, and instead of thinking coherently, he'd simply been reacting and making some very foolish decisions.

Take the episode with Daniella La Reine. He'd counted it a piece of extraordinary good luck when he'd run into his sexy former student in the French Quarter and realized that she was working as a high-class prostitute. When he'd casually mentioned Dove's aphrodisiac properties, she'd been excited about using it and had been willing to let him stay in a vacant room at the Bryant Hotel with her in exchange for a modest supply of the drug. It had even amused him that she was touting it as a voodoo potion, given the compound's origins.

But his amusement hadn't lasted for long. The talkative Daniella had spread the word about Dove too freely. The wrong people had gotten wind of the arrangement, the way they seemed to hear about everything. Now the woman had left the city in fear of her life and he was shuffling from pillar to post—and running out of money.

He thought about how he'd gotten himself into this mess. He'd devoted years to looking for the active chemical agents in the plant compounds used by voodoo healers. The most exciting line of research had been with a drug he'd labeled V-22, which had very pronounced psychoactive effects.

It had taken months to purify V-22. The process itself was tricky and even dangerous due to the unstable nature of the chemical. Finally, he'd produced enough to conduct several tests of its properties, using student volunteers. Just when he was about to proceed to the next phase, the university had cut off his funding and made it clear that further research would not be countenanced, even if he could acquire outside backing. He'd been desperate for a way to carry on with his project because it looked as if V-22 might have a salutary effect on victims of certain mental disorders. But he'd felt that could only be proven through clinical tests—which he now had no way of conducting.

The chemistry department chairman, Hank Bergman, had been sympathetic. Over drinks at the faculty club, Bergman had mentioned a place he knew about called the Blackstone Clinic down on Royale Verde. The director, Jackson Talifero, was interested in experimental drug therapy and might be willing to fund his research on V-22. Xavier had written to the man and received an invitation to visit.

Royale Verde turned out to be just the environment he was looking for. There was no government regulation to interfere with his clinical trials. And the facilities at Blackstone were fabulous. Talifero was willing to supply him with an exceptionally well-equipped lab, assistants, and access to patients who might benefit from V-22.

Talifero had been suave and persuasive. Xavier blushed now at his naiveté in accepting the man's offer without checking carefully into his background. His purposes in developing and manufacturing V-22 had been quite different from Xavier's own. Though the chemist had kept his suspicions under control for months, he'd finally been able to ignore them no longer.

Now, from his shadowy pew, he raised his head and looked at the lighted statues on the altar. Their eyes seemed to bore into Xavier, and he quickly lowered his gaze.

As a child Xavier had believed in confessing his sins and receiving his mercy. Now he doubted very strongly in that sort of metaphysical salvation. He needed to put himself under the protection of some agency with much more worldly powers—like the DEA, for instance. He didn't dare go to the local authorities. Too many people here in New Orleans had an interest in Talifero's continued well-being. He knew for a fact that some of the local police were on his payroll. The director of the Blackstone Clinic was playing in a high-stakes game.

Maybe if he told the DEA about Talifero, they'd grant him immunity from prosecution. Or maybe he'd have to spend a few years in a federal penitentiary. But even that was better than ending up dead—or back on Royale Verde in Talifero's clutches. But how was he going to put himself in touch with the federal authorities, particularly since Talifero's goons were one step behind him every move he made?

LIEUTENANT HUGH DEVINE pulled a pack of Rolaids from his desk drawer and stuck two in his mouth, adding shrimp and sausage gumbo to the list of things that gave him indigestion. Or maybe it was just this damned case.

Michael Rome had spent a couple of hours with the mug books and they'd sent a composite drawing and various fingerprints to the FBI. But they still didn't have a make on Lonnie. His dead buddy was another matter. He was a small-time crook named Joe Valenchi who'd done time in the state pen. But he hadn't had either the brains or the connections to be very high up in this organization, whatever it was.

Devine peered at his in box. On top of the office football pool folder was the list he'd been waiting for. It was an inventory of what had been found in the Bay Street house besides Joe Valenchi's corpse. Devine scanned the single-space entries and scowled. The sheet didn't contain much, considering he'd had his men go over the place with a fine-tooth comb. A check of city records had determined that the building's owner lived out of state and that the property had not been rented in over a year. Lonnie must have simply broken in and taken over the location as a site for business appointments.

When he'd come back after Michael Rome left, Lonnie had apparently removed whatever dope he had on hand. He'd forgotten the plastic hypodermic that had been kicked under the sofa during the scuffle in the living room. But it had been empty.

There wasn't much else of interest there. The search team had found little more than the remains of several carry-out meals, a rusty key, a couple of match books, some cigarette stubs, and a half-dozen porno magazines.

But there was one other item that Devine didn't know what to make of. After opening his desk drawer, he removed an envelope and turned it upside down. Onto the center of his blotter fell what looked like a blob of hardened tree gum studded with red-and-green chicken feathers and what he'd swear were a pair of black cat whiskers. It had been found tacked to the molding over the front door. Devine didn't know what the thing was, and he knew he was going to feel damned ridiculous mentioning it to Michael Rome. But the DEA agent had wanted a full report on whatever he found in that house, and he was going to get it.

Chapter Eight

Michael had just put the letters and directory entry back in the plastic bag when the phone rang. "It might be for me," he informed Jessica. "I'm expecting some information from the local police, and I gave them your number."

Crossing to the kitchen, she picked up the receiver. In a moment she turned back toward Michael. "You're right—it's a Lieutenant Devine."

She busied herself putting away some dishes while he took the call. After a few moments he turned his back to her and hunched his shoulders slightly. The move effectively ensured his privacy. Nor was there much dialogue on his part beyond an occasional "uh-huh." There was no way to tell whether he was receiving good or bad news.

"Is that it?" he finally asked. When he turned back to Jessica, there was a thoughtful look on his angular features.

"I take it there's no big break in the case," she observed.

"You've got it." He paused, his eyes narrowing. "However, they did find one interesting thing. Would you be willing to come down to the stationhouse and, uh, see if you can tell what the hell it is?"

Jessica carefully set two soup bowls in the cabinet above the stove before answering. "I haven't been in a police station for twelve years. I don't know if I can handle it."

He studied her suddenly sober features. "I know how rough that was on you."

"No, you don't!" An hour ago he'd pushed her to the limit with his probing questions about that old trauma. Was this some new attempt to manipulate her?

He saw the mistrust in her eyes. "All right, maybe I don't know. But believe me, this isn't the same thing at all. We don't have to tell anybody about your psychic ability. You're not going to be exhibit A. You're just going to be coming along as my associate."

She suspected Michael Rome was a man who didn't ordinarily make concessions in his work. Yet as she considered his proposal, another equally troubling thought crossed her mind. "Are they going to question me about Lonnie?" she asked in a low voice. She didn't want to think about that again, much less bare the disturbing particulars to strangers.

He shook his head. "Jessica, you called me a policeman, but that's not really accurate. I'm a special agent, and though I cooperate with the local authorities when it's convenient, I don't have to abide by their procedures. I gave them a very brief account of what happened with Lonnie— leaving out your name and most of the details after I took you home."

"You did that for me?"

"Yes."

She forced herself to meet his gaze. "And this other thing is important to you?"

"I wouldn't ask if it weren't important."

"Then I'll help you if I can."

"Thank you."

A wry smile flickered at the corners of her lips. "Well, if I'm going to be your associate, maybe I'd better change my clothes."

He eyed her Indian cotton shift and rope sandals. In the casual outfit with her mop of curly hair and pixie face, she looked like a kid. Devine was going to wonder if the DEA was raiding the junior high schools for agents.

"I'll only be a few minutes," she assured him.

Michael stifled the impulse to ask her to hurry. Instead he pulled a biography of Louis Armstrong from the bookcase and settled back into the easy chair in the living room. He knew very few women who could dress for a business appointment quickly.

To his surprise, however, Jessica was true to her word. Less than fifteen minutes later she emerged from the bedroom wearing a lightweight camel suit and a bittersweet crepe de chine blouse. High-heel pumps, beige stockings, and understated gold earrings completed the outfit.

Michael, who was a master at changing his own appearance, stared in amazement at the transformation. Even her bouncy curls were under control, and the subtle makeup she'd applied did wonders for her large hazel eyes.

She acknowledged his approving gaze with a slight nod of her head. "This is my buying-trip-to-New York outfit. Too bad I left my briefcase back in Annapolis."

"Oh, I think you'll do very nicely even without it," he assured her. He was so focused on this assignment that he'd almost forgotten that he'd met Jessica out of her own environment. It suddenly struck him that he had no idea what her real life was like.

On the drive down to the precinct station, he used his conversational skills to draw her out about her jewelry business. The gambit was partly to keep her mind off the upcoming appointment and partly to satisfy his own growing interest in a woman he found very appealing. But despite the conversation, he sensed her level of apprehension increasing as they pulled up in front of the drab stone building that housed the district station.

Michael helped her out of the car and then kept a steadying hold on her arm as they left the parking lot. "It's not going to take too long," he said as he escorted her up the high stone steps.

She gave him a thin smile. "I'll be okay." But her face, which had been animated only a few moments before, had become set in grim lines.

Lieutenant Devine was waiting in a cluttered little office near the end of the second-floor hall. He was a chunky man, Jessica observed, with an overhanging belly that hid the buckle of his pants.

"This is my associate, Miss Duval," Michael introduced her.

"Glad to meet you. Have a seat." The lieutenant gestured toward two metal armchairs.

To Jessica's relief, Michael had been playing straight this time. The busy detective seemed unaware of her involvement in the Bay Street incident and wasn't particularly interested in why Michael had brought her into the case.

"As I told Rome," he explained, "the lab couldn't do much with what we were able to scrounge up at the murder site. But we did find this rather nasty little artifact." Reaching into his desk, he pulled out the white legal-size envelope and dumped the contents onto the desk blotter.

Jessica stared intently at the pecan-size blob of resin with its attached feathers and whiskers. It smelled faintly of pine and decaying organic matter. She hadn't seen anything like this since the summer she and Simone had been fooling around with voodoo. They'd made some concoctions of their own. But her friend had wanted something authentic and had gone down to the old crone who lived in a shack at the edge of the swamp. She'd come back with a charm guaranteed to make them both irresistible to boys. It had smelled so offensive they'd had to throw it away.

"Do you happen to know what it is?" Michael questioned.

"A voodoo charm."

Michael's brow wrinkled. "A voodoo charm? What's it supposed to do?"

Jessica eyed the artifact with distaste. "I don't know. But I don't like the way it looks."

"Do you think—" Michael started to ask and then glanced at Devine. "We don't want to use up any more of your time. Would you mind if we took this into one of the interrogation rooms so Miss Duval could have a closer look?"

The detective shrugged. "There's an empty office right across the hall. Will that do?"

"Fine."

Michael slid the talisman back into the envelope and led her across the hall.

Jessica waited until he'd closed the door. "I suppose you want to see if my special talents can tell me anything about the charm," she observed.

"It can't hurt. Maybe if you hold it, you'll be able to tell me who made it, the way you got a picture of Harley's Pub from the napkin."

She stared up at him, wondering if she caught a note of sarcasm in his voice. "Is this an admission that you've become a believer?"

"I told you. I'm open to any possibility that can give me another lead." His tone implied that he wasn't expecting much so he wasn't going to be disappointed if nothing happened.

Sitting down again, Jessica looked at the long white envelope. Her hand reached out toward it and then stopped as if there were some sort of invisible force field sealing it off. She could almost feel the resistance against her fingertips. The napkin from Harley's was one thing. This was quite another. Touching it meant getting deeper into the kind of experiences she'd been avoiding for so long—the experiences Michael had forced her to relive.

"What are you waiting for?" he prompted.

She looked into his challenging gray eyes. He thought she wasn't up to this or that she couldn't tell him anything. With a grimace she plunged her hand into the envelope. It felt as if she'd punched through a window, a thousand shards of glass digging into her skin. She tried to scream but the sound never passed her lips. Only the instant dilation of her eyes gave any indication of her terror. She tried to counter the spell with all her strength, but her hand was pulled toward the charm with a force she couldn't control. As soon as her fingers closed around the feathers, another pain—this time white hot—seared her skin and shot up her arm to her shoulder. She gasped and was finally able to jerk her hand away.

"What's wrong?"

"It's evil," she whispered.

"How? What do you mean?"

She shook her head, still trembling from the shock. "I had the strong impression that I shouldn't touch it. As soon as I did, I felt as if I'd been branded."

"That's crazy." Michael reached for the envelope.

"Michael, don't!"

He ignored the warning and pulled out the charm, holding it in his open palm. "See, it's not doing a damned thing to me."

Silently she turned her own hand over. Where her fingers had come into contact with the feathers, angry red blisters had formed.

He stared down at the injury, hardly able to believe the evidence of his own eyes. "How the hell did that happen?"

"I tried to tell you. It burned me." Her voice was thready.

Gingerly he set the artifact down on the desk blotter. His gaze flicked from it to the welts on Jessica's fingers and back again, as if they were the paraphernalia of a magician's trick. What had just happened was totally outside his area of experience. His own skin was unaffected, yet he had seen how Jessica's flesh had been damaged by a much more tentative contact. Had her own fear conjured up the affliction? Or did the injury come from some necromancer's power within the charm? He couldn't say, but he did know he had pushed her into touching it, and he could see that both the pain and the welts were very real.

"Cold water is the best first aid for a burn," he said, helping her up and leading her out into the hall. At the end of the corridor was a water fountain. Michael stepped on the pedal and thrust Jessica's hand under the cold flow, his strong fingers gentle but firm as they cradled hers.

The icy water was numbing to his own flesh, but he didn't let go of her. They both watched as the swelling subsided slightly and became less vivid in color.

"Better?"

"Some."

He was still holding her hand. Unbidden, a memory of their steamy night together flashed into his mind once more. *Michael, why don't you want to make love to me?* He remembered the passion in her hazel eyes and his own weakness in not being able to resist what she had offered him. His gaze collided with hers and held. He didn't need to be a psychic to know that her mind was on the same dangerous wavelength.

A passing patrolman gave them a curious stare, making them both vividly aware that they were standing in the middle of a public hallway. Michael dropped her hand.

"I'm sorry." It could have been an apology for precipitating her injury. She knew it was more.

Perhaps it was better to bring it right out into the open and dismiss it. "I can pretend that night never happened, if you can," she said, knowing it was a lie.

"Under the circumstances, that's probably best." He cleared his throat. "Let's go back to that empty office."

"All right."

After closing the door, he waited until she had resumed her seat, giving them both time to get the focus of the discussion back onto the charm. "Has anything like that ever happened to you?" he asked, gesturing toward her hand.

"No." She paused, wondering how he would react to any attempted explanation on her part. "It probably doesn't make sense to you, but when I touched that thing, along with the pain, I had an overwhelming impression of malevolence."

He nodded thoughtfully, his gaze shifting to the bizarre-looking talisman. As far as he could tell, it was simply a collection of junk that could have been stuck together by a preschooler in arts and crafts class. What could have infused it with the power to scorch a woman's skin?

He looked up to see that she was trying to read his face. "Jessica, despite what you may think, sometimes I do play hunches. Let's just say that in this case, your intuition is operating on a lot stronger level than mine."

She relaxed slightly. "All right."

Michael slapped his fist into the palm of his hand. "I wouldn't have thought there was anything to this voodoo stuff. But every trail in this case keeps leading back to it."

She shrugged. "Voodoo's roots go all the way back to Africa. But here in Louisiana it developed its own traditions and practices. This may be the twentieth century, yet superstition is still a strong element in the local culture. Down in the bayou country a lot of people believe in gris-gris."

"Gris-gris?"

"Voodoo spells and charms."

"Do *you* believe in them?" he persisted.

She hesitated. "I don't even know why I seem to be 'blessed' with psychic powers. There's a lot I don't understand about the relationship between the physical world and what we can't see or touch. That means I can't help keeping my mind open to all sorts of phenomena. The only concrete thing I can tell you about this charm is that it does have a profound effect on me."

"So you really don't know much about how this particular talisman works?"

"No. Remember, I spent years trying *not* to think about things like that." Her brow wrinkled. "But my friend Simone might."

"You mentioned her before. Is she from around here?"

"Her folks lived out by my Aunt Edna. I visited there every summer, and we became best friends. As teenagers we were really into the occult—even some voodoo spells. I have the feeling she kept up the interest."

"Why do you think so?"

"She has a shop on Royal Street where she sells love potions and stuff like that."

"Then she might know who in the city could have made such a thing, and why."

"Maybe."

Michael slipped the envelope with the charm into his pocket. "Well, I assume Lieutenant Devine will let us borrow this long enough to take it down to your friend Simone for a second opinion."

WITH GREAT EFFORT, like a mountain climber pulling himself hand over hand up the side of a precipice, Jed Prentiss fought his way slowly back to consciousness. Then he fervently wished he hadn't made the effort.

His first perception was of searing pain in his chest every time he took a breath. The sensation convinced him that he was alive. Nothing else did. Fear of the unknown clawed at his insides. He could not see, or hear, or smell, or taste, or move. The isolation brought a feeling of panic that echoed in the inner chamber of his mind like a silent scream.

He realized he was injured and vulnerable. But he couldn't quite remember what had happened. And he certainly didn't know where in the hell he was now. Or if anyone was going to help him.

He dozed off and woke, slept and woke again. Still his only physical tie to the world was the pain in his ribs. It might have been minutes or hours later that he sensed the presence of someone else in the room with him and struggled to open his eyes. But his body would not obey his brain.

A gentle finger pulled up his left eyelid. He had a blurry impression of a dark female face and a white nurse's cap before she let go and the lid slipped shut again.

"I believe the patient is finally awake, sir," a soft island voice reported.

Island voice... Royale Verde. I came to Royale Verde on a mission for the Falcon.

"Good, I was beginning to wonder about the dose of phenodryl he received." The man's voice was deep and cultured. "Can you hear me, Mr. Prentiss? Jed?" he asked.

Jed struggled to give some indication that he could. None of his muscles responded to orders from his brain.

"I'm Dr. Talifero," the man continued. "You've had a cerebral accident. In laymen's terms, a stroke. You were brought to our clinic."

Cerebral accident? What the hell was that supposed to mean?

"It's not unusual, in this sort of case, to suffer from massive paralysis. It will be twenty-four to forty-eight hours before we know the extent of the damage. You also seem to have fallen and badly bruised some ribs, although they should mend satisfactorily. Other than that, I'm afraid I can't make any predictions about your prognosis. But I want you to know that we're going to do the best we can for you."

What was this guy talking about? The last thing he remembered was sneaking up on a place called the Blackstone Clinic run by a Dr. Talifero.

He struggled to remember precisely what had happened to him. He had rented a boat. That much was clear. He could recall waiting off-shore pretending to fish until nightfall. But the effort to continue piecing together the evening's activities made his head begin to throb. A stroke, the doctor had said. Was his brain damaged? Fear churned in his stomach, pressed upward against his esophagus.

"Cases like yours are often accompanied by mental confusion and even delusions," Talifero went on. "I'm afraid you may not have a clear picture of how you got here. But we'll talk about that when you're functioning a little better."

Could that be right? It seemed impossible. But would the doctor be making it all up? It was crazy. Yet the strong taint of doubt was like the taste of copper in his mouth. Some instinct toward self-preservation warned him not to trust this man despite his smooth, professional words.

On the other hand, the man had called him Jed Prentiss. Was that proof of something—or nothing?

Jed's lip trembled as he struggled to speak.

"Just relax, Mr. Prentiss," the nurse soothed. "You need to rest."

Rest, no. He needed answers. He needed to get out of this place, to get in touch with the Falcon. Or was there really an intelligence control who used that code name? For now there was simply no way to verify his memories.

Wait, don't leave. Help me. For God's sake, help me. If I can't trust my own mind, what can I trust? he tried to scream. But the words remained locked inside his skull.

He heard a light being switched off, a door closing. He was alone again, more alone than he had ever been or ever imagined that he could be. But somehow he was afraid that wasn't the worst part. A doctor named Talifero was his lifeline to reality. And that might well be his greatest danger.

Chapter Nine

As he slid behind the wheel of the car, Michael turned to Jessica. "Would you mind if we stop by my hotel room on the way to Royal Street?"

Her eyebrows arched.

"Besides the voodoo charm, the Xavier letters are the first piece of concrete evidence I have in this case. I want to send a fax of them to headquarters."

"You can send a fax from your hotel room?"

"Yeah. It's amazing what the boys in R and D can put together for the road show."

"All right, then."

He was staying at an old mansion on Esplanade that had been turned into an elegant bed and breakfast. Jessica might have elected to wait in the car, but she was curious about the accommodations he had chosen. As it turned out, he had one of the best rooms in the place—a suite on the top floor furnished entirely with Victorian antiques.

"I guess I'd pictured you at the Holiday Inn or something like that," Jessica observed, sitting down on a walnut-and-brocade sofa in the living room. Beyond partially closed French doors she could see an ornate canopy bed.

"I've lived in too many cookie-cutter Holiday Inns, thanks. When I get the chance, I look for something with a bit more individuality." The statement was made with the conviction of a man who didn't stay anywhere long enough to put down roots.

"Do you have a permanent address?"

He laughed. "I guess I sound like a real gypsy. But I do have a little ranch in Texas that I've put a downpayment on."

She could see that he had a lot more than money invested in the place. "So you're fixing it up, then?"

"Yeah, although I don't get there more than twice a year. But some day when I'm too old for fieldwork, I'm going to retire there and raise horses."

"Horses?"

"Uh-huh. My old man was on the rodeo circuit. I guess that's when traveling got into my blood." While he was talking, he unlocked an armoire and pulled out a briefcase. "Have you ever seen one of these before?" he asked, adroitly changing the subject as he opened the case.

"It looks like a personal computer to me."

"That's right. But this model has a built-in modem for connecting it to the phone lines, an onboard printer, and a fax." It also had a sophisticated encryption algorithm that ensured the security of his communiques to the Falcon.

After sending the transmission and locking the computer in the armoire again, he took out a tweed sport jacket and slipped the envelope with the charm into one of the pockets. Then he shrugged into the garment. "Come on, let's go see if we can catch your friend Simone before dinner."

Simone's shop, This Is the Place, turned out to be a small but well-appointed boutique situated between two expensive antique shops on Royal Street. The window display featured glass-and-brass etageres on which were arranged handcrafted ceramic and fabric dolls along with soaps and potions wrapped in elegant foil paper and tied with slender velvet ribbons. Like Simone, the effect was distinctive and polished.

When Michael pushed open the shop door, the proprietor was just about to hang up the closed sign. But she laid it on the counter when she saw her old friend.

"Jessica," she declared, her face registering surprise. It was not lost on Michael even though it was quickly replaced by a smile that didn't quite reach her eyes. "I didn't expect a visit from you so soon. Come in and let me show off my domain." As she gestured toward the interior of the store, the full sleeve of her burgundy caftan rippled gracefully.

"I'd like to see it," Jessica said before turning and beckoning toward her companion. "But let me introduce the two of you first. Michael Rome, this is one of my oldest friends, Simone Villard. Michael's, uh, helping me with the Aubrey thing."

"This isn't a social call, I take it."

Jessica shook her head.

Simone's attention shifted to the tall, hard-edged man at Jessica's side, giving him a careful inspection. "Are you a cop?"

"No, ma'am."

"Don't kid me," the black woman insisted, folding her arms across her chest.

"I'm with the DEA," he admitted.

"I told Jessica I wasn't going to get mixed up in anything that had to do with dope."

"We're only after some information." Michael pulled the white envelope from his pocket and shook out the voodoo talisman onto the counter.

As Simone inspected the unpleasant little artifact, Jessica was acutely aware of just how out of place it was in her friend's upscale boutique.

"This thing was found at the scene of a murder that's related to the case I'm working on. Jessica thought it was a voodoo charm and suggested that you might be able to shed some light on what it's supposed to do."

Simone's dark eyes narrowed accusingly as they fixed on the other young woman's face. "Jessica, you had no right to drag me into this."

"I'm sorry. But I remembered you were interested in this sort of thing in the old days and I thought that—"

"It's not exactly my bag now."

Jessica sensed the vehemence behind the words. She and Simone had been out of touch for a long time. Was presuming on their old friendship a mistake?

A phone rang behind the counter, and Simone's head swiveled to face it. "Now who...?" she questioned. "Please excuse me. I'll take it in the back."

Her caftan swirled around her legs as she hurried to the rear of the retail area.

"I told you not to—" Jessica and Michael heard before she firmly closed the door. They exchanged glances and Jessica shrugged.

When Simone returned, her features were carefully composed. "Now what were you saying?" she asked the DEA agent.

"We were hoping you might have some idea who might have made this thing." Michael gestured toward the charm.

Silence hung in the air of the little shop. Jessica shifted uncomfortably from one foot to the other. But Michael merely thrust his hands into his pockets and remained impassive.

Finally Simone lifted her gaze to Jessica and studied her face intently. "Well, girl, you used to be good at picking up vibrations from things. Did you get any sort of impression from that?"

"Not much. Just that it's evil." Her cheeks reddened slightly.

"Uh-huh." Simone stuck out a long finger and gingerly poked the artifact. "It sure looks evil, all right." Her nose wrinkled. "It even smells evil. I'd say that whoever made it means serious business." She gave Michael a direct look. "Now you realize that I have to live in this town. So if I get someone in trouble by helping you all, I may have to pay the consequences."

"But you know a lot of people and you understand how to make discreet inquiries," Michael guessed.

Simone turned back to Jessica. "Would finding out about this charm help Aubrey?"

"I'm not sure. Maybe he's beyond help. But if we can get the people who did it to him, it will make me feel some sense of justice."

Simone's face registered empathy and something Jessica couldn't identify. "You understand I can't promise you anything," she finally said. "But I do know a woman who lives on the other side of the city who has a reputation for this sort of thing."

"Oh, Simone, we'd really appreciate it."

"Don't thank me yet." She turned back to Michael. "Maybe you'd better give me your phone number and address, in case I need to get in touch with you."

"Fair enough." He took out a pad of paper and wrote the required information. "Or, if I'm out, you could leave a message with Lieutenant Devine at the local precinct."

"I'm sure not getting mixed up with the police."

"All right, you could call Jessica."

A few moments later they were back in the car.

"How well do you know Simone?" Michael asked.

"At one time we were best friends, but we were out of touch for years until she came over last week."

"She came to see you? How did she know you were in town?"

"The grapevine, I guess."

"Mmm."

"What are you thinking?" She remembered Simone's initial hostility today and then her reluctant agreement to make some inquiries about the charm.

"Oh, nothing really."

Michael started the engine and pulled out into the evening traffic. At the end of a long day, his mind tended to kick into overdrive. It was time to relax a little.

He looked over at Jessica. She was sitting with her head back and her eyes closed. If she were anyone else he was working with on a case, he'd ask her to dinner so they could both unwind. The idea held a lot more appeal than spending an evening in his room or taking in the sights of Bourbon Street alone. But making that kind of overture would just put a further strain on their already tense relationship. Besides, she probably wouldn't accept anyway.

"Shall I drop you back at Aubrey's apartment?" he asked.

Her eyes snapped open and she cast him a sideways glance. "That would be fine." Actually, going home alone to the empty apartment wasn't a prospect she anticipated with great excitement. For a fleeting moment she considered asking Michael to come up for dinner. But that probably wasn't really a very good idea, particularly in light of her declaration in the hallway at the police station.

"Are you going to keep me informed on your progress?" she asked.

"I should hear something tomorrow on the stuff I sent off. I'll probably be over at the university during the day, checking their files and asking some more questions. What if I give you a call around six?"

At least they seemed to have made some improvement in their working relationship. "Couldn't I go to the university with you?"

He shook his head. "No. You've already approached them. I don't want them to think this necessarily has anything to do with Aubrey."

"I guess you're right. But you will call me—for sure."

"I will."

They pulled up in front of her apartment.

For a moment she remained unmoving in her seat. Then she reached for the door handle. Before she could pull it up, he took her hand, his fingers warm and firm over hers.

"Jessica, you know Simone is right about this thing being dangerous. I want you to promise me you won't go poking around in it anymore without clearing your moves with me."

She took in the concerned look on his face. "All right, I promise. But it's going to be hard to wait around all day twiddling my thumbs."

CONSTANCE MCGUIRE glanced at her watch. It was 0800 hours, Eastern Standard Time. Jed Prentiss was already two hours late checking in after a very dangerous assignment, and she'd never known him to miss a deadline.

Outside, a steady rain fell from the overcast sky, making the usually cheery atmosphere of the solarium oppressive. Even the parrots seemed glum. Perhaps they'd caught the general mood of the morning.

Behind her, Amherst Gordon was pacing slowly back and forth, his cane tapping against the flagstones. Connie had to clamp her lips together to keep from issuing a sharp cease-and-desist order.

Last night Michael Rome had supplied the Peregrine Connection with another link in a chain of suppositions that tied a street drug called Dove to a very sinister destabilizing situation in the Caribbean. The Falcon still didn't know how everything fit together, but he'd immediately checked Gilbert Xavier's grant proposal with the National Institutes of Health. The chemist had been working on a psychoactive drug derived from swamp plants, which he hoped would benefit certain psychotic patients. Could that research have been the genesis of Dove?

The Falcon's brow wrinkled. Xavier had disappeared about nine months before Dove hit the streets. Aubrey Ballin had worked for him at Chartres University, and his sister thought someone had helped him OD on Dove to get him out of the way. Too bad Ballin was in no shape for a coherent conversation.

The Falcon shook his head. This whole business was certainly a tangled skein. While he waited for the secure phone to ring, the lines of an obscure Wordsworth poem had been running through his head. He couldn't quite remember the whole thing, but it had to do with plucking a flower from a crannied wall and marveling at how deep the roots went. Michael Rome down in New Orleans had figuratively plucked the flower, and it looked like the roots went all the way back to the Blackstone Clinic on Royale Verde.

The Falcon sighed and turned toward his assistant, realizing that he'd made a decision. "I'd like you to initiate 'missing relative' procedures with the American Consulate on Royale Verde."

"Then you think something's happened to Jed?"

"I don't believe he'd miss a check-in to go sunbathing on the beach."

"Pour yourself a cup of tea, and I'll take care of it."

Gordon pulled out a chair and sat down heavily. There was nothing he could do now but wait.

An hour and a half later Connie confirmed the bad news.

"A man answering Jed's description rented a boat last night at a marina several miles from town. It hasn't been brought back and the owner's turned in a police report. The motorbike he rented is also missing. To make matters even more interesting, someone from the Blackstone Clinic paid Jed's bill and cleared his belongings out of his hotel room."

Gordon swore. "Jed wouldn't pull a disappearing act without letting us know. He's definitely in trouble. You'd better find out who the CIA has down there."

"You're going to bring them in on this?" The Falcon's assistant knew he used that agency's network only as a last resort.

"Since time is of the essence, I'm afraid I have no choice."

After consulting the appropriate computer data base, Connie turned back to her employer. "They have an undercover operative who's an out-island tour guide on Jamaica. His name is George Holcroft."

"Nothing closer than Jamaica? What kind of show are they running down there, anyway?"

"You remember Congress cut their funding for covert operations."

The Falcon grunted. "All right, Holcroft will have to do. Patch me into the satellite link."

Ten minutes later the circuit was in place.

George Holcroft had been making final arrangements to take a group of oil company executives on a deep-sea fishing expedition when the secure phone rang. He swore. When the agency called, he had to drop everything else. Fishing was probably off the schedule for the day. "Yes?" he asked settling his short, compact frame back into his desk chair.

"This is XP 251." Gordon could hear the man on the other end of the line mentally snap to attention.

Holcroft checked the circuit authentication monitor—it really was XP 251! He'd been with the CIA for twelve years and he'd never received a call from that super-secret installation. You had to have fifteen limited-access clearances, which he didn't possess, to even know where it was. But he did know that when you received an order from XP 251, it was to be carried out expeditiously. "What are your instructions, sir?" he questioned.

"We have a possible flap on Royale Verde. It looks as if one of our special operatives, a man named Jed Prentiss, is in serious trouble. He hasn't reported back from a recon mission to the Blackstone Clinic. This morning one of the staff paid his hotel bill and claimed his belongings."

"Blackstone. The place is about as secure as Fort Knox. It's a licensed mental hospital run by Dr. Jackson Talifero. Under local law, he can hold anybody he wants for observation indefinitely."

"And he's operating pretty openly on this. The man must be damned sure of himself." Gordon's brow wrinkled. There was no use sending Holcroft into the same trap that had snared Jed. "Do you have any reliable sources of information at Blackstone?"

"I had one man. He hasn't had much to say lately. But news does travel around the island."

"Mmm. Well, it's urgent that I find out what happened to Prentiss. I want a report from you by twenty-one hundred hours."

The agent glanced at the wall clock. That wasn't a hell of a lot of time, considering it took over an hour to get over to Royale Verde by boat.

"I'll get right on it, sir." After he signed off, Holcroft finished buttoning his print shirt, pushed a hat over his short curly hair, and headed for the marina.

FELIKS GORLOV PUT DOWN his Havana cigar and took an appreciative sip of Madeira. Leaning back in the luxurious velvet wing chair, he looked around in approval at the expensive works of art casually displayed on the walls of Jackson Talifero's living room. Despite the austerity of the Soviet way of life, Gorlov was a man who enjoyed comfort and opulence. The Blackstone Clinic had both of those in abundance. After his initial visit to the clinic, Talifero had invited him to move out here from Queenstown and he'd accepted. Of course, some people might not like being confined to the grounds of a mental hospital—no matter how plush. But even that had its advantages, the Soviet KGB agent had discovered, when the director of the clinic was as resourceful and progressive as Jackson Talifero in providing personal services to honored guests.

Gorlov took another sip of the strong, white drink. Naturally, all of his assignments weren't quite this pleasant. His last diplomatic posting to Madrid had almost cost him a one-way trip to Siberia. He'd been caught dabbling in some private drug deals. But he'd managed to turn the discovery to his advantage by claiming he had intended to remit the bulk of the proceeds to the state all along. The ploy had worked better than he'd dared to hope, possibly because the top boys in the department had been busy with more pressing matters. One of his colleagues in Madrid, a major in the KGB named Aleksei Rozonov, had defected, and a lot of effort had gone into minimizing the damage.

Gorlov himself had laid low and ended up with only a minor reprimand for exceeding his authority and also with quite a bit of secret respect for his resourcefulness. He'd also attained the status of a bona fide KGB drug expert—which was why he had been selected for this particular mission.

He'd spent several days going over Talifero's reports on a new drug called V-22, street name Dove. It had remarkable properties and a huge potential for illegal profit. What's more, Talifero had no qualms about turning the destructive force of the drug on his fellow Americans. It would wreak havoc in every U.S. city where it was distributed. That was just the sort of double punch that Moscow liked to throw.

BLACKSTONE'S DIRECTOR entered the room and Gorlov glanced up.

"Sorry I had to leave you for a few minutes," Talifero apologized. "I needed to look in on a new patient who's recovering from a cerebral accident. He's extremely disoriented and the staff wanted some guidance on appropriate medication." He had no intention of explaining that his men had caught a suspected American agent sneaking on to the grounds.

"Oh, that's quite all right. I was enjoying your art collection." And your wine and cigars.

The doctor smiled expansively. Out of the corner of his eye he took in Gorlov's carefully slicked-down hair, expensive dinner jacket, and black patent leather shoes. With difficulty, he repressed a guffaw. The Russian looked as if he'd stepped out of a 1930s gangster movie. But he needed to play the congenial host with this man and, in fact, handling Gorlov wasn't all that difficult. You simply had to play to his vanity and his singular tastes.

But the Russian was part of a much larger problem that was threatening to get out of hand. What if he couldn't fulfill his bargain with the Kremlin after all? That would mean the end of his political aspirations and maybe even his life. Very few double-crossed Moscow and lived to tell about it.

"I'm sorry your chemist has been so busy. I'm really anxious to meet him," Gorlov remarked.

Talifero chuckled and shook his head as if they were discussing a very intelligent but recalcitrant child. "You know how these dedicated researchers are. He's just about to make a critical breakthrough on his latest project, and he won't be interrupted. But I think I can get him to give us some time in a few days." Crossing to the sideboard, he picked up a crystal decanter and poured himself a generous glass of island rum. "And when do you expect my shipment of merchandise?" he inquired, changing the subject.

"It's already arrived in Cuba. I can guarantee delivery here a week after we have your first payment."

"That should be very shortly. You understand it takes a little bit of time to get that much capital together." Privately he was wondering if he could use his paintings as collateral on a loan—at least until the pipeline to New Orleans was operative again.

Until Gorlov had shown up unannounced, he'd counted on more time to get Xavier back and the drug production going again. And he'd thought the dozen people combing New Orleans would have been able to unearth the little twerp by this time. Now he had to rely on that bitch Moonshadow. He didn't dare think about what would happen if the woman couldn't accomplish that vital task for him.

After taking a stiff swallow of the rum, he turned back to his guest. "But let's not talk about business any more this evening. I'm sure you're tired of reading status reports on V-22. I've arranged a demonstration that will give you some 'hands-on' experience of what the drug can do."

Gorlov's eyes lit up. Ever since he'd first read about Dove and Jackson Talifero, he'd been looking forward to just such an opportunity. He knew quite a bit about the effects of various psychoactive substances. As part of the training for his higher-level job, he'd spent a month on the staff of a secret facility where dissidents "volunteered" for drug experiments. The doctors there were a bunch of typical Soviet prudes. They didn't care whether they destroyed people's minds, but they observed all the proprieties while it was happening. He knew from his dossier on his host that Talifero didn't have any such proletarian qualms.

"As you've undoubtedly read, on certain types of psychotics V-22 has a very rationalizing effect. But on other individuals it sweeps away inhibitions while stimulating strong sexual cravings."

"Yes. I'd be very interested in seeing that."

"Well, I was about to administer the drug to one of our females. There are two possible candidates—both quite attractive, by the way. Perhaps you'd help me decide which one should receive our special attention tonight."

"I'd be honored," Gorlov managed.

"Good. Then come along. I think you'll be impressed with the special facilities we have here."

Chapter Ten

The enclave of seafood restaurants at the edge of Lake Pontchartrain wasn't exactly her milieu, Moonshadow thought as she stepped out of the cab and looked toward Bruning's. But Gilbert Xavier had insisted on meeting her out there. More correctly, she had subtly planted in his mind the compulsion that he needed to meet with her. As insurance, she'd prepared a special charm using a few drops of his blood she'd stored from his visit to her house. Perhaps she should have suggested a place too. But at this stage of the game, it was best to indulge him. So she had dressed conservatively in a dark paisley foulard dress. Instead of covering her hair with her usual African turban, she'd smoothed it back into a neat chignon.

Of course there was precedent for a voodoo priestess coming out to the lake, she reminded herself. In early nineteenth-century New Orleans, the great Marie Laveau had conducted arcane services on these very shores. She considered herself Marie's spiritual descendant with a potential to be even greater than the legendary voodoo queen.

Pausing, she looked around the rather unprepossessing restaurant. Though she'd never patronized the place herself, she remembered that in the old days, Gilbert had come here at least once a week for spicy shrimp and crawfish. Perhaps he'd enjoyed the view as well as the food. The establishment's most notable feature was the wall of windows that offered a panoramic vista of the lake.

Since it was too late for the luncheon crowd and much too early for dinner, the dining room was almost deserted. Someone had turned the TV over the bar to the Cable Christian Network and a sincere-looking fundamentalist was making an impassioned appeal for funds to carry on his mission.

Moonshadow grimaced. Everybody needed money, even her. That's how Jackson Talifero had gotten a hold over her in the first place. The women in her family had scrubbed the floors in the Talifero plantation for generations. But her own relationship with Jackson hadn't been quite that class conscious. In the more liberal atmosphere of the New South, they'd become quite good friends when she was in her late teens and he was over forty. A man that age interested in a teenager. She now saw the relationship for what it was. Then she'd been flattered. He'd even generously offered to finance some of her first business ventures in exchange for samples of her voodoo potions. Young and too heady with her own power to recognize the danger of entailing obligations, she'd accepted.

She cursed the day she'd ever taken his money. The man knew too much about her illegal activities and had threatened on numerous occasions to use the knowledge if she didn't provide him with certain services and information. Now, although he'd moved to Royale Verde and she had a legitimate front behind which to hide her more questionable pursuits, she was still afraid of discovery. Two years ago she'd hoped that telling Talifero about Gilbert Xavier's remarkable talent as a chemist would have gotten him off her back. For a few months the ploy looked as if it was going to work. Now she was in deeper trouble than she'd ever been before. She had the horrible premonition that it was going to take something drastic to bring it all to an end.

The chemist had not yet appeared, so she selected a table in the corner where she could watch the door and ordered a Perrier with lime. Shortly after her drink arrived, she saw him hurry through the door, glancing over his shoulder to make sure no one had followed. The man hadn't even bothered to put on a clean shirt. She made an effort to keep her nose from wrinkling. He reminded her of a mouse scurrying for cover. His apprehension made it more likely that he was going to run right into a trap.

When he saw her sitting calmly in the corner, a look of relief washed over his pasty features.

"You don't know how much I appreciate your meeting me here," he avowed, pulling out a chair and sitting down.

"What can I do to help you, my friend?" she asked solicitously.

"I've decided I can't take this anymore. I've got to turn myself in."

She struggled to contain her astonishment. "To Talifero?"

"God, no! I think I'm only going to be safe if I go to the feds—even if I have to go to prison."

Her gaze narrowed. "The feds? And what were you planning to tell them about me?"

"Oh, I promise to keep your name out of it."

Moonshadow took a sip of her drink. She'd been playing the risky game of stalling Blackstone's director while she toyed with the idea of forming an alliance with Xavier. The maneuver could break Talifero's hold on both of them, but now she wondered if the strategy was really too dangerous. When she'd told Talifero the chemist was about to crack, she'd only half believed her words. Now he seemed to be falling to pieces before her eyes.

A plan began to form in her mind, one that might well save her own skin and would have the added advantage of taking care of several loose ends at the same time.

"What did you want from me?" she asked softly.

"The whole city's full of Talifero's men, and I have to lie low. I was hoping you could arrange a meeting for me with a federal agent."

"Hardly the company I usually keep."

Xavier's face fell.

"But my sources tell me that there is someone in town trying to find out where your drug—Dove—is coming from," she continued. "Perhaps he'd be willing to offer you protection for evidence against Talifero."

Despite his avowed intentions, Xavier couldn't repress a flash of fear. To give himself time to think, he took off his wire-frame glasses and set them on the table, then rubbed the bridge of his nose. He hadn't dreamed the federal government was already on the case.

Moonshadow caught the note of panic in his eyes. She was going to have to act quickly before the man had second thoughts. Repressing her own distaste, she reached out and put her hand gently over his, the red nails a striking contrast to his anemic-looking skin. "Don't worry, Gilbert. Leave everything to me. I think I can even set up a meeting for this evening. You'll feel better once this is all resolved."

"What do I have to do?" God, he wanted to believe she could make everything all right.

"Call me at five and I'll tell you the arrangements."

MICHAEL'S DAY at the university had been rather frustrating. Wearily he inserted the old-fashioned skeleton key in the lock of his hotel room door. The chancellor had made it clear that the university records were not going to be opened to him without a federal warrant. Even with the Falcon's connections, that would take a couple of days to secure—given the sketchy evidence he could provide as justification. The only measure of success he'd salvaged had been at the college library. Perhaps because it was located in New Orleans, Chartres University had a surprisingly complete collection of books on the occult. Even though he still couldn't make heads or tails of the charm he'd left with Jessica's friend, he now knew quite a bit about the subject of voodoo.

Before unlocking his room and removing the Do Not Disturb sign, he carefully inspected the door. Since the Dove case was heating up, he'd left a telltale sign that would alert him if anyone entered the suite while he was gone. He'd used various devices in the past. This one was simply a small straight pin inserted one thumb length above the bottom hinge. If anyone opened the door, it would drop out of position.

After noting that the pin was still in place, he entered his room and shrugged out of his tweed jacket. He was about to toss it onto the bed when he stopped abruptly. In the middle of the blue bedspread was a folded sheet of heavy cream-color paper. But the object on top was what riveted his attention. It was a severed cockscomb pierced with a long thorn tipped in red. More gris-gris, he thought with a sigh. How the devil had the thing gotten in there? he wondered, glancing at the window. His third-floor suite looked out onto Esplanade, and he couldn't quite imagine anyone climbing the drainpipe in broad daylight. Besides, the windows were locked.

Though he wasn't one to bow to superstition, he dislodged the note gingerly from under the talisman and broke the wax seal. Inside, old-fashioned black script slanted across the page.

Mr. X, who holds the key to your search, wants to meet you at the old Lafayette Cemetery, plot 105, at sundown tonight. You must come alone and tell no one. If you disobey, the charm on top of this note will bring you a painful death.

Michael didn't like receiving threatening summonses—or ones that appeared mysteriously in locked rooms. Naturally, anyone with the right tools could have opened the door. And of course, the housekeeping staff had ready access. But noticing the pin and replacing it exactly where he had left it was another matter. Someone wanted him to think it had been accomplished by magic. It was easier to believe a well-trained operative had been given the assignment—which tended to confirm the Falcon's original assessment that the scope of this problem was much larger than it appeared. It also meant that the voodoo charm had only been added for local color and wasn't going to make his coronary arteries start constricting if he didn't follow directions.

He stuffed the note in his shirt pocket, knowing he'd have to deal with it later. Right now there was other business to take care of. Before going to bed last night, he'd made a comprehensive report on the day's activities as a follow-up to the transmission of the letters. Now he needed to see if the Falcon had come up with anything and if he had any more instructions.

After booting up the computer, he accessed a protected electronic mailbox. Immediately a screenful of information appeared on his terminal.

Michael paged down through the amber-and-black text and then went back over the material more carefully. The National Institutes of Health verified his supposition about the direction of Xavier's research. There was a good possibility that, if he could find Xavier, he would find the source of Dove.

The rest of the message concerned Royale Verde and another agent named Jed Prentiss. A good man, Michael recalled. They'd worked together several years ago to bust a Brazilian cocaine connection and had gotten to be friends. Jed had gone off to get a closer look at the Blackstone Clinic and hadn't returned. The Falcon suspected he was either dead or being held captive. Michael cringed at the grim alternatives.

He considered making a hard copy of the transmission. But after the mysterious entry into his room, he decided to rely on his memory. After switching off the computer, he looked at the note again. The Mr. X referred to might well be Xavier. Or somebody wanted him to think so and was setting up a trap. Either way, he was going to have to keep that meeting. But he wasn't stupid enough to heed the warning in the note. In a quick call to the stationhouse, he left a message for Lieutenant Devine explaining where he was going but asking the officer not to interfere, as the informant he was meeting was very nervous. If Michael didn't check in by ten-thirty, the lieutenant was to look for him at burial site 105 in the old Lafayette Cemetery.

He had just strapped on the shoulder holster for his Colt Mark IV when he remembered Jessica. He'd promised to call her around six. Maybe he'd just make it early. Though he let the phone ring half a dozen times, she didn't answer. Glancing impatiently at his watch, he decided he really didn't have time to talk even if she were home. He wanted to get to the cemetery well before the appointed time. He'd just have to get back to her later.

The old Lafayette Cemetery was located on Washington Avenue in the Garden District, an area of large mansions built by the English settlers. Michael parked a block from the main gate and walked along the whitewashed wall, trying to get a feel for the area.

His first stop was at the caretaker's cottage, where he explained that he was a historian doing some research on the unique form of interment in the region. The old man, who introduced himself as Luke Gillespie, probably didn't have much company. Glad to be of assistance, he showed Michael a map, on which he easily located plot 105 near the center of the grounds.

"Feel free to have a look around, but remember that the gates close at sundown," Gillespie warned. "Most folks don't like to get locked in here after dark."

"Me included," Michael assured him. He wouldn't have picked this place for a rendezvous, but that was probably precisely the point.

The lengthening late-afternoon shadows made the cemetery all the more foreboding, Michael thought as he shoved his hands in the pockets of his jeans and ambled off. When he reached a grassy lane between two rows of small mausoleums that resembled miniature Gothic and Romanesque churches, he had to repress the impulse to glance over his shoulder.

He'd never been in a New Orleans cemetery before, but he'd heard about them. Because the soil was marshy, the community had turned to above-ground burial. Poorer families purchased vaults in the graveyard wall or in group memorial buildings. The rich built their own. The more sturdy were of stone. A good number, however, were constructed of local brick covered with plaster, which tended to crumble with age.

Michael made a wide circle around plot 105, verifying that this section of the cemetery was deserted—except for an infirm-looking white-haired couple who had come to put a red rose in a vase in front of a granite sepulcher.

He made a careful inspection of the tomb. It was a small granite building with a Gothic roof and the usual white slab covering the entrance. Michael could see nothing out of the ordinary about the tomb. After checking out the area immediately around it, he withdrew to a spot where he could observe anyone approaching. It was now almost dark, and the old couple didn't see him as they shuffled by on the path heading toward the front gate.

The sky was overcast, blocking out most of the pinks and oranges of the sunset. As the last rays of light sank toward the horizon, the temperature dropped several degrees, and a little breeze sprang up, rustling the leaves in the tall trees that dotted the area. The faint swishing sound was the only noise he could hear. The isolation was a bit unnerving, and he couldn't help thinking about all the ghost stories he'd heard around rodeo campfires late at night.

He waited five, ten, fifteen minutes, his back pressed against cold stone. Dim lights at the cemetery's major crossroads came on, but they were few and far between. What was Xavier waiting for? he wondered. Or was this all a wild goose chase designed to frighten him off the case?

He was straining his ears trying to hear some sound of life when uncertain footfalls from the direction of the gate drew his attention. Pressing back against the crypt, he watched a short, thin man approach the designated plot and look around nervously. Then he coughed, as if that might attract attention.

Michael tensed, listening for evidence that the man was being followed. There was none. Nor could he see anything. But in this gloom, that wasn't surprising.

Drawing his gun, he waited several minutes longer before calling out. "All right, put your hands in the air and turn around."

The man froze, then obeyed. "I can't see you," he complained.

"That's the way I want it."

"Are you from the DEA?"

"Yes."

"Thank God."

"Who are you, and what do you want?" Michael questioned.

"Gilbert Xavier. I want to turn myself in."

"Why?"

"I need protection." Xavier's voice rose pleadingly.

Michael stepped forward and frisked the little man. He wasn't carrying a weapon. Up close, he looked like a frightened weasel. "And why should I be interested in you?"

"I'm the chemist who made the street drug called Dove." He eyed Michael's gun. "Could you put that away?"

"All right."

Michael holstered the weapon. "Go on."

"What do you want to know?"

"Who do you want protection from?"

The words came out in a rush like the confession of a mortal sin. "Jackson Talifero. He lured me down to Royale Verde. Offered me a lab, test subjects, anything I wanted. I thought the man was interested in finding new drug therapies for certain psychoses. But that's not his purpose at all. He wants to produce Dove to finance a takeover of the island. He's a devil, a madman. I got away, but he has thugs out looking for me. I don't want to go back. That's why I want to turn myself in to you."

Though the information was riveting, Michael's face remained impassive.

"Don't you believe me?" Xavier questioned.

Michael didn't answer. "How did you come up with this particular meeting place?"

"She suggested it."

"Who?"

"The priestess. The one who first came to me at the university with the idea of purifying some of her plant compounds."

"What priestess? What are you talking about?"

"She told me she was going to contact you."

"We didn't meet."

He was about to ask another question when the white slab in front of tomb 105 gave way with a resounding crash. Blinding light spilled forth from the interior. One of Michael's hands went to his eyes, the other reached for the gun under his arm, but he couldn't see to shoot. Xavier screamed but the sound was choked off abruptly, as if someone had wrapped a hand around his windpipe.

Whoever had been in the crypt was counting heavily on the element of surprise and the blinding light. Dark, crouching figures came at him, but Michael could see nothing distinctly. He tried to turn away from the brilliance, but a large hand grabbed his throat, pulling him back. Instinctively he kicked out with his foot and felt his shoe connect with soft flesh. He had the satisfaction of hearing a low groan as his would-be assailant went down.

"Watch it," an excited voice warned. "He fights like Jhoon Rhee."

Michael recognized his old friend Lonnie. He also heard the shuffle of several pairs of feet closing in around him. He turned away from the light, but it didn't help much. It was as if a hundred flash bulbs had gone off in his face. Still, his hand groped toward the holster.

"Pull the gun and you're a dead man, Rome," another voice advised. "We have you boxed in."

He was still too blinded to see them, but somehow he doubted his adversaries were bluffing.

"Toss your piece on the ground—nice and easy—and put your hands up," Lonnie ordered.

Under the circumstances there seemed no alternative. "I'll surrender if you turn off the spots."

"You don't have a choice." But someone cut all but a dim light.

That gave him a chance, at least. Maybe, when his vision cleared, he could fight them off and rescue Xavier, if the chemist were still alive. With a sigh of resignation, Michael tossed the gun onto the ground and raised his hands. Immediately one of the thugs behind him aimed a kick at the small of his back. He pitched forward, unable to see the ground, yet he was able to break his fall with the palms of his hands.

"That's something on account for what I owe you," Lonnie grated.

Michael groaned. Let them think he'd been hurt.

Lonnie's foot kicked him in the ribs, turning him over. It was all Michael could do to keep from grabbing the bastard's leg and sending him sprawling. But his vision was coming back. He could see five or six men around him. Two looked like bouncers. In any case, as soon as the bright spots cleared, he was going to attack.

In the background, Xavier found his voice; but it was half an octave higher than it had been two minutes ago. "What are you going to do to us?" he quavered.

"You're going back to continue your vacation on Royale Verde. The narc's going to have a quiet rest here."

Michael didn't like the sound of that. If he were going to be dead either way, he might as well go down fighting. As one of the bouncers leaned down toward him, his body tensed. Grabbing the man's massive shoulders, he flipped him over in such a way that the thug landed between him and the rest of the group.

In the darkness Lonnie cursed. "Cut out the fun and games, Rome," he advised.

The man Michael had surprised came back to life. In the next moment they were wrestling on the ground. Others circled the adversaries, ready to take Michael on if he emerged victorious. He didn't get a chance to find out how many challenges he could have withstood.

"Hold him still for a second, Jack," a voice commanded. The bouncer redoubled his efforts, pinning Michael to the ground. He was getting ready to throw off the hold when he heard a whooshing sound and felt a sharp stinging pain in his hip. His body went limp and, almost simultaneously, his senses dulled. It was an effort to hold on to consciousness.

In the next moment Lonnie was squatting beside him. Reaching down, he took Michael's slack jaw in his hand and jerked his face up. "You're going to die, Rome. But it's going to be slow. You'll have a lot of time to think about what you got yourself involved in down here."

Michael's vision swam. They had given him some sort of powerful paralytic. When he tried to squeeze his fingers into a fist, they remained lifeless at his side.

"We're going to give you a proper New Orleans-style burial. But it won't be in the vault we came out of. That one's too nice and dry and airy because it's been a drug drop for the last year. No, we're going to put you in a real crypt in the old part of the graveyard."

Lonnie snarled out an order and the other bouncer picked Michael up like a sack of grain and slung him over his shoulder. His head banged against the man's back with every step, but he didn't have enough strength in his neck to stop the motion. The helplessness brought a feeling of panic. They were going to bury him alive, and there was nothing he could do about it.

Finally he was deposited roughly on the ground. When Lonnie leaned down again, Michael could only stare back blankly. "How do you feel now, Mr. DEA hot shot? In case you're wondering, you've had a low dose of phenodryl. It will start to wear off in a couple of hours so you can enjoy all the sensations of suffocating. Pleasant dreams."

Michael felt himself hoisted up again. Though his senses were dulled, he could tell that he had been set down on a cold slab. The clouds had dissipated so that he could see the open dark sky. The points of light were like comets with tails. Though he strained to see more clearly, they slowly faded from his vision. Then abruptly the stars were gone and he felt suffocating dankness close in around him. Stone grated against stone just before he was encased in total blackness. He tried to curse, but nothing came out of his mouth.

Chapter Eleven

Jessica threw down the science fiction novel she'd been staring at for the past fifteen minutes. She couldn't concentrate on slug invaders from Titan when she was worried about Michael.

It was very possible that he'd called her early. At least the phone had been ringing when she'd come up the steps around five-thirty with a heavy bag of groceries. By the time she'd unlocked the door and made it into the kitchen, there was nothing on the other end of the line but a dial tone.

After wasting ten minutes debating whether she should bother him, she fished his number out of her pocketbook and dialed. There was no answer, and the woman at the desk finally volunteered that Mr. Rome had left in a hurry just minutes before. He might have been keeping an urgent appointment at the university. But somehow Jessica didn't think so.

Two hours later she couldn't shake the conviction that Michael was in some sort of trouble. Was she operating on intuition or raw emotion? she asked herself. And why should her emotions be tied up with Michael Rome's safety? She barely knew the man. Yet when fate had catapulted her into his arms, he had kept her from falling into the abyss. Though neither one of them had been able to acknowledge it, the experience had forged a bond between them. He'd cared about what happened to her that night, and she cared very strongly about what happened to him now.

She'd been closer to him than she had to most other human beings. Did that give her some sort of special access to his consciousness? Could she conjure up a vision of where he'd gone? Taking a deep breath, she closed her eyes and cleared the screen of her mind. When it was blank, she brought a picture of Michael into focus and watched as he closed the door of his hotel room and walked down the curved staircase to the lobby. She could see him getting into his car and driving away. But the images had no reality. She knew she was simply manufacturing them from her own imagination. For a moment she admitted defeat. She was about to get up and try the phone again when a feeling of helpless terror so powerful swept over her that she gasped and clutched the arms of her chair as if to anchor herself to the here and now.

The room around her swirled into blackness. Her skin grew clammy, and her sense of fear increased. It was as if damp, suffocating walls were closing in around her. For a moment it was a struggle simply to draw air into her lungs. She might have screamed if she hadn't been panting for breath. Then as quickly as it had come over her, the terrible sensation was gone. The room snapped back into focus. Disoriented, Jessica looked around. She felt drained, shaken, and frustrated. What she had just experienced had not been a product of her own imagination. Somehow it was connected to Michael. She was as sure of that as she'd been sure the image of his getting into the car came from her own mind. Dread surged through her. He was in trouble and she had to go to him. Quickly—if she could only figure out where he was.

Her head was throbbing as she tried to think about what to do. Would Michael have gone off on a dangerous mission without informing anyone? She couldn't imagine that he'd be that remiss. But who would he tell? The question brought to mind Lieutenant Devine. She got up and pulled a phone book from one of the lower kitchen cabinets. But after she'd located the precinct number, her hand hesitated over the dial, as she thought about opening herself up to the kind of ridicule she'd experienced twelve years ago? Yet, she had to do it for Michael.

The lieutenant was still at his desk when the phone rang. "Devine speaking," he answered.

"This is Jessica Duval, Michael Rome's associate."

"Oh, yes, Ms. Duval. Has Michael checked in with you?"

"Actually, I think I missed his call. But I'm worried about him."

"Did he leave you a message about the old Lafayette Cemetery?"

Her heart skipped a beat, but she forced her voice to remain calm. "He told me to call you if he didn't get back to me," she improvised.

"Yes, well, his message said the informant he's meeting there is nervous. He wants me to stay out of it."

Jessica closed her eyes for a second. "Lieutenant, I'm *sure* Michael is in trouble. We have to go over there."

"Now wait a minute. He was very clear on that. He said to wait until ten-thirty."

"That will be too late!"

"Really, Ms. Duval, I don't have to tell you Michael Rome is a very competent agent. He knows what he's doing."

Jessica fought down a wave of nausea. "Lieutenant, did Michael tell you why he was working with me on this case?"

"What do you mean?"

She had to force out the words. "I'm a psychic. I provided him with some important leads. Tonight I had a feeling of being closed in, suffocating. I know it was coming from Michael. If you won't help, I'm going over there alone."

"To a graveyard? Alone? At night?"

"Yes."

Devine sighed. He'd been looking forward to going home to a Hungry Man TV dinner and a bag of microwave popcorn. He'd been too busy to pay much attention to Ms. Duval when they'd met before. He wished he had. Right now, on the face of it, she sounded like a nut—but a sincere nut, he had to admit. So she claimed to be a psychic. He'd never worked with one. But what he'd told her about Michael Rome was still true. The man was a seasoned professional, and if he'd gotten some leads from Jessica Duval, maybe she knew something that he didn't.

"Okay, give me your address," he said. "I'll be right over to pick you up."

"Thank you, Lieutenant."

Fifteen minutes later Hugh Devine pulled up in front of the house. Jessica, who had been waiting on the steps, stood up and looked uncertainly at the black-and-white police car. The last time he'd seen her, her outfit had projected a professional image.

This evening her appearance told another story. She was wearing jeans and a dark turtleneck. With her tousled hair and pale face, she seemed very young and vulnerable. She'd told him she was in a hurry, yet her feet seemed to be weighted down with lead as she approached the police car.

He was definitely getting mixed signals from her. Had she changed her mind after all? Or maybe she felt uncomfortable working with the police. Many people did. When she opened the door, she hesitated for a moment and then slid onto the vinyl seat and closed the door.

"I think we'd better stop by Michael's hotel room," she said, her voice not quite steady.

"I thought you were in a hurry to get to the cemetery?"

"I am. But I have the feeling we should stop at his place first to look for—to look for..." She glanced down at the hands, clasped tightly in her lap. "I don't know exactly for what. But I know it's there."

"Do you have Rome's address?"

She supplied it but didn't say anything else on the drive to the hotel.

Devine debated asking her what was wrong or maybe chucking the whole thing. But he was curious, and Ms. Duval's obvious anxiety had aroused his detective's instincts.

Jessica was glad Devine was with her to speak to the woman at the desk. His voice and manner conveyed gruff authority. In surprisingly short order, they were standing in the middle of Michael's suite. Jessica peered around, feeling foolish that she didn't know what she was searching for and yet confident that she would find it.

When her gaze collided with the cockscomb on the dresser, she drew in her breath sharply.

"Another voodoo charm?" the lieutenant questioned, following the direction of her eyes.

Jessica nodded and tiptoed over. Like the other talisman, this one fairly radiated a sense of evil. She didn't want to touch it, but she knew she must.

"Lieutenant," she said, "I have to ask a favor."

"Yeah?" He was prepared for almost anything now.

She sat down on the Victorian couch. "I know this is going to sound strange, but could you pick up the charm and put it in my hand?"

"Why?"

"I had a reaction to the last one. I'd rather be sitting down."

Devine shrugged. Jessica forgot to breathe as he carried the talisman toward her. Silently she opened her hand, palm up. This time there was no burning sensation. But the moment the shriveled piece of animal tissue touched her flesh, her senses began to swirl and she slumped sideways on the couch.

Devine had been watching her with guarded interest. Now he sprang reflexively into action. "What?" he snapped, trying to snatch the charm away. But her fingers closed tightly around the grisly artifact. She didn't feel her body jerk convulsively as the thorn embedded in the cockscomb pierced her flesh. All she knew was that her body and mind were somehow being torn apart. She was here on the couch but she was also in a dark, musty enclosed place at the old Lafayette Cemetery, her limp form resting heavily on a cold slab of stone. A tomb—she was in a tomb. The smell of death made her retch. But then she was also somewhere else. In a dimly lit hospital room, the hot humid air weighing

down on her immobile limbs, her mind screaming silently
for help.

Another man, not Michael. Jed. The name came to her.
He was in grave danger. But he was too far away for her to
reach. Michael was here. In the musty, smothering darkness. She had to focus on that.

"For God's sake. Ms. Duval—Jessica. For God's sake,
snap out of it." Devine's urgent voice drifted toward her as
though from a dream.

Her mind refused to acknowledge the interruption. She
had to concentrate on where Michael was. Not the enclosed
place. The exterior. She must look for some landmark to tell
her where he was. Doggedly she tried to bring the total scene
into focus the way she had with the bookstore, or with Harley's. But the graveyard was dark and shadowy. She could
see rows and rows of little buildings that all looked the same
except for a few obscure architectural details. But in front
of one an onyx stone angel was sitting pensively with its chin
resting on her hand. It was near Michael.

Michael. She was brought back more sharply to him
again. He was trapped, suffocating, the charnel house all
around him. She had to get to him before the black angel
carried him away.

Her eyes snapped open, and the anxious face of Lieutenant Devine swam into her vision.

"What in hell happened to you?" he demanded, uncurl-
ing her fingers from around the cockscomb. A drop of
blood glistened in her palm.

"Don't worry about me." Her voice was gritty. "He's the
one that's dying," she whispered.

"Who?"

"Jed. No, Michael." Why was a man named Jed mixed
up in this?

Devine stared at her chalky face. "Let me get something
for your hand."

She squeezed the injury, bringing fresh blood to the surface to cleanse the wound. "This will have to do. Please,

Lieutenant. Don't you understand? We've got to get to the cemetery right now.''

IN HIS DANK PRISON Michael's senses returned slowly. His arms and legs had the pins-and-needles feeling of having been asleep. Only he felt as if they'd been moribund for a hundred years. It took intense concentration to even move his fingers.

Lonnie had told him what drug they'd injected him with. Phenodryl. He recognized the name. It was a powerful animal tranquilizer. Illegal. Used by poachers who stole stock for zoos. A large dose would keep a water buffalo quiet for hours or reduce a man to a near comatose state. It must have slowed down his metabolism. But the fact that he was beginning to think clearly again meant they hadn't given him very much. The recovery process, however, was unpredictable. It still might be hours before he got back the use of his large muscles.

His sense of smell and touch hadn't been totally obliterated. Now they returned. He didn't know about his hearing or vision. His eyes strained against the darkness. Either he was blind or not a sliver of light was getting into the vault. If the latter were true, that probably meant no air was getting in either.

He could feel cold and dampness seeping up from beneath the stone platform on which he lay. His mind served up a piece of information he'd rather not have remembered. These old sepulchers were designed to be used over and over. When the tomb was needed again, the previous body was simply pushed to the back where it fell into a pit. That probably explained the fetid smell rising from below him.

If he could have vomited, he probably would have. If he thought any more about his desperate situation, he would go crazy. Was there any hope that he might be rescued? Certainly not from the Peregrine Connection. He hadn't even told the Falcon where he was going.

How ironic that he should die in a crypt in New Orleans, of all places. He'd parachuted behind enemy lines and crawled through tunnels in Southeast Asia, survived days in a rubber boat in shark-infested waters when drug smugglers had blown up his craft off the Florida Keys... But then he'd been able to take some action to save himself. Now he could only lie here like a corpse on a slab in the morgue.

Devine would probably show up after ten-thirty, but he would go to plot 105, find the dope warehouse, and assume they'd taken him somewhere else. That left Jessica. Until the voodoo charm had burned her hand, he'd scoffed at her psychic ability. Now his mind clung to the tenuous hope that it might save him.

The image of her that came to him was not from the last time he'd seen her. He wanted to escape from this vault. The only route was through his imagination. He remembered the way she'd looked that morning when he'd awakened next to her. The covers had slipped down, exposing her creamy shoulders and the tops of her high, firm breasts. Even as he'd admired her beauty, he'd noted the innocence and exhaustion that mingled on her sleeping features. A feeling of protectiveness had welled up inside his chest at the same time he'd acknowledged that the lower part of his body was hardening with a more basic response. He'd had to climb out of bed to keep from pulling her into his arms. Since then his emotions and his intellect had been at war. Keeping her at a distance was imperative for his own peace of mind. But so was bringing her close—and never more than at this moment.

But not even thoughts of Jessica could hold reality at bay. The air in his prison was getting thicker. Every breath was becoming an effort.

Jessica, Jessica, Jessica. Despite his conviction that the effort was probably useless, he called out to her in silent entreaty. That was the only hope he had to cling to.

HUGH DEVINE POUNDED on the door to the caretaker's cottage, wondering if the cemetery custodian was as dead as everybody else around there. Finally Luke Gillespie appeared at the door in a gray chenille robe. His eyes were half closed, but the lieutenant's police badge woke him up in a hurry.

"We need to find plot 105 on the double," Devine explained.

"There was a fellow around here earlier looking for that plot. Young guy."

Quickly Jessica described Michael.

"Yeah, that's him, but he said he'd leave the grounds before I closed up."

"Was there anyone else around?" Devine questioned.

"Mourners, you know."

The fear that they were wasting precious time clawed at the inside of Jessica's chest. Why were they standing there talking? She peered into the darkened cemetery, wanting to charge off in search of Michael. She'd never find her way by herself.

"We need to find the black angel," she said.

Devine shot her a quizzical look. What was she talking about?

But she had already turned to the old man in the bathrobe. "Do you know a grave that has a statue of an angel carved from black stone?"

Gillespie's wrinkled brow creased even more deeply. "Let me think about that. Angels are pretty popular around here. But most of them are white marble or granite. I do recollect an onyx one, though."

Jessica wanted to shake his bony shoulders. "Where?"

He pursed his lips thoughtfully. "It's in that section." He pointed toward the northwest.

"Do you have a flashlight?" she asked.

"Sure do. A good one. Sometimes we need it when we have vandals around here at night," the old man said, turning back towards his little cottage.

"Bring a crowbar too," Devine called out.

In a few moments the man had returned with the required items.

Jessica snapped the powerful torch on and moved it experimentally back and forth. The beam cast a strong stream of brilliance into the eerie darkness, illuminating the rows of little structures that made up the necropolis.

Devine sighed. Logic argued that they check plot 105 first. But he'd seen what had happened to Jessica back in Michael's room. Maybe she was operating on something stronger than logic. Even without supporting evidence, it was almost impossible to discount the sense of conviction she conveyed.

"I can show you the quickest way," Gillespie volunteered.

"Thank you."

They started off at a much brisker pace than would have been possible on their own. It wasn't hard to keep up with the old man, yet Jessica found her breath coming in short pants.

"Ms. Duval, are you all right?" Devine questioned.

"I don't know. Michael isn't." Please keep him alive, she prayed silently.

Though it seemed as if they tramped through the darkness for hours, it couldn't have been more than minutes. Finally the caretaker swung the light, illuminating the angel. Still panting, Jessica stared at it and then around at the nearby crypts. They were in the area of the cemetery she had seen in her vision, but she hadn't a clue in which direction to turn.

"Michael," she called. "Michael, can you hear me? Where are you?"

There was no answer in the silent graveyard.

GOD, DID HE HEAR HER calling him, or was that just lack of oxygen making his thoughts giddy? Jessica, Jessica. No sound came out of his mouth. But could he move somehow? Give her a signal? With every bit of strength he could muster, he struggled to lift his foot. The heel of his shoe scraped against rough stone.

"HE'S SOMEWHERE over there." Jessica pointed to the right of the angel. "He needs me. Right now."

Devine moved in that direction. A faint scraping noise caught his attention. "Rome, if that's you, do that again."

They strained their ears. For long moments there was only silence. Finally the noise was repeated, but more faintly.

"It's this one," Devine shouted, slapping the granite wall of a Gothic tomb.

Jessica was at Devine's side, flattening her hands against the cold stone. Somehow it was like a direct connection to Michael. She could feel the life slipping out of his body. "He's barely alive. We've got to get the vault open." Seeking closer contact, she pressed her cheek against the granite. "Michael, hold on. We're here. We'll get you out."

Gillespie offered the crowbar. "We have to open these things every time there's a funeral. There's a notch at the bottom of the slab. I'll show you where to put it, but my back's too weak to do you any good. It usually takes two men."

Devine swore under his breath. A few inches of stone separated him from the trapped man, but if he couldn't move it, it might as well be a mile.

Wielding the instrument as directed, he pressed his 250 pounds of weight down. In the light of the torch, Jessica could see his muscles bulge and perspiration break out on his wide forehead. The heavy slab groaned but didn't move. Putting his foot on the bar, the officer pressed down with all his strength. The stone still didn't give.

Jessica sprang to his side and added her weight to the lever. The slab protested and then fell forward. Both Jessica and Devine instinctively jumped out of the way. The massive rectangle broke as it hit the steps in front of the vault. Before the dust settled, Devine was pushing his shoulders inside the opening. He began to cough, but at the same time he pulled the slab forward. Michael tumbled out onto the ground.

Jessica knelt over him, listening for the sound of his breathing and feeling the pulse in his neck. Thank God, she thought, he was alive.

She looked at his face. His lips were blue from the cold and lack of oxygen. His eyes were open and staring at her.

"Are you all right?" she whispered.

His lids closed for a second and then reopened. She could see that he was straining to move his lips.

"It's all right. Don't talk," she reassured him. "You're safe now."

Devine knelt on the other side of the man they'd literally snatched from the grave. She followed his hands as they made a quick assessment of injury, checking for broken bones or wounds.

"He's in one piece. Nothing broken," the officer reported. "My guess is he's been drugged. It looks as though they've given him a paralytic."

Michael's lips formed the word *phenodryl* but neither one of them knew what he was trying to say.

Devine took off his jacket and laid it across Michael's chest.

Jessica pushed back his matted hair and uncovered an abrasion. Her fingers stroked tenderly down his cheek. His gaze was focused on her face, and she smiled reassuringly.

"Do you want me to call an ambulance?" Gillespie questioned.

"Please." She threaded her fingers through Michael's, pressing them tightly, trying to give him her warmth and comfort. Was it her imagination, or did he return the pressure?

It was a joy to be able to touch him and know that he was alive. Thank God they'd been in time! Tears glistened in her eyes. She'd been through some terrifying experiences, but she'd never been more afraid than when she'd thought she wasn't going to find Michael Rome.

Chapter Twelve

"How are we feeling this evening, Mr. Prentiss?" the solicitous voice asked.

So it hadn't been a nightmare. The man was real. Cautiously Jed opened his eyes. It was still an effort. The lids felt as if they'd been glued down. He found himself staring at a tall white-haired man dressed in a linen suit. His face was carefully neutral, yet Jed detected an edgy look around the eyes that made him wary.

"Do you remember meeting me when you were first brought here? I'm Dr. Talifero."

When Jed tried to answer, his voice came out in a harsh growl.

"It may be a bit rusty at first, but that's to be expected in these cases," the doctor reassured.

"What...am...I...doing here?" Jed managed.

"I explained all that before, but a section of your memory has apparently been distorted. In addition to your bruised ribs, you've had a stroke. But I won't be able to tell how much brain damage you've suffered until we can do an evaluation."

Brain damage? The man in the bed struggled to sit up and fell back. The IV tube connected to his arm swayed dangerously. Glucose, or something more potent?

Talifero came to his side, steadying the plastic line. "Just take it easy. I'll get the nurse to come in and crank up your bed in a few moments. But since you're awake, I'd like to talk now."

Jed nodded cautiously. He tried to shift his position but every move made his chest ache more.

"I've found with cases like yours that the last forty-eight hours preceding the cerebral accident are sometimes wiped out or even replaced with false memories. What I'd like you to do is tell me what you recollect from that period. If it will help, you can even start with what you remember before you came to Royale Verde."

The patient licked his lips. His recent memories were very clear now. If they were accurate, telling them to Talifero would be suicidal. But suppose the man was speaking the truth? Then what? The effort to puzzle it out made his head throb. Brain damage? Or the effect of a drug?

"Mr. Prentiss, I can't help you if you're not willing to help yourself," Talifero said encouragingly, yet there was an element in his voice that suggested this interview held considerable importance to him.

It would certainly be a novel interrogation technique to convince an agent that he'd had a stroke and get him to spill his guts in the name of therapy, Jed thought. But was he an agent? Or was that some fantasy his injured mind had glommed on to as a way to stave off reality? He'd just have to try and play for time until he could sort the truth from the fiction. "I was on vacation—fishing—when I got lost in the dark."

Talifero's jaw tightened. "I'm afraid that may not be entirely accurate. My contacts in town report that you were asking rather probing questions for a casual tourist."

"I'm thinking about buying beach property down here," Jed clarified.

"Let's try another approach. Can you remember any of your friends or relatives? Is there anyone we should notify about your accident?"

The question was probably a trap, but was there some way he could use it to contact the Falcon? There was the dead-drop post-office box that Peregrine used. But until he knew the situation better here, he didn't even dare try that. "No one," he answered.

The doctor gave him a thoughtful look. "Mr. Prentiss, I'm glad you were planning on a long stay in the area. However, I'm not sure you realize it, but this is a psychiatric sanitarium, and I have the absolute power to keep patients here as long as I feel it necessary. If you can't provide us any clues to your real purpose on Royale Verde, you're not going to get any better, and I'll have no option but to transfer you to the disturbed wing where the care is, of necessity, a little less gentle. Why don't you see if that prospect will jog your memory? We'll talk again later."

Before the patient could answer, he turned on his Italian leather heels and left the room.

IT WAS FOUR in the morning before the resident who had examined Michael was willing to release him. The doctor wanted to keep him in the hospital for twenty-four hours for observation, but Michael flatly refused.

"With phenodryl there might be some aftereffects, like muscle spasms, headache, or dizziness," the intern argued. "And I can't take responsibility for letting you leave unless someone else will agree to stay with you for at least the next twelve hours."

Jessica, who had been waiting outside the curtained-off cubicle, heard Michael swear.

"You can sign him out to me," she volunteered.

The doctor parted the curtains, and she noted that Michael was back in his somewhat-the-worse-for-wear street clothes. He looked up as she entered. "I want to be alone." God, he'd been buried alive. That was bad enough, but he'd been stupid enough to walk into a trap and then lose the man who was the key to solving this damn case.

"Staying by yourself is completely unacceptable," the resident insisted.

Michael sighed. "All right then, just let me out of here. And don't order a wheelchair to take me to the door. I can walk."

After hours of lying in the tomb and then on this damn examining table, he wanted to move around. But an orderly had to help him off the table and he could only lift his legs enough to shuffle as he made his way down the deserted corridor.

As Jessica slowed her pace to match his, she ached to take his arm and steady him. But she understood he was too independent to accept any help. She'd been elated at his quick physical recovery, yet the physician's efforts to get him to talk about the ordeal had been rebuffed. He was like a clam whose shell snapped closed every time its vulnerable interior was probed. She suspected that meant the experience had been traumatic even for someone as calloused as Michael Rome.

In the cab, he moved to the corner near the window and turned his head away from her. When they drew up in front of the hotel, he opened the door and got out as quickly as possible. "Okay, you've done your duty. Go home."

She gave him an incredulous look. "You've got to be kidding." After stuffing some bills into the driver's hand, she hopped out and slammed the door behind her.

His look was thunderous as he started off toward the dimly lit lobby. Even in the last twenty minutes he could feel that his physical strength had increased. But mentally he'd been barely holding himself together for hours, and he didn't know how much longer he could do it. He certainly didn't want an audience if he came unglued.

However, Jessica was right beside him as he inserted the key in the lock. If his reflexes had been up to par, he would have closed the door before she could get inside. Instead, she came into the sitting room.

"Can't you leave me alone!" he rasped.

She put a gentle hand on his arm. "You've been through a horrible ordeal. It's all right to need help."

"Don't touch me!"

"Why not?"

"I've been in a grave, for God's sake. All I want to do is stand under the shower and scrub the stench of death off."

She put her arms around him and he started to shake. Her embrace tightened. For long minutes she simply held him, willing him to accept what comfort she could give. But he was still fighting himself and couldn't accept the solace she offered. "Jessica, get out of here," he tried one more time. But the note of conviction in his voice was missing.

"Let's get you into the shower."

"I'm a big boy. I can do it by myself."

"Okay, but if you need me, I'll be right outside."

"Suit yourself."

The bathroom was in a little hall off the sitting room. "Don't lock the door."

He didn't answer, but he didn't snap the catch either.

Jessica sat down on the couch. She was exhausted from the mental anguish of trying to find him and the waiting at the hospital. She listened for the sound of the water, but he hadn't turned it on.

"Are you all right?"

The muffled reply could have been either yes or no.

Tentatively she turned the knob and peered inside. Michael had taken off his shoes and shirt and unzipped his pants, but he was leaning against the wall, his wide shoulders and head pressed backward as if he needed the contact with something solid. Her eyes took in the familiar expanse of his naked chest and then traveled back to his half-closed eyes. His face was drained of color.

"Michael, what's wrong?"

"Dizzy. It's going away."

"Maybe a shower isn't such a good idea right now."

"Don't you understand, damn it? I've got to get clean!"

"Yes, I understand." She reached behind the curtain and turned on the water, adjusting the temperature. Then she turned back to Michael. "Let me help you finish getting undressed."

Before he could object, she hooked her thumbs in the belt loops of his pants and pulled them down. After a moment's hesitation she did the same with his briefs, being careful to appear as impersonal as the doctor who had examined him in the emergency room. Yet she was vividly aware of every muscle in his strong, trim body. There was a bruise at his waist and another on his ribs.

Turning quickly away, she held the curtain aside and waited while he stepped under the spray of water. She could see more bruises on his back. So they'd roughed him up before they'd shoved him in that crypt. Remembering the way he'd fought in Lonnie's living room, she wondered how many men it had taken to overpower him.

But he wasn't in fighting shape now. His foot slipped and he caught himself by grabbing the shower head. Reaching inside, she steadied his shoulder. She should never have let him get in there. He might fall and hit his head.

When his body hit the side of the shower, she winced. This was ridiculous, she thought, reaching for the buttons of her own shirt. Stripping down to her bra and panties, she stepped behind the curtain.

Water was streaming down Michael's face, but his half-closed eyes snapped open. "What the hell are you doing?"

"Keeping you from killing yourself in here."

"I should never have let you come home with me."

"You couldn't prevent it." Michael had readjusted the water so that it was hotter. Where it hit her body, it almost burned. "Listen, if you're worried about your reputation as a macho loner, it's safe with me. I'm not going to tell anyone about this."

He gave her a scathing look. "If I had the strength, I'd kick you out of here." Then he pointedly looked away from her. It was obvious that the next best thing to getting rid of her was pretending she wasn't there.

If the performance was designed to make her angry, it didn't work. She knew he was in pain, if not physically, then mentally. She wanted to fold him into her arms again. Knowing that he still wouldn't allow that, she picked up the bar of soap and worked up a lather in her hands. Then she began to smooth her fingers across his chest. After a few strokes he closed his eyes and some of the tension went out of his shoulders. Encouraged, she washed his neck and chest. The feel of his firm skin sliding under her soapy hands was erotic, but she tried not to think about it. She worked up more lather and coasted her soapy palms across his flat belly but didn't dare go any lower. "Turn around and let me do your back," she directed instead, her voice husky.

He shifted his position, bracing his hands against the wall. Now that he was facing away from her, she allowed herself the luxury of drinking in the uncompromising masculinity of his form. Muscles corded in his arms and shoulders, and his body tapered down to a narrow waist and tightly rounded buttocks. Her soapy fingers trembled slightly as they slid across his waterslick skin. The bruises she skimmed over with the barest touch.

"Bend your head back so I can do your hair," she instructed.

For a moment he hesitated, then complied. She poured out a dollop of his green shampoo into her palm and inhaled the fresh pine scent. Her fingers combed through his hair, appreciating its slightly rough texture. When she worked the lather into his scalp, he muttered something unintelligible.

He straightened and thrust his head directly under the stream from the shower. The water seemed to have had a reviving effect. She could see new tension in the set of his shoulders.

"I can finish this by myself."

"I don't think that's very smart."

"Believe me, it's very smart." There was a gritty edge to his voice. "You might have come in here with good intentions, but I'm afraid having an almost naked woman in the shower running her hands over my body is more than I can handle right now."

"I'm sorry," she tried to apologize

"If you won't get out, I will." He pulled the curtain aside and stepped from the cubicle, leaving her under the cascading water. She took a steadying breath. Touching him had aroused her too.

Reaching out, she turned off the taps. She was now standing in the shower in her dripping underwear. "At least give me something to dry off with."

A large hand thrust inside the curtain and offered a white towel. Jessica hung it over the faucets while she removed her soaking panties and bra. Then she wrapped the bath sheet around her body. When she stepped out of the shower, Michael had a towel draped around his waist and was drying his hair with another. The hesitation was gone from his movements. Physically he seemed to have recovered. But the pain of the ordeal was still etched into his features.

She looked at him, her heart aching. Then, without giving herself time to reconsider, she walked over and wrapped her arms around his waist. His whole body stiffened.

"Don't."

She pressed her cheek against his shoulder and began to speak very quickly. "Michael, when you disappeared this evening, I knew something terrible had happened to you. I made Devine take me to your room. When I saw the cockscomb, I was afraid to touch it, but I forced myself. Michael, it was horrible because I knew exactly what you were feeling." She paused, drawing in a steadying breath. "I couldn't be sure if we were going to get there in time. Please don't shut me out now."

For several heartbeats he didn't move. Then, as if against his will, his arms came up to pull her closer, and he buried his face in her neck. When he'd been afraid he was dying, his thoughts had been on her. She'd heard him calling her, even when he couldn't utter a sound. She'd given him back his life, and now she was stirring his body to the ultimate affirmation of life. He focused on her, her skin flushed from the heat of the shower, her hair a mass of damp auburn curls, her eyes pleading with him to accept her comfort.

"Baby. Oh, baby."

"Make love to me, Michael."

She had asked that of him once before, and he hadn't been able to refuse. It was beyond his power to walk away from her now.

He moved back slightly and tipped her face up so that he could look into the hazel depths of her eyes. "Are you sure this is what you want?"

"Very sure."

Her fingers moved up to clasp the back of his head, pulling his face down to hers. When their lips met, it was as if she was bringing the warmth back to his body that even the hot water hadn't been able to restore.

Her mouth opened under his, and he accepted the invitation, tasting her with the fervor of a man who had thought he would be denied all sweetness forever.

He took her lower lip between his teeth, nibbling it with careful, erotic little bites.

His hands moved down her back, sliding up under the towel to cup her hips and cradle them against his. She reeled from the pleasure of the contact, alive with the heady sensation of being in his arms again.

When he had held her like this before, it had been in a drug-induced dream. Her senses had been mixed up, her mind confused. But this was real. Now she was responding because she wanted to, not because she couldn't help herself. She moved against him, a little moan escaping from her.

He had told himself over and over that her reactions before had come from Dove, that they had nothing to do with him. Now that she was in his arms again, there was no denying the eagerness with which she met his passion. That meant a great deal to him. Everything.

All at once he wanted to wrap her warmth around himself, devour her, make love to her every way that a man could make love to a woman.

"Yes, Michael, everything." Her hands tangled in his hair, stroked across his back and shoulders. She couldn't get enough of him. She would never be able to get enough of him.

He stripped the towel off her body and tugged the other one from around his waist. With a deep groan, he pulled her into his arms again. The feel of her naked flesh against his was exquisite, almost more than he could stand. He hadn't asked to want her like this. He had fought that desire with all his resources. Now, suddenly, his need for her went beyond urgency. He wanted her this moment. Right here. Standing in the steamy bathroom. Yet he remembered the way he had taken her before. He had been rough and quick. It wasn't going to be that way this time.

He forced himself to catch his breath.

"Jess."

"Mmm."

"Come to bed with me."

She twined her fingers with his. "That's an offer I can't refuse."

He laughed softly, led her down the hall, watched mesmerized as she folded back the covers and slipped between the sheets. When she held out her arms to him, he came into them with a sigh of pleasure.

His lips explored the satin skin of her shoulder, the tender curl of her ear. "You're so sweet."

Her eager fingers stroked the hard muscles of his arms, counted his ribs. "And you're a very sexy man. But I've already told you that."

"I remember."

"It was different that night. I was on fire, but it was... artificial." She strove to keep her voice steady. "Michael, I'm on fire now. I think I want you as much as a woman could possibly want a man."

His fingers stroked through her hair, then tilted her face up and glided his lips across her cheek, finding her mouth again. He cherished her tenderly, holding his passion back, wanting more than anything to meet her needs as well as his own.

When his hands began to stroke her again, he was sensitive to her reactions. He hadn't known it, but there was a basic honesty about her that the drug had only heightened. And the way her hands moved over his body told him as much as the desire he read in her eyes. Last time she had been like someone caught on a roller coaster, helpless to get off until the ride was over. This time he sensed that she wanted to enjoy every hill and dip for its own thrill.

"Michael, I love the way you touch me," she whispered.

The knowledge that she was responding so strongly to him increased his own excitement. He cupped his hands around her breasts, intrigued by the contrast of his dark skin against the cream of hers and fascinated by the rapture on her face when he caressed her.

When he sucked one taut nipple into his mouth, her nails dug urgently into the flesh of his back.

His hands stroked between her legs, feeling her readiness. She made little pleading sounds as she moved against him.

Her fingers slid down his body and closed around him. With that invitation, he knew he couldn't hold back any longer. Groaning, he slid deep into her warm velvety softness. He could feel her contract around him.

"Oh, that's so good." She sighed as he began to move within her.

"More than good. Incredible."

Her hands clasped his shoulders as she matched her rhythm to his. She was tuned to him in a way that she would never have believed possible. It was as if he were another part of her that had always been missing. They moved in concert, each stoking the other's fire until, in the white-hot heat of their climax, they crossed the last barrier that separated them.

For a moment in time they were truly one.

The waves of ecstasy subsided slowly, but still he clasped her to him. Rolling to his side, he brought her up against the length of his body.

When he finally spoke, his voice was husky. "Jess, you saved my life tonight. I was too angry and upset to acknowledge that."

"It's all right. I know what you went through." She reached up to stroke his cheek. "You were there when I needed you. It hurt that you didn't want to let me be here for you. But I understood."

"I was a real bastard tonight."

"I'm too sleepy to argue about that now."

He was relieved that she didn't want to discuss it any further. The experience in the tomb had opened up emotional wounds that he still couldn't cope with. "Yeah, it's late. We'd better get to sleep."

Settling himself more comfortably, he tucked the covers around their shoulders before cradling her head in the crook of his arm. It had been a long time since he had wanted to share the whole night with a woman. But there was a rightness to having Jessica lie beside him.

She must have sensed it too. He could feel her body relaxing as her eyelids feathered closed.

He waited until he was sure she was asleep. Then his lips pressed softly against her face. "I don't deserve you, Jess."

Chapter Thirteen

They had gotten to sleep so late that it was just after noon when Michael woke up. He found Jessica curled beside him, her silky skin warm against his own. He didn't want to wake her, but he couldn't resist stroking his fingers across her shoulder and down her arm. She smiled in her sleep and her eyes opened slowly. After a moment of disorientation, she snuggled closer, an affectionate kitten purring contentment.

"Good morning," she finally murmured.

"Good afternoon, you mean."

"Mmm." Her arms slid around his waist and tightened. "Do we have to get up?"

He certainly didn't want to. Maybe they could have breakfast sent up and later dinner. The thought of spending the day in bed with her was infinitely appealing. His body was already beginning to respond very positively to the idea.

"Perhaps not for a while."

She nuzzled her face against his chest. "Good."

Still, he did have responsibilities. "I have to talk to Devine sometime and report in to my supervisor."

"To the Falcon?" The question slipped out before she realized he hadn't told her the name.

Michael tensed.

She raised her head, hazel eyes large and serious. "I don't know his real name. But I can tell he's important to you. I'm sorry. I can't help it."

"I understand that." His voice indicated that he didn't like it.

"You're a man with secrets."

"And responsibilities. It's not up to me to decide whether to share them."

She nodded sadly.

"I've had to live this way for a long time."

But you were close to someone named Laura. You're not going to tell me about her, are you? And I'm not going to ask.

He took her hand. "Jess, you're an extraordinary woman."

"And a threat to the barren life you've chosen."

His face hardened. "It's not what the average person would want, but it's not exactly barren either. The Falcon convinced me I was needed. Every assignment I've accepted from him has reinforced that conviction and brought its own satisfaction."

"So where does that leave us?"

He didn't answer the question. "Jess, I tried to hold you at arm's length. I couldn't do it. But that can't be a factor in the decisions I have to make."

Would it make a difference if I told you I've fallen in love with you, Michael?

"Well, I guess that's my cue to fade out of your life." She started to swing her legs off the bed, but he pulled her back.

"Don't make me feel any worse than I already do."

"What do you want from me, Michael? You've already told me you don't have room for excess baggage."

He wrapped his arms around her and held her. "Don't call yourself that. That's not really the point, anyway. Jess, there's another agent working on this case. He's in trouble. Maybe dead. You know damn well it could just as easily have been me."

"Jed."

He swore. "What do you know about Jed?"

"Hardly anything."

"What?" His voice was harsh.

"Michael, when I open my mind up, it's like a radio receiver. I can't control what comes in. Last night when I was looking for you, I could see you lying in that tomb. But it was mixed with another scene. Jed was trapped too." She paused, recalling the picture. "In a hospital room. I think someone gave him the same drug they gave you. That's why his image was like an overlay on yours."

"The Falcon's going to need to know that right away."

"And you have to have some privacy."

"Yes. Jess, I'm sorry."

"I know. I understand."

She wanted to cling to him, argue with him. There was so much they hadn't said to each other. Instinctively she knew that words wouldn't do any good. Instead she pressed her face against his hard shoulder. For the briefest moment, she opened her lips, wanting to taste the warmth of his skin one last time. Suddenly she realized that if she didn't leave at once, she was going to break down in front of him.

Without looking back at the bed, she got up stiffly and walked down the hall to the bathroom. After finding her underwear was still wet, she rolled it in a towel and pulled on her jeans and shirt. The clothing was damp and rumpled and she felt like a mess. But it wouldn't be a very long cab ride home.

When she came back to the bedroom, Michael had pulled on a pair of fresh jeans.

"Jess," he began.

"Anything you say is just going to make it worse. Goodbye." She didn't trust herself to speak above a whisper or even to raise her eyes to his.

He clenched his fists, holding himself stiff and tight. Instead of striding across the room and pulling her into his arms again, he watched her walk out the door and close it. He hadn't felt this devastated since they'd told him about Laura. But that just made him more sure than ever that he had to let Jessica go, even if it tore him apart. With someone else, maybe he could have had a relationship and kept it separate from his work. But with Jessica, every secret that he knew would put both of them in jeopardy.

IT WOULD BE IMPOSSIBLE to feel any worse, Jessica thought as she dragged herself up the steps toward Aubrey's apartment. But she was mistaken. No sooner had she closed the door than the phone began to ring.

"Ms. Duval?"

Her heart skipped a beat. "Yes."

"This is Dr. Frederickson."

She knew what he was going to say.

"I'm afraid I have some bad news."

Maybe she was wrong. *Please God, let me be wrong, just this once.*

"I'm sorry, but your brother expired this morning. I've been trying to reach you."

She sank down into one of the kitchen chairs, struggling to catch her breath.

"Ms. Duval, are you all right?"

"Yes. What happened?"

"I'd rather not go into it over the phone."

Blood. A lot of blood, red and pooled on the tile floor of a bathroom.

"Did he kill himself?"

"Uh—yes," the doctor confirmed reluctantly. "Ms. Duval, he was very disturbed. We had him under very close observation, but—"

"I know you did everything you could, Dr. Frederickson. I'll be down there in about forty-five minutes."

SHE COULDN'T FACE going to the cemetery, not after her recent experience. The very idea of opening up her family crypt was too close to the nightmare of a few days ago. So, after a lot of private soul searching, she had Aubrey's body cremated.

A few students and some of the university faculty came
to the quiet memorial service conducted by a minister recommended by the mortuary. It surprised her that Simone
didn't come. Maybe the grapevine had failed her old friend
this time, or perhaps she was still afraid of getting involved. At the very least Jessica had expected a note of
condolence. But it didn't really make any difference. No
matter who showed up to tell her they were sorry about the
tragedy, taking care of Aubrey's last needs was a very lonely
job.

The only other person she'd really wanted to see was Michael Rome. But when she'd called his room after her visit
to Dr. Frederickson, he'd already checked out. She'd
thought about getting in touch with Lieutenant Devine to
see if he knew where to reach Michael, but somehow she
never seemed to be able to work up the courage.

It took only a few days to wrap up Aubrey's affairs. Jessica was glad that there wasn't a great deal to do, because she
wasn't capable of much physical or mental activity. Depression had settled around her shoulders like a gray shroud,
and she considered it a major accomplishment if she could
drag herself out of bed in the morning and get dressed.
She'd lost her only close relative, and that was a hard
enough blow to cope with. Losing Michael on the same afternoon made things that much worse. Falling in love with
a man she hardly knew had been a terrible mistake.

She'd never felt quite so rudderless. When she called
Carrie, her manager back in Annapolis, she found that her
business was still running smoothly. Carrie urged her to
consider taking a vacation before coming back to work. The
idea had some merit. There was no reason to stay in Louisiana, and there was no reason to go home. But making a decision about what to do next was almost beyond her
capability.

Jessica was occupying her usual chair in the living room
when the doorbell rang. She looked with little real interest
toward the door, wondering vaguely who it could possibly
be coming around. Maybe it was one of those enterprising

individuals who encased obituary notices in plastic and sold them to relatives of the deceased. However, when she finally opened the door, the rather pretty young woman standing in the hallway didn't look as if she were playing that role. Her blue eyes were too perceptive and the style of her light-brown hair too chic.

"Jessica Duval?" she questioned.

"Yes."

"My name is Eden Sommers. May I come in and talk to you for a few minutes?"

Jessica hesitated, searching the woman's face. She was a person who radiated confidence—and determination. She was there because she wanted something. But it was difficult for Jessica to pick up what it was; it seemed as if the woman were deliberately channeling her mind away from the real reason for her visit.

"I don't know."

"Please. It's important."

"All right." With a sigh, she stepped aside and motioned toward the living room.

Jessica returned to her chair. After looking around for a moment, the blue-eyed young woman settled herself gracefully on the couch.

"May I call you Jessica? I've heard a lot about you."

"From whom?"

"From Michael. From the Falcon."

"Oh."

"Aren't you wondering why I'm here?"

"Does it really matter?"

Eden's eyes were sympathetic. "Jessica, I heard about your brother. I'm sorry."

"One of those things.

"We've already discovered it wasn't."

"What do you mean?"

"Your brother stumbled into a hornet's nest at Chartres University. After Michael sent us those letters Aubrey had hidden, we began a thorough investigation into the chemistry department and Henry Bergman. This morning the administration agreed to relieve Bergman of his duties as chairman of the department, pending a hearing. But the whole affair is still being kept quiet over there.''

"What whole affair? What are you talking about?"

"It will be weeks before we have the full story, but apparently Bergman not only steered Xavier to the Blackstone Clinic, he was also allowing the campus labs to be used to manufacture illegal substances. Incidentally, he was also diverting federal grant money to his own purposes."

For days Jessica had been numb, not wanting to probe any further into the intrigue that had led to Aubrey's death. She still didn't know how Ms. Sommers fit into this, but suddenly she was interested in hearing what the woman had to say. "Is that why everyone on campus gave me the cold shoulder when I tried to find out about my brother?"

"I imagine so. Bergman was running scared. Over the last few months a number of outspoken students had been roughed up by thugs."

"So if Aubrey stumbled on to something questionable, he would have wanted to keep quiet about it while he gathered the proof he needed."

"That's what we surmise. Unfortunately someone got to him before he had enough evidence to prove anything. We still don't know the details of Bergman's connection to Lonnie, but we're working on it."

"Thank you for telling me all this."

"We owe you that much at least."

Jessica sighed. "With Bergman under investigation, something good came of this horrible ordeal."

Eden's eyes were full of compassion. The information she'd just imparted would give Jessica some measure of peace, but that hadn't been her primary reason for coming to New Orleans.

"Your brother's role in the Dove case isn't the only thing I came to talk to you about. I'd also like to discuss your involvement."

"I'm done with it!"

The two women confronted each other in silence. Eden could see Jessica's distress. Jessica could sense Eden's strength of mind.

"Don't turn away from Michael," she finally said.

"What do you mean, turn away? He's done everything he could to drive me away."

Eden locked her hands together in her lap. The white knuckles revealed that this was difficult for her too. "In many ways Michael's like my husband, Mark Bradley. Long before we were married, he walked out on me because he wanted to protect me from the dangerous life he led."

"But he wasn't afraid of you. You didn't make him feel as if his head were glass and you were reading all his secrets."

"Actually, I did."

Jessica looked up sharply. "You aren't . . . ?"

"No, I'm not a psychic. The next worst thing, a psychologist."

Despite herself, Jessica laughed. Then her expression sobered again. "Why are you here?"

Eden gave her a direct look. "I work for the Falcon."

"Sure. The Falcon."

"I'm sorry to be so mysterious. I really can't tell you very much about our work. But our director feels you could be very valuable on this case."

"What does Michael think?"

"The possibility of bringing you back hasn't been broached to him. I argued that until we talked to you, there was no use—"

"Antagonizing him," Jessica finished.

Eden smiled. "You know him very well, don't you? But so do I. He's an old friend, and I have a lot of respect for his integrity."

Jessica nodded.

"Would you object to working with him again?"

"I think you've guessed there's been some personal involvement between us, and I'm afraid it would get in the way."

"But what if he were in danger? Wouldn't you want to help him?" Eden asked.

"He's going to try to rescue Jed!"

Eden's eyes widened. "Michael said your perceptions were uncanny. How did you pick that up from me? I was trying not to think about it."

Jessica shrugged. "Sometimes I just know."

"Particularly when it has to do with someone you care about."

"Yes."

The two women stared at each other. Finally Eden spoke. "I first got involved with the Falcon under less than ideal circumstances. He used my love for Mark to guarantee my cooperation on a top-security mission. At the time, I didn't feel that I had a choice. But I don't want to use coercive tactics on you."

"If you're telling me that Michael's life may be in danger and that my working with him might make the difference, then there's no way I can refuse."

"I was hoping you'd feel that way. Michael Rome is a very lucky man, even if he's too stubborn to realize it right now."

"ALL RIGHT, MR. PRENTISS it's time to stop playing games."

Jed pushed himself to a sitting position against the pillows. "What games? I don't follow you, Doctor."

"Oh, I think you do. You are down here on Royale Verde working for some American intelligence organization. I want to know which one and what your specific interest is in me."

"Didn't you tell me that I was recovering from a stroke?"

The doctor sighed. "Unfortunately, I don't believe you ever bought that story, although it would have made things a great deal easier on both of us."

Jed stared back at Talifero, wondering what his chances were of escaping from this fortress of a sanitarium. Not very good, he guessed. The windows were barred, the grounds were patrolled, and the guards outside his door were armed. And then there was the doctor's sudden change in tactics. He wouldn't be tipping his hand if he thought Jed Prentiss was going anywhere.

"Now, let us be frank with each other, Mr. Prentiss. I have gone through your personal possessions with considerable care. You are quite well equipped for espionage. What was your mission exactly?"

"I had no mission. I am simply a tourist." So *something* good was coming out of this. At least he knew he wasn't crazy—or brain damaged. The doctor's assessment of his role matched his memories perfectly.

"Oh, come now. My police informants kept me apprised of your activities since the moment you arrived on Royale Verde. You were apprehended sneaking onto my property with a knapsack full of bugging equipment."

When Jed made no reply, the doctor slipped his hands into his trouser pockets and took a step back, regarding his prisoner with some interest. "As I told you before," he murmured, "this is a psychiatric hospital. We're well equipped with many different kinds of experimental medications. I think we will have to try using some of them on you."

Jed met his gaze levelly.

"Given in high dosages, some of them actually do cause stroke and brain damage. Others loosen the tongue. Although I have the feeling that in your case, your cover story has been drummed into your head so effectively that it would take several interrogations to shake your account. That's unfortunate for you. It means I'm better off starting with something a bit more traditional. Pain."

"You don't frighten me, Talifero."

"No? What a pity. But you will probably have changed your attitude by tomorrow morning." He paused and opened the door.

Two large men wearing white uniforms and gun belts walked in and stood with their arms folded across their chests. "I'd like Mr. Prentiss moved to a soundproof cell in the maximum security wing. Strap him down and give him fifty milligrams of tricarbotane.''

The guard sucked in his breath and gave Jed an incredulous look. ''Fifty milligrams?''

''Are you questioning my orders?''

''No, sir.''

Talifero turned back to the man on the bed. ''I don't want to keep my dinner guests waiting. But I'll be looking in on you later just to see how you're doing.''

THE TURBAN OF GOLD CLOTH would go nicely with her burgundy-and-gold caftan, Moonshadow thought as she held the flowing silk fabric up against her naked body. She was admiring her tawny reflection in the mirrored wall of the bedroom Jackson Talifero had settled her into yesterday morning.

Now that she was down there on Royale Verde, she was feeling quite a bit more optimistic about her relationship with Blackstone's director. Though he'd tried to hide it, the man had been clearly relieved at getting his chemist back. Since she had been the agent for accomplishing the recapture, a great deal of Talifero's goodwill toward her had been restored, and she felt more confident that she would be able to handle him—or discover what he was really up to so she could have a stronger weapon to use against him if she needed it.

She, Gilbert Xavier, and Lonnie Milstead, along with two silent security guards, had arrived on Royale Verde by seaplane from Key West the day before. She had been down here on a few other occasions to conduct special voodoo rituals and remembered the opulence well. She supposed it compensated somewhat for the prison atmosphere. Of course, she knew about the hidden television cameras all over the place. But she had a justifiable pride in her sleek body and didn't mind putting on a show whether she was alone or not. If that improved Jackson's mood, so much the better.

Too bad for Xavier; he wasn't having quite such a relaxing time. He'd been under guard ever since they'd captured him in the cemetery. Talifero had given orders that he wasn't allowed in the bathroom by himself until he was safely back in the Blackstone compound. As soon as he had arrived, the pale and shaken chemist had been frog-marched directly to the lab complex for a series of very frank conversations with Blackstone's chief of staff. Moonshadow hadn't seen him since, but she suspected he was going to cooperate for the moment. The conjecture had been confirmed when a servant had arrived a half hour ago with a hand-written note from Talifero. Her host explained that a dinner was being held in honor of Franco Garcia, who had come especially to meet Dr. Xavier. If the chemist were being trotted out for such an occasion, then the man-to-man talks must have been quite successful. But then Talifero had the enviable ability to inspire fear in the heart of just about anyone when it suited him.

Blackstone's director was serving cocktails on the terrace. When Moonshadow made her entrance, the other guests were already assembled under the striped canopy festive with softly glowing lanterns. Xavier was talking to Barahona, the chief of police. Though the expression on the chemist's face was carefully neutral, his tension was betrayed in the death grip he had on his highball glass.

The other three men who, like Xavier were all in white dinner jackets, turned appreciatively in her direction as she stepped through the French doors. She gave them a slight nod, acknowledging their admiration as her due. The guest she didn't know must be Franco Garcia. She had learned from the maid who made up her room that he was a Brazilian planter. However, if Jackson was trying to impress the man, he must be more than that, and she wanted to know what he was doing here.

From under long ebony lashes, she studied him with a mixture of curiosity and anticipation. Obligingly he returned her interest with an avaricious smile. She wasn't vain, but she knew few men could refuse what she set her mind on getting from them.

The byplay wasn't lost on Talifero. Coming over, he took Moonshadow's arm and escorted her across the patio.

"My dear, I'd like you to meet our guest of honor." The introductions were made graciously. "Franco is quite interested in your exceptional talents."

I'll bet he is, the priestess thought.

Gorlov took her offered hand and raised it to his lips. He rather liked playing the role of the South American aristocrat. It was a damn sight more gratifying than haggling over Soviet wheat deals, which had been the cover assignment in Madrid that hid his role of a KGB operative.

"Jackson has told me you'll be performing a special ceremony for us. I'm looking forward to it."

She allowed herself a side glance at Talifero's impassive face. This was the first she'd heard of a voodoo ceremony. What else had Jackson promised this man? But her well-modulated contralto conveyed none of her inner speculation. "I'm sure you won't be disappointed."

Talifero nodded approvingly and took a long swallow of his planter's punch. Now that he had Moonshadow where he could keep an eye on her, he was a lot more confident of his ability to keep her in line. He wasn't even particularly concerned that she was discreetly starting to pump Gorlov for information. What did it matter now really? Things were back on track.

Even if he did have to sell a couple of Renoirs to make the first payment to the Russians, he had Xavier back in the fold. The little bastard was going to make up for his defection by working twenty-four hours a day from now on. Too bad producing Dove was such a delicate procedure. If the stuff had lent itself readily to mass production, he'd have jettisoned the obstreperous chemist months ago. But whatever Xavier's faults, he wasn't a liar. If the process wasn't handled with kid gloves, half the island—and all of his ambitions—could go up in flames.

Chapter Fourteen

The trip from New Orleans to Washington was one that Jessica would never forget. Once she'd agreed to become part of the operation the Falcon was conducting, it was like being initiated into some sort of secret society. Only this society was a hush-hush intelligence organization called the Peregrine Connection.

On the small private jet, Eden gave her a very comprehensive overview of the Dove case. It was fascinating to see how the details she and Michael had uncovered were intertwined with the intrigue at the Blackstone Clinic on Royale Verde.

But Jessica got more out of the discussions with the sympathetic psychologist than mere information. There'd been no one she could talk to about her relationship with Michael. Now, under Eden's gentle questioning, she found herself opening up to a surprising degree. Even though she held back some of the details, it was evident that Eden understood her dilemma, and Jessica felt better after unburdening herself. They had just begun to talk about how she might cope with her problems when the copilot opened the cockpit door to tell them the Falcon was waiting to speak to them via microwave link.

In addition to its plush customized interior, the plane contained sophisticated teleconferencing equipment. A panel in the front of the cabin slid up to reveal a large TV screen on which the Falcon's imposing visage appeared. It was like watching a news program on which a commentator in New York interviewed a guest in the Los Angeles studio—only now Jessica was part of the action.

The silver-haired man, who introduced himself as Amherst Gordon, projected an aura of gruff charisma and keen intelligence. As he spoke, Jessica sensed that he'd sacrificed any sort of normal private life for the cause of freedom he believed in so strongly. It wasn't hard to see why he inspired such personal loyalty among his staff.

"Ms. Duval, your help has already been invaluable," he summed up. "And I'd like to officially welcome you to the team."

"Thank you."

"Now that I know you're on board, I'll bring Michael up to date on the new developments, and we will be prepared to move on as soon as you arrive."

Shortly after he'd signed off, the plane landed at Dulles International Airport, where Jessica and Eden were met by the Aviary's courtesy van and driven to the Peregrine's Berryville headquarters.

As a resident of the carefully preserved city of Annapolis, which had become a thriving center of commerce more than two hundred years ago, Jessica was no stranger to colonial charm. But she still wasn't quite prepared for the splendor of the Aviary, which rivaled the best Maryland's capital had to offer. Even more impressive, she knew from Eden that the country inn had been restored with strictly private funds.

The Peregrine staffer had also been quite good at providing a thumbnail sketch of Constance McGuire, Gordon's assistant and confidante. When the willowy, gray-haired woman came down the steps to greet them, Jessica felt almost as if they'd already met.

Connie's first words were for the psychologist. "So, Eden, your persuasive talents are still intact," she remarked.

Turning to Jessica, she offered her hand. "Let me add my welcome to the one I know Amherst has already extended."

Inside the Georgian mansion, the atmosphere wasn't quite so cordial. As Constance led them down the wide center hall, Jessica could hear an angry voice. It belonged to Michael Rome.

"I think it's a stupid idea to send an amateur like her into that jungle down there."

"Michael, you're not thinking—you're just reacting."

As Jessica entered the conference room, the DEA agent caught sight of her, and his face softened for just a moment.

The newcomers pulled up seats at the large table where the two men sat. After a moment's hesitation Jessica took the chair opposite Michael.

It was impossible for him to keep his eyes off her. She wore the navy-and-yellow Indian print dress and distinctive brass necklace that he had first seen her in. Over the past few days she'd been on his mind a lot, and not just because he was writing reports that included the information she'd given him. But until a half hour ago, he'd been telling himself that it was best for her if he never saw her again.

Now, here she was back in his life, as fresh-faced and appealing as she'd ever been. Damn. He was suddenly irrationally happy, buoyant. He squared his shoulders, struggling to suppress his emotions.

"How are you, Jess?" His voice was strained and a bit husky.

"All right. And you?" She studied the face that was so familiar and yet so remote. In this elegant setting, he'd chosen to wear faded jeans and a chambray work shirt with sleeves rolled up to his elbows. The outfit made him appear more uncompromising than ever. Yet the way his gray eyes darkened when he looked at her told her as much as the tense set of his shoulders.

"I'm okay. I'm sorry I couldn't come to your brother's funeral."

"I understand. Eden explained that you were called back here."

They were both very aware that the other people in the room were observing the encounter.

"We were just discussing your role in this operation," Gordon informed her. "I think we all agree that our first priority is to rescue Jed Prentiss—and Gilbert Xavier, if possible. And since you've already established a link with Jed, I'm hoping you'll be able to fill us in on some of our intelligence gaps."

"It wasn't much of a link," Michael cut in. "Just something that was mixed in with what was happening with me. Maybe she's lost it. And if she has, there's no reason to involve her further."

The Falcon gave his operative a considering look. "A good point. Perhaps we should test the hypothesis right now." He turned back to Jessica. "Would you be willing to try to reestablish communication with our agent on Royale Verde?"

Jessica looked around at the four faces registering various states of curiosity and anxiety. "I'm really not used to—"

"An audience," Eden supplied. "I'm sure you'd be more comfortable in my office."

"Quite right." The Falcon turned back to Jessica. "I understand you like to work with personal possessions of the individual you're trying to envision."

"Yes." She appreciated his straightforward approach. This wasn't like working with the police who'd been half in awe, half suspicious of her.

"Apparently Talifero had Jed's luggage taken from his room. But he'd left his passport at the hotel desk, and I had an agent down there retrieve and send it." He reached into his breast pocket and pulled out a small blue book with the gold U.S. seal. "Would you like to use it?"

"Thank you. That should be very helpful."

The Falcon looked at Jessica expectantly, but she didn't reach for the document.

"I, uh, I'd rather not touch it until I've been able to clear my mind."

Eden took the passport. "Maybe we're pushing you too hard. Do you want to rest for a while?"

"I'd like her to do it now while she's under some stress," Michael cut in.

In response to his combative tone, everyone's head swung in his direction.

He shrugged. "Out in the field she's not going to be able to take a nap when we need some information."

Jessica gave him a measured look. "All right, I'll see what I can do now."

"I'll come along," Michael insisted.

Eden raised an eyebrow.

"I've seen what can happen when she does this. You haven't," he answered her unspoken question.

"Is that all right with you?" Eden asked Jessica.

She nodded.

The psychologist led the way down to the lower level of the building that housed Peregrine support activities. Her office was off a cheerful sitting room at the end of the hall.

"I'd like you to wait outside," she informed Michael, gesturing toward one of the leather armchairs.

"Keep the door ajar."

Eden hesitated.

"I won't interfere unless I'm needed," the DEA agent assured her.

Eden glanced at Jessica. Again, the other woman nodded her assent.

Looking resigned, Michael lowered his angular frame into one of the chairs and reached for a magazine on the coffee table.

Inside Eden's office, Jessica glanced around with interest. In addition to the wide desk and leather swivel chair, there were several padded armchairs and a comfortable-looking couch.

Eden pulled the door almost closed. "Where would you like to sit?"

"A chair would be fine."

"It would be helpful if I could record this. Would you mind?"

"I don't think it will interfere."

Jessica seated herself in a light-green armchair. Eden put the passport on the table beside her. "Whenever you're ready, then."

The other young woman looked at the document and flexed her fingers. They felt hot and tingly, and the same sense of apprehension that had assailed her when she'd seen the voodoo charms washed over her now. She took a deep breath and exhaled it slowly, making her mind a blank. Then she reached out and picked up the small blue book.

When there was no immediate reaction, the tight muscles in her shoulders relaxed a bit. Maybe Michael was right. Maybe her thoughts of Jed Prentiss had been just a fluke. Opening her mind, she tried to coax a picture. She had the feeling of great distance.

"He's so far away," she murmured. "There are miles of water between us—and walls and barriers."

None of her previous psychic experiences had been like this. All at once she felt as if she were traveling above the earth, not in an airplane but on the very air currents themselves. She saw ocean waves lapping gently on a curved shoreline. After what seemed a long while, she swooped closer to the ground where she looked down on white stucco walls surrounded by tropical vegetation and armed guards. Then she was sailing over the walls and moving toward a two-story Spanish-style building with a red tile roof.

Unaccountably, her vision seemed to take her right through the wall of the building and into a stuffy, windowless room furnished only with a padded table. She felt as if she were hovering somewhere near the ceiling, looking down on the empty scene.

As she watched, the door was flung open and two burly attendants dragged a prisoner into the room. He was a tall man with light-brown hair and broad shoulders. When he struggled against his guards, one held his arms while the other casually delivered a blow to his abdomen with a billy stick. Though she had never seen the prisoner before, she knew immediately that it was Jed Prentiss.

It took a rain of blows to quiet him. But finally the two men strapped him down on the table with his arms and legs secured to metal rings at the corners. The sight of his athlete's body abused so harshly made her want to squeeze her eyes shut. But she wasn't seeing this with her eyes.

One of the guards left and returned a moment later with a hypodermic.

"This is your last chance, buddy. Are you sure you don't want to talk?"

The prisoner shook his head.

"The tricarbotane will make you wish you had." With that he swabbed some alcohol on the man's arm and plunged the needle into his vein.

The door closed with a loud clank. The man on the table was alone, and Jessica felt her disembodied self descending toward him. Some instinct toward self-preservation made her struggle against the contact. She watched in horror as his features contorted in a grimace of pain. His teeth clamped together, and she knew it was to hold back a scream.

But the need to help him pulled her forward. She had to reach out toward him. As she did, an invisible barrier gave way, and all at once she felt herself sucked forward with a rush. Her own face contorted as her consciousness merged with his. There was no thought in his mind—in her mind— except agony. And it swallowed her up as well. God, her whole body was on fire from the inside out. Acid was pumping through her veins. She felt herself drowning in it, consumed.

A piercing scream escaped from her throat and her hand clenched around the passport. Eden was on the other side of the desk in an instant. But as quickly as she moved, she didn't get to Jessica before Michael had burst through the door.

He swore and grasped her by the shoulders. "Jess, what's happening? Come back."

She screamed again, spasms sweeping over her in giant waves. Her eyes were wide and staring, but she saw neither Michael nor Eden.

"Let go of the damned passport," he ordered. She was incapable of obeying.

Steely fingers grasped her hand and pried the twisted document from her grasp. As he pulled it free, the pain stopped abruptly and she sagged in the chair. Reaching down, he scooped her up and took her to the couch, cradling her on his lap.

Even as he held her close against him and soothed his fingers across her back and shoulders, he was looking accusingly at Eden. "Can't you see what this kind of thing does to her?" he rasped.

Jessica stirred against him.

"It's all right. Relax. You're safe now," he murmured.

She closed her eyes and burrowed into his warmth, rubbed her face against his shirt, inhaled the familiar scent of his body.

"Michael."

"What is it?"

"Thank you."

For several more minutes he simply held her. Then he shifted her body so that he could search her face. He waited until her breathing had returned almost to normal.

"Can you tell me what happened?" he questioned softly.

"Jed. I found Jed. It was horrible."

"What?"

"They injected him with something called tricarbotane."

"Bastards!"

"Tricarbotane?" Eden questioned.

"A drug the Russians developed in the sixties," Michael answered, his voice scathing. "The substance has no medical value. It puts victims in agony for hours but doesn't leave any physical effects—except an urge to talk to prevent further treatments."

Eden rubbed her forehead. "I didn't know the name, but I've heard the experience described." She knelt beside Jessica. "Are you all right?"

"I saw them give it to Jed. I wanted to help him, but I couldn't do anything except feel his pain."

"Your mind merged with his?" Eden asked.

"Yes. I couldn't stop myself."

Michael swore. "That's all the more reason why you should stay out of this, Jessica."

The woman he held cradled in his arms raised her flushed face so that she could meet his eyes. "It doesn't matter whether or not I go down there with you, Michael. I'm already in it."

THE TROPICAL EVENING was rich with the fragrance of island flowers. Moonshadow had wandered out into the garden, sure that the guest of honor would follow.

He caught up with her beside a small pond where bronze pelicans dipped their large beaks between the lily pads.

"I've been intrigued by you all evening," he murmured.

"I think the feeling is mutual."

She leaned over to trail her graceful fingers in the water. When a large goldfish came up to investigate her ruby nails, she laughed softly, her voice like silver bells in the moonlight.

Gorlov sat down beside her on the low stone wall, inhaling her intoxicating scent.

Through long dark lashes, she gazed up at him. "But you're such a man of mystery."

"How so?"

"I sense that you have more power than you pretend, and I'm attracted to power."

He didn't deny her supposition. "And I am attracted to beauty. Yours matches that of any goddess." He was surprised at the poetry she had inspired. But then he'd been thinking all evening that he'd like to slide the caftan off her bronze shoulders and find out if she were as beautiful all over as he suspected. "I've never met a woman quite like you," he added.

"And you are beyond my experience too. Different. Very intellectual. Quite foreign, I think. You're not really from Brazil, are you?"

He hesitated.

"I never make love to a man unless I know his real name." As she spoke, she reached up to run a ruby nail down the ruffles of his dress shirt. She sensed the instant reaction of his body to both the words and the intimate gesture.

"Feliks," he supplied.

"A Slavic name?" Her dark eyes held his gaze and her hands smoothed more firmly across the front of his shirt, a cellist tuning a new instrument.

"No. Russian." His voice was thick and husky.

Russian. Now she could hear the accent that years of training had hidden. Very interesting, she thought. Through the ruffles, her fingers traced tiny circles on his bare chest. She could feel his level of sensual tension increasing.

"Feliks, I believe that you and I will become very good friends tonight."

Impatiently he reached for her, his mouth descending to hers like a vulture. In that moment she knew that he was going to be a selfish lover. But her own pleasure was of little importance tonight. This man had some kind of hold over Talifero, and she was going to call upon all her powers to find out what it was.

"Shall we go back to your room?" he questioned huskily.

So he wasn't aware of the TV cameras. She didn't care who might be watching, but she didn't want anyone to hear what they might say. "No," she whispered, taking his hand. "Come down into the summer house where the magic of the night and the fragrance of the garden will be all around us."

MICHAEL'S SHOULDERS were rigid as he turned back to face Eden. "Don't I get any say in who I work with on this rescue operation? I don't want Jessica along."

"Why not, Michael?" she whispered.

He didn't answer.

"There's more working here than your concern for her safety," Eden interjected.

"Don't push me," he warned the psychologist.

Eden sighed. "Michael Rome, you're one of Peregrine's best operatives, but you're not being very logical about this mission. I can see now that I made a mistake by not getting you to tell me more about what happened in Greece three years ago."

Michael started toward the door.

Before he reached it, Jessica jumped up and put a restraining hand on his shoulder. "It has to do with Laura, doesn't it?" she asked quietly.

He whirled to face her. "Damn it, stay out of my head."

"Then tell us about it."

His hands balled into fists, and he sucked air into his lungs. For several moments the room was silent. Then he looked from one woman to the other. "All right, if it will make you understand how crazy this idea is, I will."

"Michael, I don't want to just hear your filtered version," Jessica said softly.

"What other kind of version is there? She's dead. I don't suppose you communicate with ghosts. Or shall we all hold hands and conduct a seance?"

She shook her head tightly. "No. I don't do that sort of thing. But I'm getting better at projecting my mind. If you don't put up a barrier against it, I think I can go back there with you and see for myself what happened."

He closed his eyes. "Jessica, haven't you had enough torture for one afternoon?"

"I want to help you." She sat down on the couch again. "Come back here beside me."

Wearily he obeyed. "I don't think you're going to get very far." He gave Eden a quick glance. "You see, I don't remember exactly what happened."

"Michael, I suspected that. It's not unusual. It's a trick the mind uses to protect itself from trauma. But unfortunately, the pain comes out in other ways."

He pressed his lips together.

Jessica took his hand. It was ice cold.

"Try to relax. Think about the mission—and how it ended."

"You're not going to like it."

"That's not important," Eden interjected.

"I can't fight both of you. If you two signed up as an interrogation team, you could break any Soviet agent alive."

Jessica laughed hollowly. "I'm not trying to break you, Michael. I'm just trying to understand what makes working with me so threatening to you."

"All right," he snapped. "You can have what you asked for." Squeezing his eyes closed, he forced himself to think about that day three years ago. He and Laura Atkins had been on a mission for the Falcon in Greece. She was a linguist, and this was her first time in the field. Michael hadn't thought she was ready, but he'd enjoyed her company and rationalized that the assignment was really not all that dangerous.

They were meeting a defector named Balinski who had escaped from Bulgaria and was hiding in the hills around Elasson. Posing as a married couple on vacation, they took several days traveling from Athens. They stopped at little taverns to enjoy the spicy Greek food, walked hand in hand through historic villages, and enthusiastically continued the charade of being married in the bedrooms of charming country inns.

But as the rendezvous drew closer, Michael sensed Laura's nervousness. They were to meet Balinski in the ruins west of town. Michael would have left her in Elasson, but she was the one who spoke the man's language.

He forced his mind to picture the scene once again. The rocky hills. The dry grass. The gnarled olive trees. Balinski, dressed like a hiker emerging from behind the remains of a small temple and whistling two low notes.

Despite the innocence of the scene, it was a death trap. The man was more important than even the Falcon had suspected. He knew too much to be allowed to escape to the West, and the Bulgarian secret police were already closing in.

Armed men surrounded the defector. When one shouted a warning, he broke for cover. They cut him down in a hail of automatic fire. Michael remembered instinctively ducking behind the rocks. He had never been able to bring any more of it into focus. Yet some part of him remembered. Here in this quiet room at the Aviary, sweat broke out on his brow and his temples throbbed.

The grim images had come to Jessica very clearly, like a movie projected on the screen of her mind. She felt the tension in Michael's body and squeezed his hand.

"Damn it," he spat out. "I saved my own neck and let them kill her. She died, and it's my fault."

"That's not what happened, Michael."

"How the hell would you know?" His voice was harsh with self-accusation.

"Even if you can't see the end of it, I can. It's there in your subconscious."

"I can't face it, Jess. I never should have let them send her on that assignment. She was too green." He turned his face and shoulders toward the wall. He needed to be alone with this, had always needed to be alone with it.

"Taking her on the assignment wasn't your decision." Eden interjected.

"Why couldn't I save her?"

"You tried," Jessica soothed, gently reaching over to bring him back toward her. "You pulled her down with you and held on to her. When one of the Bulgarians started in your direction you reached for your gun. Laura panicked and ran. That's how she was shot. It wasn't your fault."

"So why didn't they get *me?*"

"They must have assumed she was the only contact and didn't come looking for you. She was already dead, and you did what you were supposed to do. You came back to report what had happened to the defector."

Michael's blue shirt was soaked with perspiration. His head felt as though an eighteen-wheeler were roaring through the middle of his skull. Yanking his hand away from Jessica's, he covered his face.

"Don't you believe me?" she questioned.

"I don't know."

"Michael, it wasn't your fault." Eden added her assurance to Jessica's.

"It's hard to accept what you're telling me. But then, you already know that."

"Guilt does strange things," the psychologist added. If she only had the time to put Michael into six months of therapy, she could help him work through this properly. As it was, she felt like a front-line medic patching up a soldier and sending him back to the front. But with Jed's life hanging in the balance, there was no time for extensive therapy. Despite their personal problems, Michael Rome and Jessica Duval were the best shot Gordon had at successfully pulling off the rescue. Whether she liked it or not, her job was to get them in shape to do it.

She came over and put her hand on Jessica's shoulder. "I think we should leave him alone with this for now."

Jessica didn't want to go. But she deferred to the psychologist's judgment. Before standing up, she leaned over and brushed her lips against Michael's cheek. "It must have been terrible to carry that around with you."

He didn't answer. He was slumped on the sofa, wrung out and exhausted, his mind still struggling with the new information that he must have known all along but refused to acknowledge. They were right. He needed to be alone with his feelings about Laura. Whether he had been technically responsible for her death or not, it was hard to stop blaming himself. And the old guilt was mixed up with his current anxieties over Jessica.

He didn't look up as the two women left the room.

Chapter Fifteen

Jessica put down the thick briefing folder and leaned her head back against the leather couch in the library. It was almost eleven o'clock and she knew she should be in bed, but she was still too unsettled to sleep.

She'd taken a sheaf of background material downstairs to read and made herself a cup of herb tea. But it was impossible to keep her mind on the Blackstone Clinic and Royale Verde. Michael had steered clear of her since the confrontation in Eden's office. The raw emotions she'd last seen on his face continued to haunt her. When he hadn't appeared at dinner, the psychologist had taken her aside for a few reassuring words.

"Michael has the facts now. But he still must deal with them in his own way, Jessica," she'd explained.

"I know that. I hope he comes to the right conclusion."

Now, despite Eden's admonition, she had the feeling that he needed her. Would it help if she went and talked to him? she wondered, glancing at her watch. But it was late. He was probably in bed, and she certainly didn't want to walk in on him there.

She was just closing the folder when the feeling of being watched made her look toward the doorway. Michael was standing with his hands in the pockets of his jeans, regarding her with intense gray eyes.

"Doing your homework?" he questioned.

"Trying to. There's a lot to absorb."

"So you're still determined to go?"

"Yes."

"Laura and I were sleeping together," he said abruptly.

She gave him a measured look. "And whose idea was that?"

"Hers, although I wasn't averse to going along with it. However, as the senior agent, I should have known better."

"How did you feel about her?" *Did you love her, Michael?* Her fingers gripped the folder as she waited for his answer.

He looked toward the darkened windows. "I liked her. I shouldn't have used her as a safety valve to let off steam."

"Maybe she was using you. Did you ever think about that?"

"Agents on assignment aren't supposed to get sexually involved with each other," Michael insisted.

"Are you trying to say that if you hadn't been lovers, she wouldn't have gotten killed? That's nonsense. How would that have prevented the ambush?"

"Maybe if I had been thinking a little more clearly, I would have seen the trap."

"You're still looking for a way to blame yourself."

"No, I'm looking for a way to keep it from happening to you."

She heard the anguish in his voice, knew that his concern for her was more than superficial. "Michael, I care a lot about you too. If I didn't think I could help you, I wouldn't be coming along."

He moved into the room and took a seat at the other end of the couch. His gaze caressed her face, but he didn't dare touch her.

"Jess, don't you understand the risks? These people are ruthless. They didn't hesitate to get your brother hooked on Dove. They tried to kill you—and me."

"You can't scare me off of this."

"I wish I could. I have a job to do, and I can't afford to worry about you too."

"Then don't. I'll take care of myself."

He sighed. "You know that's only part of it. There's a friend of mine down there on Royale Verde being tortured. I've got to help him, and I should be putting all my concentration on that assignment. But I can't stop thinking about the session we had with Eden." He paused. "And how much I'd like to escape to a very quiet bedroom and spend the night making love to you."

She leaned toward him slightly. She ached for that too.

Their eyes locked for several heartbeats.

"Michael, you can't help Jed until you know the situation down there. All you can do tonight is speculate and make contingency plans that will probably be worthless in the long run."

"I'd still feel better if I could concentrate on the problem without so many distractions."

She had to clench her hands together to stop herself from reaching out toward him. He'd had to cope with so much recently. "Accepting what comfort I could give you doesn't mean you're betraying Jed," she finally said.

His gaze focused on her lips as if contemplating their taste and texture. She had spoken of comfort. It was much more than that. She'd awakened deep emotional needs he hadn't wanted to admit existed. "Jess," he began.

The temptation to draw him into her arms threatened to sweep her away. She loved this man deeply. But he wasn't ready to deal with that now. If she surrendered to her desire for him, she'd be giving him the proof of his own doubts, and he'd use that against her in the morning.

"You're a man of tremendous willpower," she finished the sentence for him.

"Jess, I wish things were different."

"I'll see you at breakfast."

He stood up and turned away. She had won a victory. But what had she lost?

THE NEXT DAY Jessica found out just how quickly the Peregrine Connection could put its plans into action. The morning was taken up with several intensive briefing ses-

sions. The Falcon's strategy was to strike quickly before
Talifero realized that a rescue mission had been mounted.
To do that, he was counting on Jessica to supply Michael
with inside information he would ordinarily be unable to
obtain.

After being outfitted with suitcases that had everything
from summer vacation clothes and black camouflage fatigues to electronics equipment and plastic explosives, the
pair left that afternoon for Jamaica. That evening they had
made contact with the CIA man, George Holcroft. His
deep-sea fishing cruiser, the *Sea Turtle,* took them to Royale Verde. The name of the craft was deceptive because it
had a powerful motor that could outrun any patrol boat. It
also carried sensitive eavesdropping equipment that could
pick up signals from twenty miles offshore.

The boat made short work of the distance between Jamaica and Royale Verde. By very early Friday morning they
were tied up at a half-moon-shaped harbor at the south end
of the island.

Jessica had been given the small forward stateroom while
the men bunked down in the main cabin, which also served
as a galley and sitting room. When she awoke to the gentle
slapping of waves against the side of the craft, she was disoriented for a moment. Yesterday she had been in Virginia.
The day before that, New Orleans.

Swinging her legs over the side of the bunk, she scrambled down and pulled on a pair of white cropped-cut pants
and a knit top. When she emerged from the hatchway, the
two men were already on deck studying a map of the island. Jessica was once more struck with how well the ver-
satile Mr. Rome could adapt to a given environment. At the
university he'd projected the image of street-wise student;
near Harley's he could have passed as a dock worker. Here
on the *Sea Turtle,* dressed in a white polo shirt and shorts,
Michael looked like a man who could tie a very competent
reef knot and hold the helm steady even in stormy seas.

He glanced up and caught her staring. The coolly assessing expression in his gray eyes gave no hint of their compli-

cated relationship. Without sparing the subject even a word, he'd made it clear he was going to block out their unfinished personal business for the duration of the assignment. She hoped she could match his professional demeanor.

Yet she could still discern an element of protectiveness in his actions. Last night, though he'd been anxious to assess the current situation at the Blackstone Clinic, he'd seen her exhaustion and sent her to bed without putting her psychic talents to any further test.

"How did you sleep?" he asked.

"Fine."

"Good, because we're going to need you in a little while."

George waved her toward the galley refrigerator. "There's some fruit and muffins in the fridge. Make yourself at home."

"Thanks." She looked out over the bay full of pleasure craft bobbing in the gentle waves. It didn't seem like the departure point for a commando raid. Along the shore was a fishing village of white stucco houses with red tile roofs. It was terraced into the hillside that protected the harbor. The sky was a clear blue and the water an incredible aqua.

Jessica helped herself to a banana muffin and a slice of fresh pineapple and carried them back on deck where Michael and George were deep in discussion about the best way to make an assault on the clinic.

After she'd finished her light meal, Michael turned to her. "Now that we're closer, I'd like your impressions of what's going on in that compound." His matter-of-fact tone of voice told Jessica he no longer doubted her ability to pick up information he had no other way of acquiring and that, since she had insisted on coming, he was going to make use of the talent.

Holcroft looked from the seasoned operative back to the young woman in a T-shirt and pedal pushers. He'd been assured Ms. Duval was a psychic and had already made some sort of contact with the agent being held by Talifero. That kind of claim didn't impress him. There was a lot of mumbo jumbo that went on down on these islands. Most of it was for the benefit of the tourists. He wasn't going to put his faith in clairvoyant intelligence gathering until he saw some proof.

"Perhaps we'd better go down to the main cabin," Jessica suggested. "Do you have anything from the Blackstone Clinic?" she asked Holcroft.

He laughed. "How about the brochure they use to lure jetsetters with nutty relatives?" Opening another compartment, he pulled out a glossy booklet.

The color picture on the cover made her shiver slightly. It depicted one of the buildings she'd seen in her vision two days ago. "That should do."

Down in the lounge, Michael waited while she made herself comfortable on one of the built-in couches. "I'd like to know whether Jed is still alive, where he and Xavier are being held, and what Talifero is planning for them." There was one piece of information he wasn't going to share with her. His main concerns were rescuing Jed and stopping the production of Dove. If they could get Xavier out, fine. If they couldn't, he'd simply have to be abandoned.

She took a deep breath. Despite her insistence on coming along, she was still afraid of opening herself up to the aura of evil that clung to the Blackstone Clinic. Yet if it would help save Jed, she'd have to take that risk. "I'll do my best."

"I know." Was her best going to be good enough this time? he wondered. And what was the personal risk to her? "Don't go in too far," he added softly.

Her eyes were pulled to his for just a moment. The mixture of worry and expectation she found in their gray depths gave her the strength to reach for the brochure.

This time, when she took the folder in her hand, the clairvoyant perception came faster and surer than it ever had before. Her eyes were open, yet the boat lounge and the men before her disappeared from view. They were replaced by the beautifully manicured grounds of the private psychiatric clinic. The heavy, sweet fragrance of tropical flowers enveloped her. Two men were standing below the terrace shaded by the shiny leaves of a lemon tree. One she recognized from

the Falcon's briefing file as Jackson Talifero. The other was
a tall black man who stood silently, his face slightly averted.
Jessica sensed that he was struggling to hold back anger.

"You will prepare the ritual site for the usual Saturday
evening service," Talifero directed. "But I will be making
some changes in the normal procedures. The American
mambo is with us again. She will serve as priestess and you
will assist her. Is that understood?"

"Yes."

"See that she has everything she needs. She will probably want to prepare the American spy herself."

The voodoo priest nodded, even as he clenched his fist
behind his back. He was *hungan* on this estate, and he
should be the one to decide whom to offer to the great *loa*.
The American priestess had not earned that honor—or the
respect of his followers. Yet he couldn't protest if the doctor chose to give her his prerogative. The ceremony tomorrow, like so many conducted on the estate, was illegal. The
special rites were possible only because of Talifero's protection, and that put the ultimate power in his hands.

Jessica shuddered violently.

"What is it?" Michael demanded.

The picture snapped and the garden scene vanished. She
was back on the boat, feeling Michael's urgent hands on her
shoulders.

"What happened?" he repeated.

She swallowed convulsively. "They were talking about an
American spy. Jed, I assume."

"*Who* was talking?"

"Talifero and his *hungan*—his voodoo priest."

"So what did they say?" George Holcroft interjected. His
tone of voice indicated that he didn't attach much importance to voodoo priests.

"Talifero was giving the man instructions to prepare Jed
for a ceremony tomorrow night." She paused and frowned.
"Most of what I got was from their conversation. But I did
pick up something from the priest's mind—maybe because
he was so angry. The ceremony tomorrow night is illegal."

Michael turned to George. "What would that mean?"

The CIA agent swallowed. "About the only thing they don't allow down here in those ceremonies is human sacrifice."

Michael swore. "With Jed as the main event. We've got to get him out of there, and it looks as if we only have about thirty-six hours to do it."

"Which means we don't have time to bring in an American team. Relying on local talent can be tricky," Holcroft muttered.

"I'll put a unit on stand-by in case we have some time," Michael suggested. "But let's proceed on the assumption we have to move quickly. Who's available on the island?"

"A lot of people here are afraid of Talifero. But there are some who would welcome the opportunity to oust him. I do have the names of a few contacts."

Jessica put a hand on his arm. "There's one more thing that may be important."

"Yes?"

"Talifero and the priest were talking about an American voodoo *mambo*—a priestess." She paused. "I don't know why, but that gave me a really odd feeling."

"Do you think it's related to those voodoo charms we found back in New Orleans?"

"Maybe. But I think it's more than that. Something that's connected to me personally."

Michael studied her pale complexion. "Perhaps because you had such a strong reaction to the charms."

She nodded reluctantly. "That could be it." But deep inside she knew it was something she was afraid to delve into right then.

Michael turned back to George. "What else do you know about the services held on Talifero's estate?"

"They've got the island gripped in fear." He looked thoughtful. "However, there may be one factor in our favor. The ceremonies are by invitation only, but if you run with the right sort of crowd, invitations aren't that hard to come by."

"I take it you're not talking about us," Michael said. "We certainly couldn't pass as natives."

George agreed. "Right. But with my connections, we ought to be able to get a few allies at the site."

Michael nodded. "Then we'd better start getting the arrangements in place."

"What can I do to help?" Jessica asked.

"Stay here out of sight. When we come back I want you to help us figure out the layout of the estate."

"Perhaps I could try to project myself over there again while you're gone."

"No!"

The vehemence of the syllable made George's head whip around, but the Peregrine agent didn't notice.

Jessica's eyes challenged Michael's to a silent tug-of-war. "Why not?" she finally asked.

"Sometimes you can't get back by yourself, and I don't want to take any chances."

"You're right," she acquiesced. "This is new to me, too."

Michael looked at his watch. "If we're not back in three hours, use George's transmitter to call headquarters."

"You're not anticipating any trouble, are you?"

"No. But you never can tell."

Jessica pressed her hands against her sides to keep from reaching toward Michael and begging him not to go. She had the feeling that something wasn't going to work out the way he was anticipating, but she knew a vague warning wouldn't keep him from leaving. Besides, he and George could hardly stay there hiding when Jed's life was hanging in the balance.

"Take care," she whispered.

"You too. And don't get off the boat."

After they left Jessica washed the breakfast dishes and straightened the lounge before opening a day-old newspaper from Jamaica. It didn't hold her interest. Wandering up on deck, she unfolded a canvas chair and dragged it into the shade from the cabin. Though fairly well screened from prying eyes, she had a good view of the harbor. The dock was busy. Local merchants had set up an open-air market on the quay and were doing a brisk business in fresh produce and souvenirs. A native woman deftly weaving baskets caught her interest, and she wanted to go over for a closer look. Yet Michael's warning kept her on the boat. Standing up, she moved to the rail and leaned toward the shore. A small black boy wearing a score of shell necklaces saw her and came scurrying over.

"You want beautiful jewelry?" he asked in French.

The curly-haired little salesman looked so eager to please that she smiled, but shrugged. "I don't understand French."

He repeated the question in English. Jessica immediately asked, "How much?"

He removed several of the strands and held them out to her, naming a modest figure.

Jessica reached over and accepted them. They were made of tiny pearlaceous shells carefully strung on a long piece of nylon thread. "Did you make these yourself?" she asked.

"My sister."

From the shadow of a nearby building along the dock, another figure watched the interchange with interest. He'd been treated like a second-class citizen by Talifero ever since he'd arrived down there. He hadn't even gotten an invitation to the fancy dinner last night, and this morning he'd been sent out like one of the hired hands to keep an eye on the wharf. Already tired of the duty, he'd been about to find a café where he could get a cool drink. Now he was glad that he had remained on the scene. It looked as if he'd just found the trump card that was going to make Talifero take him seriously.

"I only have American money," the woman was saying.

"I give you best exchange rate." The boy grinned. He knew when he had a prospect hooked.

"You're quite a salesman. Let me get my purse." Jessica turned and ducked down the companionway to the lounge. When she reappeared, the man in the shadows watched her buy three shell necklaces and then resume her seat. It didn't look as if she were going anywhere, and it wouldn't take him more than fifteen minutes to go call in reinforcements.

MOONSHADOW SET DOWN her teacup and walked toward the bedroom window. Outside in the morning sunshine she could see Talifero talking to the *hungan,* Piers Lavintelle. She could imagine that the voodoo priest was unhappy about her presence. She certainly wouldn't like her power usurped by an interloper. But there was no other choice. Conducting tomorrow night's ceremony was a crucial part of the plan she was formulating.

She smiled with satisfaction. Her liaison in the garden last night with Gorlov—or Garcia, if he wanted to keep up the pretense—had been most informative. She'd given the man a great deal of pleasure. Afterward, while he was relaxed and vulnerable, she'd used a subtle hypnotic technique that had made him very talkative. Though he now remembered nothing of the conversation, he'd told her about Talifero's plan to turn the island into a Soviet-backed dictatorship—financed in large part from U.S. sales of Dove. Moscow would get another foothold in the Caribbean and Talifero would get the kind of power he craved.

The Soviets weren't willing to put up the initial money, but if Talifero proved he could pull off the coup, they were going to cement the relationship with foreign aid. Already communist military advisors and arms were in Cuba waiting for Gorlov to give the go-ahead for their embarkation. Now that Moscow's representative had met Xavier and toured the chemist's laboratory, he was very close to giving the order.

Gorlov had been very pleased with the idea of flooding the U.S. market with Dove. It would be a very disruptive influence. But Moonshadow knew that the pain would be felt most intensely in the lower-class community where drugs were a way of holding the realities of a harsh life at bay.

The prospect sickened her. So did Talifero's plans for Royale Verde. As absolute master of Blackstone he was formidable enough. As the absolute ruler of a Caribbean

island, he would be the scourge of the native population—
and very dangerous to her personally. She suspected that he
had plans to keep her here. If his island takeover proceeded
as anticipated, there would be no way to get out from under his thumb.

Her only option was to stop his bid for power while she
still could. But to carry off her escape plan, she would need
Xavier's help. Even after her previous betrayal, she was sure
she could get the chemist to cooperate with her. After all,
she would be offering him a way out of his dilemma. And
if logic didn't work, she'd make up another charm to bring
him around using the vial of his blood that she'd brought
with her from New Orleans. Yes, in the end he'd do her
bidding. The only real problem was his stability. Though he
was putting up a good front, she knew he was in worse shape
than he'd been in New Orleans. If he went to pieces at the
wrong time, he could get both of them killed.

THE MORNING HAD GONE well, Michael thought as he and
Holcroft strode back down the quay toward the *Sea Turtle*.
The Peregrine agent was eager to tell Jessica about the local
men they'd recruited and share some of the firsthand information he'd picked up.

The underground opposition to Talifero was more organized than he'd suspected. Several of the recruits had actually attended voodoo services at Blackstone in order to
assess Talifero's strength.

Another dissident who hadn't been willing to go along
had still been a very valuable source of information. He had
worked briefly as a gardener at the estate and had provided
a crude map of the compound. The lab was outside the main
wall and not too far from the place where the voodoo rituals were held. But Michael wanted Jessica to fill in more
details and particularly to pinpoint where Talifero was
holding Jed.

"She must be below," Holcroft observed as they drew
close to the craft. Pulling the mooring rope, he brought the

bow up to the edge of the wooden pier and stepped across onto the deck.

"Jessica?" Michael called as he followed the CIA agent. There was no answer.

"Jessica?" he tried again. When his foot crunched against something on the deck, he looked down. It was a little pile of pink fragments that must have been a seashell, judging from the other shells that were scattered across the painted boards.

Holcroft stooped down and picked up a strand of nylon thread on which a few shells were still strung. Flung into the corner was another strand, still intact. "It looks as if she bought a couple of necklaces from one of the local vendors," he observed.

"I told her not to get off the boat," Michael muttered.

"She didn't have to. The boys often come right up to the boat hawking their wares."

"That doesn't explain where she is now."

"Maybe she went to get her money back. We can check the dock if you're worried," Holcroft offered.

Michael looked down at the broken strand. "I'm worried."

As he started back down the wharf, a small black boy wearing a dozen shell necklaces detached himself from the crowd and scurried into a side street. Michael sprinted in his direction and caught up easily. "Wait a minute. I want to talk to you."

"I didn't do nothing, boss."

"Did you see a lady on the boat?"

The boy's dark eyes slid away from the man's penetrating gaze.

"Did you see where she went?"

Michael fished in his pocket for some coins. "Tell me."

The boy licked his lips and looked at the money. "She left with two white men. I don't think she wanted to go."

Michael drew in a deep breath. "Can you describe them?"

"Most white men look alike to me, boss. But one, he had an ugly scar on his face. It was shaped like a star."

"On his left cheek?"

"You see him too, boss?"

Michael swore. He only knew one man with a scar like that—Lonnie, the dope distributor who had given the Dove to Jessica and been in charge of the recapture of Xavier. If he'd taken Jessica away, there was only one place she could be now: the Blackstone Clinic.

"How long ago did they leave with her?" he rasped.

The boy shrugged. "It's been a while."

"Thanks." Handing the kid the money, Michael turned away, a sick feeling churning in his stomach. Christ, Jessica in Lonnie's hands again! He remembered what that bastard had had in mind for her last time—and what he had tried to do to him as well. The thought made him want to go pound on the gates of the Blackstone Clinic and demand entrance. But he couldn't do that. He'd just end up the way Jed had, and that wasn't going to do anybody any good. He had to think clearly and not let his emotions trick him into doing something that was going to lose the whole shooting match for everybody.

Chapter Sixteen

Lonnie and his friend had waited patiently in the shadows until the boy left. Then, when Jessica had turned back to the companionway stairs to put the necklaces away, the drug dealer had made his way quickly down the dock and vaulted onto the deck of the *Sea Turtle*. After grabbing Jessica from behind, he'd wrestled her quickly out of sight into the lounge, where the other man had joined them. In a few succinct sentences, the man from New Orleans had explained what would happen to her if she screamed in the public dock area or tried to make a break for it.

In very short order the three of them were making their way down the quay, Lonnie holding firmly to Jessica's arm and shielding the gun in her back with his body. As she passed, she tried desperately to catch the eye of the boy who had sold her the shell necklaces. He gave her a quick frightened look and turned his head away.

When Jessica and her captors reached a battered Ford parked on a narrow side street, Lonnie shoved her down into the backseat and gagged her with a handkerchief. After securing her hands and ankles with cord, the two men covered her with a dusty blanket. One of them remained in the backseat with her while the other drove.

It was hot and stuffy under the cover. With the gag in her mouth she could hardly breathe. She was half lying, half sitting. Whoever was driving was in a hurry, and the car swayed along winding roads, throwing her alternately against the locked door and the man who sat next to her. But the discomfort was nothing compared to her fear. The memory of Jed strapped to that table with acid pumping through his veins leapt into her mind. Convulsively she thrust it away. God, what was in store for her?

"Lie still," the man next to her hissed. For emphasis his fingers closed around her arm in a vicelike grip. Escape seemed all the more impossible. Where were they taking her? The Blackstone Clinic was the most likely destination. The only hope she could cling to was that Michael was already mounting a rescue operation for Jed and Xavier.

They stopped only once, at what she assumed was a guard post. There was a hurried conversation in guttural French and then the clank of a heavy metal gate. On the other side was a crushed stone drive. The car swung off to the right and lurched to a stop. Jessica was pulled roughly from the seat. Someone untied her feet. But the other restraints remained. The blanket still over her head, she was marched through a doorway into an air-conditioned building. She could see only her feet and a small circle of polished tile floor. The man who had been in the backseat with her still kept a punishing grip on her arms. But her own terror numbed the sensation. Her heart was pounding in her ears and she could feel the vibrations throughout her body.

The conversation on the other side of the door came to her as waves of sound that she couldn't decipher. She only knew the speakers might well be deciding her fate. When the barrier finally opened, she was shoved inside.

"What have we here?" a cultured male voice inquired as the blanket was pulled off her head.

The sudden brightness of the room made her blink. When her vision cleared she found herself staring at the white-haired man who had been giving orders in the garden. It was Jackson Talifero. His cold tone of command had frightened her in the vision. The reality of standing in the same room with him was far worse.

"It's the bitch who was messing with our operation in New Orleans," Lonnie supplied.

"Hmm," Talifero murmured. He studied Jessica with the keen interest of a scientist fascinated with a new biological specimen.

She tried not to flinch. But as he removed the gag from her mouth, her heart began to pound even harder.

Tousled auburn hair, pixie face, enormous hazel eyes, white ankle pants, and a T-shirt. She didn't look much like an intelligence agent. It was probably a carefully cultivated persona. Though she was frightened, she was putting up a brave front. "What are you doing down here?" he snapped.

She looked away. It was useless to try the cover story Constance McGuire had prepared for her. Lonnie had already recognized her.

"Well?" Talifero prompted, his voice taking on a biting edge.

When she didn't answer, he slapped her hard across the face. Her eyes stung and she bit back a scream.

"We'll find out why you're here, whether you cooperate or not," he promised. The confidence of his tone wasn't reassuring. She didn't know if she could survive what he'd done to Jed.

Talifero addressed his next question to Lonnie. "Did you search the boat?"

The pale man shook his head apologetically. "No. I thought I should bring her right here to you."

"I want to know who she's working for."

"She was with that DEA agent, Michael Rome, in New Orleans. We took care of him back there."

"I hope so, for your sake," the director said with a growl. "You should have asked for instructions. Now I'm going to have to get Barahona's men on the job, if it's not already too late."

What a mess, Talifero thought. He hadn't let on to Gorlov that the captive starring in the ceremony tomorrow was an intelligence agent. Now this girl turned up. If the Russian suspected Blackstone was being stalked, Moscow might well withdraw their support.

Talifero turned away toward the window, his hands clasped easily behind his back. But his mind was racing. *All right, think it through calmly, don't panic. Probably she knows Prentiss. The man hadn't broken under torture. But perhaps if you put them together, he may respond to a friendly face from home. Maybe they'll talk to each other. And if they don't, you can always get rid of her at the ceremony with him.*

Lonnie cleared his throat. "Doctor."

Talifero swung back to face the drug distributor. "Yes."

"She's the chick who got that shot of Dove back in New Orleans. Only Rome came in and messed things up for me."

The director's eyes held a speculative gleam as he ran his fingers down her bare arm. "And what happened after that?" he murmured. "Was Mr. Rome the benefactor of Lonnie's largesse?"

She pressed her lips together.

"I was wondering if you might let me, uh, take up where I left off with her when Rome interrupted us," the drug dealer put in.

Talifero laughed. "Now that's an idea! We do have the facilities for it."

Jessica clenched her fingers together behind her back, her nails digging into her palms.

The director turned to her. "Would you tell me whom you're working for if I promised not to turn you over to Lonnie?"

"No." The syllable was the most difficult Jessica had ever uttered. But Talifero's question hadn't given her any hope. She saw no reason why he would keep his word.

"Well, maybe I'll let you think about it for a while."

At that moment there was a knock at the door. Talifero glanced at his watch. He'd forgotten that he'd made an appointment with Moonshadow to discuss tomorrow's ceremony. Well, she was going to have to know about this new development sooner or later.

"Come in," he called out.

The priestess took several paces into the room but stopped abruptly when she saw the young woman with her hands tied behind her back.

"No, my dear. You don't have to leave. I was just interrogating another prisoner. Maybe you could give me some suggestions on how to make her more cooperative."

The director put a hand on Jessica's shoulder and turned her roughly around. She found herself facing an extremely attractive and very self-contained black woman dressed in a flowing jade caftan and matching turban. Unwillingly her eyes were drawn to the smooth tawny features, heavily accented with makeup. Her eyes squeezed shut to block out the image. An illusion. Oh, God, let it be a mistake! When she opened them again and stared at the self-possessed woman, she felt a chill freeze her heart. My God, Simone! Jessica gasped.

The priestess drew on years of discipline. Her face betrayed nothing.

Talifero's gaze flicked from one woman to the other. Was there something here below the surface that he didn't understand? "You seem to have startled Ms. Duval, Moonshadow. Do the two of you know each other?"

Jessica held her breath, her mind reeling from the shock of the unexpected meeting—here at the Blackstone Clinic of all places. She'd seen Simone in New Orleans only last week. What words would come out of the woman's mouth? she wondered. She seemed to be an ally of Talifero. He called her Moonshadow. She'd never heard that name. What else didn't she know about Simone?

"Ms. Duval and Michael Rome consulted me about the voodoo charm the police found at Lonnie's."

"Quite a coincidence. Where do you suppose they got your name?"

The black woman shrugged imperiously. "I am well known around New Orleans as being an authority on such matters. Quite probably someone recommended me to Rome."

"I see." The director stroked his chin. "I'm thinking about having her join Prentiss tomorrow evening at the ceremony you'll be conducting. Would you have any objections to offering two sacrifices to your gods?"

"None whatsoever." The assurance in her voice was matched by the cool indifference in the depths of her ebony eyes.

"GET READY TO CAST OFF right now," Michael snapped as he jumped aboard the boat.

Holcroft looked up, startled. He and Rome had only been back at the wharf for a few minutes. "You're not going to wait and see if Jessica turns up?"

"She'd not going to turn up. One of Talifero's men got her."

Holcroft swore. "Are you sure?"

"Absolutely. The kid she bought the necklaces from described him to me. He's the candy man from New Orleans who tried to kill me. He must have brought Xavier back."

"And you think someone's coming back for us?"

"Exactly."

Holcroft was already untying the line at the bow. Michael cast off the one at the stern. "I assume you can change the name on this tub," he said as the CIA agent started the engine.

"Naturally. I'll take care of it as soon as we get out to sea."

Neither man spoke until they had cleared the crowded harbor.

"I'd better put in a call to headquarters," Michael said, heading for the lounge.

"Yeah." And ask XP 251 what we're supposed to do now, Holcroft added silently.

A BURLY ATTENDANT opened the metal door of the dimly lit little room and shoved Jessica inside. She landed on the cement floor in a heap. For a moment she lay still, struggling to catch her breath. Her head was still spinning.

Her old friend Simone was there, apparently working with Talifero and mixed up in this drug thing. It was hard to believe, but it must be true. Suddenly pieces of a puzzle fell into place. She remembered the day Simone had come to Aubrey's apartment. She'd tried to talk Jessica out of probing into the drug scene. The words had sounded so earnest. But she hadn't been worried about her old friend at all. She'd been protecting her own interests.

When she'd failed with Jessica, she'd set the trap for Michael at the cemetery. And Jessica had unwittingly helped Simone by introducing her to Michael. The thought made her head throb. Why hadn't she been able to read Simone's duplicity? The answer was all too clear now. The woman was a voodoo priestess. She had probably fashioned the talisman that had burned her, which meant she had powers beyond Jessica's wildest dreams. She hadn't come around or written after Aubrey's death because she was already down here with Talifero.

Now Jessica knew why she had reacted in her vision to the director's reference to the visiting voodoo *mambo*. He'd been talking about Simone.

For a long time she was too heartsick and disoriented to move. When she finally raised her face and glanced around her cell, she was startled to see that she wasn't alone. In the corner of the room, sitting on a narrow mattress that rested directly on the floor, was a broad-shouldered man. He was wearing only a pair of faded jeans. His hair was matted and his skin was pale. There were rope burns around his wrists and ankles and cuts across his broad chest. Jed. So he was still alive. Thank God for that at least.

She stared at him, remembering how she had been drawn into his mind, wanting to comfort him when he'd been in pain. Now, though battered by his captives, he appeared completely unapproachable on any sort of personal level.

He regarded her with cynical interest. "Well, what have we here?" he questioned.

"I—"

"It was just a rhetorical question, honey," he cut her off abruptly, his look condescending. This was probably just another one of Talifero's tricks. "They've put you in here for some purpose. Probably to get me to talk."

He'd suffered through that tricarbotane torture without talking. He certainly wasn't going to give anything away to this woman—no matter how innocent she looked. "Maybe you don't know it, but we're live on TV right now." He pointed toward a small round opening near the ceiling.

Jessica gulped and nodded.

"So, whether you're one of the unfortunate inmates of this asylum, or one of Talifero's confederates, or even a fellow prisoner, I don't have anything to say to you." He crossed his arms and looked toward the cinderblock wall.

Jessica closed her eyes for a moment, struggling to assimilate his defiant words. Jed. He'd gone through so much, and he was still fighting them. Would she have that kind of courage when they tortured her? And how could she get through to him now?

"Do I have to sit on the cold floor?" she finally asked him.

He shrugged and moved to one end of the mattress. "I guess not."

Jessica scooted over beside him. For several minutes they sat in silence. She had to communicate with him, tell him what was happening. But how? They couldn't talk. It would be suicidal to let Talifero in on Michael's plans. God, if she could only project her thoughts. But that power was beyond her.

"I'm frightened," she murmured, trying to reach him with her eyes as much as her voice. That was no lie. She was terrified, more than ever now that she knew about Simone.

"I don't particularly want to hear about it."

Another long silence followed. She might as well have not been in the room. She used the time to think of and discard ideas. Could they communicate in some sort of code?

A workable plan began to form in her mind. After shooting Jed another quick look, she reached out and clasped his hand so that her fingers were against his large palm. When he tried to pull away, she covered his hand with her other one. "Please," she whispered. She felt the tension in his body.

Angling herself so that their hands were hidden from the camera, she scratched her thumb down his palm.

From under hooded lashes, he gave her a questioning look.

"Please, I'm frightened. Just let me hold on to you," she repeated.

He said nothing, but he didn't withdraw from the contact.

She scored his skin again. This time, instead of a straight line, she made a letter "F."

He nodded almost imperceptibly. He understood what she was doing.

Slowly, writing with her thumb, she spelled out the word "Falcon."

She heard him draw in his breath. His blue eyes probed her face.

With their hands still hidden from the camera, he reversed the process, spelling out a word in her palm.

"How?"

"Rome."

For the first time, hope flickered in his eyes. He studied her face, then shifted so that she could lean more comfortably against him.

"When?"

She rested her head against his shoulder, glad for the simple human comfort.

"Tomorrow."

"You?"

"Jessica."

Had he met her before? He didn't think so. Yet there was something familiar about her, as if he somehow knew her. The Falcon must have sent her and Michael down there. He could only assume that she had gotten captured or let herself be taken in order to facilitate the rescue. But there was another explanation for her presence in this cell, he reminded himself. If Talifero had somehow gotten hold of the word *Falcon,* it could all be a clever trap. But then he'd also have to know about Michael Rome.

Jed closed his eyes, not wanting her to read his sudden vulnerability. There were a thousand questions he wanted, needed to ask—questions that would take all day to spell out in the palm of her hand. But then it looked as though neither one of them was going anywhere.

"DUVAL AND PRENTISS have been locked in that cell together for six hours now. They're sitting huddled together like two dogs trying to keep warm. But as far as I can tell, they've hardly said a word." Talifero walked over to the sideboard and poured himself a drink. Then he turned back to Simone. "I have half a mind to take Lonnie up on his offer. Maybe after an hour or so with him, our new prisoner will be willing to talk."

The priestess shook her head. "I can't allow that."

"What do you mean *you* can't allow it? I give the orders down here."

"In the old days, a woman used in the ceremony would have been a virgin."

Talifero laughed. "I assume it's a little late for that with Ms. Duval."

"But still, she must be as pure as possible. Letting an animal like Lonnie defile her so soon before the ceremony would make her entirely unacceptable to the great *loa.* "

Talifero muttered an oath. "Do you honestly believe that nonsense?"

Moonshadow drew herself up straighter in her chair. "So you consider my religion nonsense."

"Your religion! It's just a tool you use to make your living."

"You have a rather distorted view of me, Jackson."

"Oh, no, my dear, I have a very clear perception of you. But for some reason of your own, you obviously have your heart set on making tomorrow's ritual authentic, so I won't stand in your way." He was willing to humor the woman for the moment. He didn't want one of her tantrums messing things up with Gorlov, and until he had control of the island, she was still a threat. But as soon as the coup was over, he was going to take personal pleasure in breaking her.

The priestess inclined her head slightly. "In that case, I'd appreciate it if you'd move her to a cell by herself for the night."

"I was going to do that anyway."

JESSICA SHIFTED on her mattress and tried to get comfortable. Though it was dark and quiet in her tiny cell, sleep eluded her. She tried to mentally detach herself from the claustrophobic surroundings—let her mind find Michael. But some force seemed to hold her spirit bound as effectively as the locked door kept her body from escaping.

When two of Talifero's goons had come to separate her from Jed, she'd struggled violently, terrified that she was going to be handed over to Lonnie. But she'd simply been taken to a solitary room and left with a bowl of water and some thin stew for dinner. She'd been afraid the food might be drugged. But after a few cautious tastes, she'd been hungry enough to finish the stuff. If that was what the patients there got regularly, she felt damned sorry for them.

There was a metal clank at the door of her cell, and Jessica tensed. Were they coming to get her after all?

"Jessica?" a voice whispered in the darkness. "I must talk to you."

She sat up. The voice was Simone's.

"Come over here and put your face near the crack in the door. Hurry. I must turn on the TV camera again very soon, before someone suspects."

"I have nothing to say to you."

"Hurry. I'm trying to save your life."

Stiffly she got up and moved to the door. "Why should I believe you?" she whispered.

"It's your only hope of survival. But if I'm going to help you, I must know who came down here with you."

So that was it. A trap for Michael. Jessica pressed her lips together.

"Jessica!"

"I have nothing to say to you. Go away and leave me alone."

"Don't you understand? The ceremony tomorrow will be a human sacrifice. You and Jed."

"You're on Talifero's side. Why should you do anything for me?"

"I tried to warn you off. I never intended for you to get mixed up in this, but Talifero is a powerful man. I had to obey him."

"Then how can you defy him now?"

"A calculated risk. I believe I can defeat him once and for all."

"Why do you need to know who I came here with?"

"So they can rescue you."

"I find that hard to believe."

"Trust me."

Jessica squeezed her eyes shut for a moment. She wanted to believe, but it was impossible. "I can't."

THERE WAS NO WAY he could get to sleep, Michael thought, shifting uncomfortably on the narrow bunk. He already knew what they had done to Jed. He wondered what they might be doing to Jessica and clenched his fists.

Jessica! Had he really walked away from her in the library back at the Aviary? He remembered when she'd needed him, how her body had moved frantically against his, how his arms had tightened around her, soothed her. He remembered the taste of her mouth, her sweetness, her insistence that she was responding to him, not just the drug. Then later, when she had almost literally brought him back from the dead, how she had held him in turn, comforted him, given him everything that a woman could give a man. Given him her love.

Her love. He pictured her face that night, the tenderness in her eyes mixed with the passion. She *had* given him more than he was willing to accept. Though she had been afraid to tell him how she felt, she had still given. Unselfishly, without reserve. He had repaid her with rejection.

Jess, he thought. *Oh, God, Jess. You mean so much to me, and I never got a chance to tell you. I was afraid to open myself up to you, terrified I was just going to hurt you. I'm going to try to get you out of there. If I can, Jess. If I can.*

Suddenly the cabin was too oppressive, too closed in. He had to get out into the open air. Swinging his legs over the side, he eased himself down to the deck. A quick glance told him Holcroft was sleeping. Moving quietly so as not to disturb the agent, he climbed the stairs to the aft deck and stood looking back toward the dark shoreline. He felt as if something was searching for him in the night, and he must respond.

The disembodied presence came across the dark water seeking him, tentatively at first and then with more assurance. He felt something—no, someone—touch his mind and knew that he was neither dreaming nor fully awake.

Michael Rome! I dared not hope to find you here. But I should have known.

He didn't exactly hear words, but his mind turned the disembodied thoughts into language. "Who are you?" His heart leapt. "Jess?"

Not Jessica. A friend.

The sound that wasn't sound solidified in his mind. A woman. He knew her and yet he didn't. He tried to bring her image into focus. She blocked his efforts.

Better not to see me. Don't waste time trying. I can communicate like this only briefly.

"How did you find me?"

You were thinking of Jessica. Strong thoughts. Loving thoughts. Despairing thoughts.

"Why are you here?"

The ceremony tomorrow. Jessica is to be part of it—with Jed.

He cursed softly. He had been afraid of that.

Do not despair. You can rescue them. Directions came to him in staccato phrases and sentences. *Don't come by water. Circle Blackstone to the west and approach the ceremonial grounds from the back. Fewer guards. It will seem that your friends are being slain. A sham. There will be a diversion. Wait until then to make your move.*

"Who are you? Why are you telling me this?"

Together we can stop Talifero.

He felt her disengaging, slipping away. "Wait. I need to know more."

But the presence had already vanished into the darkness of the night.

Chapter Seventeen

Gilbert Xavier looked around the well-equipped laboratory and sneered, his lips drawing back into a canine parody of a smile. Talifero had supplied him with everything from a spectrophotometer to an electron microscope that had its own special AC generator. It was a work environment to rival anything found at the top research universities. But instead of being shared by dozens of chemists, it was his alone. Today that didn't excite him the way it had when he'd first arrived at the Blackstone Clinic. He'd come to realize that the expensive facility was a Venus flytrap, and he was the fly that had become enmeshed in its sticky poison.

He picked up several of the expensive quartz tubes for the spectrophotometer and let them slip through his fingers to the polished granite of the lab table where they splintered into nasty-looking shards. Too bad there wasn't a spare gun in the supply cabinet along with the extra tubes. In his present frame of mind, he could almost imagine himself confronting Talifero, demanding his freedom, and shooting the man if he didn't let him go.

It had taken him years to develop the exacting process that turned swamp plants into V-22. When he'd run away before, he'd taken his notes. Lonnie and his men had brought them back to Blackstone. Talifero had made sure that they weren't going to leave the grounds again. So if he did what Simone wanted tonight, he really would be giving up everything. What's more, the element of risk was absurdly high. It was hard to picture himself coming out of this alive. But what did it matter? His situation was untenable. Better dead than red, he thought, remembering the details Simone had given him about Franco Garcia—or, more properly, Feliks Gorlov. Xavier began to giggle. Once he started, it was hard to stop.

He found that tears were streaming down his face and wiped them away with the back of his hand. He'd better get a grip on himself. If he was going to carry out Simone's instructions, he had work to do. Opening the cabinet where the glassware was kept, he removed a large retort and several beakers. Then he took out the key to the reagent storage room.

MICHAEL SAT UP in the bunk and shook his head. He'd had a crazy dream last night, probably the product of his own desperation. A disembodied phantom had come to him in the night, promising that he could save Jed and Jessica and giving him instructions. It had all been very real at the time. But in the light of day, it seemed preposterous. He could hardly rely on that kind of aid. Go by land instead of sea. It sounded like a line from Henry Wadsworth Longfellow.

But he wasn't the only one making the raid on Blackstone that night. Even if he were willing to risk his neck on the advice of a mysterious voice inside his head, he could hardly ask Holcroft and his local men to do the same.

That made him doubly surprised when the CIA man himself broached the subject of the approach to the clinic as they sat with mugs of morning coffee in the lounge of the boat that had been hastily rechristened *Star Fish*.

"You know," the agent mused, "I've been giving tonight's mission a lot of thought. Your man Prentiss went in by boat. I would have done the same thing. But he got caught. I assume he knew what he was doing. So either that access is heavily patrolled, or he was damned unlucky." He took a sip of his coffee. "I'd like to make sure we don't get pulled in by the same net."

"What do you think about coming up the main road and circling the grounds?" Michael asked cautiously.

"Risky. But in light of our present intelligence, maybe it makes sense. Talifero is no dummy. He knows Jessica can't be working alone. In addition to his usual guards, he's undoubtedly prepared to fight off a rescue attempt. But let's try to duplicate his thinking. He probably figures the least likely approach anyone would make is along the main road. So that may very well be the weak spot in his defenses."

"I was wondering about that myself. Unfortunately, I was hoping Jessica could supply a better map of the place."

Holcroft gave the other agent a considering look. Rome seemed like a pretty stable guy, yet he'd taken the girl's vision yesterday damned seriously. "Tell me honestly," he asked, "do you really believe in that psychic stuff?"

Michael took a sip of his own cooling coffee. The question meant Holcroft didn't give Jessica's abilities much credence. All the more reason to keep quiet about last night's private "vision." If he spilled that, Holcroft would probably turn the boat in the other direction and head for Jamaica. Michael shrugged. "Her hunches seem more on target than most people's. But I'll let you know what I think for sure when this is over."

Holcroft laughed. "Yeah. You and me both. Too bad she can't pick locks with her mind. Then she could get Prentiss, and the two of them could walk right out of that place so we wouldn't have to risk our necks going in."

Don't I wish, Michael thought.

"It would help if we knew what Talifero was planning for Jessica," he said aloud, wondering if the specter had been right about that too. "I hate to think we have to hit the ceremonial grounds and two of the buildings."

"The local guys may well have some information on that. News travels fast around here."

"Right. Let's get going."

The two men had arranged to meet their team of half a dozen local dissidents at a small inlet about ten miles up the coast from their original mooring.

By the time they arrived at midmorning, the little group had already assembled and were waiting out of sight in a clump of trees. Michael and Holcroft anchored the *Star Fish* a hundred yards out in the bay and rowed in. After stowing the small boat in the underbrush, they joined the local recruits.

"We had to be very careful," one of them commented. "Barahona has extra men out around the island—like he's expecting trouble."

Holcroft nodded and filled the group in on what had happened since their last meeting.

"Not good for the girl," a young man commented. "I hear they like to jolt up the sisters and have some fun with them."

"No, I heard from my cousin who delivered vegetables out there this morning that the white woman's going to be saved for the ritual," another corrected.

Michael's jaw clenched and he looked away. God, he hoped the man was right, but what a thing to hope for. Pretending that he was still concerned about the rowboat, he walked over and rearranged the vines that had been thrown over the top. The man's news was more confirmation that last night's strange message was right. He straightened and took several deep breaths. When he turned back to the group a few minutes later, his face was impassive.

"All right, what can you tell me about Blackstone and the ceremonies?" he continued the questioning.

A lithe, very dark-skinned man named Jon Bequi seemed to know the most about the clinic. Though he was no voodoo worshiper, he had attended several rituals in order to pick up useful information.

"Do they search for weapons?" Michael asked.

"Sure do, mon. And they only let local people in. No spies."

"Then the three of you attending the service will have to go in unarmed. We'll carry extra pistols and ammunition for you."

"How large a crowd can we expect?" Holcroft wanted to know.

"Maybe forty people. Maybe eighty. This is a big event. But you wait a couple of hours into the service. They be on the ground writhing around. Won't even know you're there."

"We may not be able to wait that long."

"When does the priest, uh, make the sacrifice?"

"He likes to wait until the people are pretty charged up. It depends."

They asked more questions and were not necessarily pleased by the answers. But at least they were able to pick up a good deal more information about the setup at Blackstone.

The key to the rescue lay in the regulation military-issue C-4 plastic explosives they'd had brought along from the Aviary. Michael wasn't going to wait for some specter's diversion. He was going to create his own. The men on the team would be needed to help set the charges at various locations around the clearing. Since they had no idea when the murders would take place, the C-4 couldn't be set off with timing devices. Instead they would have to use antennas and transmitters and be within a quarter of a mile of the blast sites. That made their possible discovery all the more likely. But they had to be close in to pull Jessica and Jed out anyway.

Jon Bequi suggested that they approach the compound during the afternoon. "They don't expect anyone to come in broad daylight," he pointed out. "My brother sometimes goes up there to sell them fresh fish. He had a good catch yesterday. We could ride in the back of the van."

"Does Barahona have a checkpoint on the road to the sanitarium? Will his men want to have a look in the truck?" Michael asked.

Bequi shrugged. "The driver will slip them some money and tell them we're in a hurry. To make the point, we'll stow some rotten fish in the back."

Michael and Holcroft exchanged glances. So they were going to be riding to Blackstone in a truck with rotten fish. Well, if that was the best way to get there, so be it.

But they planned an alternate way to get out. Two of the men would bring the *Star Fish* to Devil's Point and wait off the coast for a signal if needed.

THERE WAS ONLY WEAK TEA for breakfast and no lunch. Jessica huddled in her dark cell, wondering what was going to happen next. In the middle of the afternoon, three muscular female attendants came for her. Two pulled her up by the arms and led her out of the cell. The other stood by in case of trouble.

When she asked where she was being taken, rough hands simply shoved her down the hall. After that she kept her mouth shut and tried to stay calm. The first stop was a shower room where her clothing was summarily stripped off. Then she was thrust under a spray of water where her hair and body were washed. The attendants dried her with a large towel, rubbing her hair so vigorously that her scalp stung. It felt good to be clean. Yet the very impersonal way the women were treating her—almost as if she were an object, not a person—was disconcerting. What were they preparing her for? She didn't want to examine the possibilities.

One of the women threw a long cotton robe over her shoulders, and she shrugged her arms into the sleeves, glad to cover her nakedness once more. Clutching the front closed, she was hustled barefoot down a flight of stairs to a hall with a vaulted stone ceiling. The guard who wasn't gripping one of her arms knocked on a wide mahogany door.

"Enter," a voice instructed.

Jessica was thrust inside to find herself facing Simone. The priestess was dressed in a simple white shift and turban. She pointed toward a wooden table similar to the one where Jed had been strapped down when he had been given the tricarbotane.

"No!" Jessica was powerless to hold the plea back.

"Quiet," an attendant commanded.

Though Jessica put up a struggle, it wasn't difficult for the muscular woman to strip off the robe and strap her naked to the table. Simone casually laid a piece of coarse linen across her middle, slipped it under her hips, and tied it at one side to make a sort of short sarong. Then she turned back to the attendants. "You may leave me now."

"The doctor has asked me to wait outside the door," the tallest of the three announced.

"That will be satisfactory. But this part of the ritual only I may witness."

The three women withdrew, leaving Jessica alone with the priestess.

Simone eyed the almost-naked woman strapped to the table. She could see the terror in Jessica's eyes and the tension in her body as she tested the bonds that held her arms and legs to the corners of the table.

"This is the only place in Blackstone besides Talifero's bedroom that's not on his closed-circuit system," she whispered. "But I can believe the woman out there has her ear pressed to the door."

Jessica closed her eyes for a moment, then opened them again to study the face of the woman she had thought was her friend. "What are you going to do to me?" she asked, unable to keep her voice steady but wanting to know the worst.

"Prepare you—as I did your friend Jed an hour ago—for the voodoo ceremony. The two of you are to be sacrificed to the gods tonight."

The casual way the words were uttered was numbing. So she was going to die here. What else was in store for her first? "After Lonnie's had me?" she asked quietly.

"I've made sure he won't touch you."

"Thank you for that, at least."

Simone sighed and moved very close to the table, observing her captive's face. "Jessica, the *hungan* will be with me at the ceremony. He must read your terror, know that it is real."

"What—what are you talking about?"

"I'm sorry, old friend. Sorry that you got yourself involved in this. It was your old psychic powers that pulled you in."

Jessica nodded tightly.

"You had a lot of ability, even as a teenager. But what happened this time may be partly my fault."

Jessica stared at her wide-eyed. "How?"

"I was focused on you when you came back. The connection between us may have helped awaken your buried powers."

"Then please," Jessica appealed. "Please just let me go."

"You wouldn't make it across the grounds. Now, stop talking to me or I will be forced to put a gag in your mouth. I'm sorry for what happened, but there's nothing more I can do."

The thought of another choking gag made Jessica's stomach knot. She clamped her lips together. Last night Simone had come to her and pretended that she was trying to help her. Thank God she hadn't grasped at that straw. At least she had told the priestess nothing. She could comfort herself with that.

It had been a long time since she'd thought of religion in any positive sense. Now she found a remembered psalm from her childhood running through her head. The words helped to soothe her a bit.

Moving to the shelves against the wall, Simone opened a jar of fragrant oil. She rubbed it on Jessica's wrists and feet and the sides of her breasts, releasing a strong jasmine odor into the room.

Next she took a pot of red pigment and began stirring it with a small stick. Coming back to Jessica, she dipped a brush into the jar and drew a small circle around the pulse point at the base of her neck. A soft chant flowed from her lips as she worked.

Jessica closed her eyes and gritted her teeth. Her arms jerked at the bonds, but her struggle had no effect.

"Lie still," Moonshadow commanded. "You'll only hurt yourself."

Intoning all the while, the priestess painted outward from her original circle, fashioning a chain of similar circles, which she filled in with black and white. Other designs were blue, green, and yellow.

Jessica could feel her heart thumping against her ribs. The sensation of the brush smoothing across her flesh and the priestess's lulling singsong were not unpleasant, but the implications were. The design became more elaborate as the priestess worked, spreading up the captive's neck, down her arms, and across her breasts, turning her white flesh into an exotic work of pagan art.

On her hands and fingers the strokes grew more delicate, like a fretwork of painted lace. The ritual itself was mesmerizing, almost blocking out the horror that was to be its culmination. Jessica's eyes closed, her mind drifting. If only they were Michael's fingers touching her, not Simone's. She wanted to reach out to him, tell him what was happening to her. See him one last time. Let him know how much she loved him. The unspoken words burned in the back of her throat now, like unshed tears.

Where was he now? she wondered. Her mind reached outward, wanting, needing him. Abruptly she felt Simone's hand on her shoulder, shaking her from her reverie.

"No!" the priestess commanded. "You must stay here. You belong to me now."

Jessica's eyes snapped open. "What are you doing to me?" she cried out.

"I'm doing what is necessary. It won't be long before the ceremony now."

There was a basket of small white orchids on the shelf. Moonshadow brought it down and began to stud the delicate flowers into the curls of Jessica's hair.

When she finished, she stepped back to admire her handiwork. "You really do look quite lovely," she murmured.

"But I must go robe myself now. We will meet again very shortly." Simone turned and left the room.

In the basement chamber, Jessica had lost all track of time. Now she could hear the sound of drums coming from the jungle. With great effort, she raised her head and looked down at her painted body and knew a fear that reached to the very depths of her soul.

JACKSON TALIFERO rarely attended the voodoo ceremonies, but when he paid the worshipers that honor, he occupied a special seat on a platform at the right of the altar where he had an excellent view of the proceedings. Tonight his guest, Feliks Gorlov, was sitting beside him. With the flickering torchlight, pulsing drums, and colorfully dressed participants, it was really quite a spectacular show, he thought. Not to mention the *hungan* prancing around in his feather costume waving his arms about like a great bird of prey as he exhorted the faithful. Tourists would probably pay premium prices to see something like this, but the ceremonies held behind the Blackstone Clinic were reserved for the true believers and a few privileged voyeurs. It was a mark of Talifero's status on the island that the ritual was conducted on his property and that his presence and that of his guest was accepted. Any other white man who tried to sneak in would be treated to the same painful reception that Jed Prentiss had experienced. Too bad the American agent hadn't broken, Blackstone's director mused. But with the Dove deal shifting into gear and his own political aspirations, getting rid of the man was probably just as effective.

The crowd was large tonight, Talifero thought, looking around with satisfaction at the islanders who had assembled for the ceremony. True believers, he mused, or those who came because it was prudent to pay their respect to him.

At the edge of the clearing, the drummers provided a steady rhythmic beat. The tempo was still fairly slow, and the dancers were still in control of their gestures. But he knew from experience that soon the pace would quicken until the flow of the moving bodies became frantic. Some would fall out on the ground, victims of exhaustion. Incredibly, others would stay in frenzied motion for hours.

He spared a glance at Gorlov. Earlier in the evening the Russian had been jovial, almost boisterous. Now he was pale and wide-eyed, his body stiffly perched on the edge of his seat. Talifero couldn't tell whether he was excited or frightened. Probably both. At any rate, he'd have an entertaining story to tell back in Moscow—if anybody believed him.

Gorlov fought to loosen the iron fist that gripped the pit of his stomach. Up until now he'd been enjoying Talifero's rather extraordinary hospitality. Yet here in the darkened jungle with the drums and savages, he was suddenly aware of how powerful the man was. He had decreed ritual murder, and these people were enthusiastically carrying out his edict.

The *hungan* glided toward the center of the altar and turned his head, giving the honored guests a silhouette of his mask with its enormous bird's beak. It was part of the threatening persona he chose to project. Talifero knew that Moonshadow preferred direct eye contact with her worshipers—and victims.

She was already at the ritual grounds, but she had decided not to appear during the early part of the proceedings. The doctor shifted slightly so that he could see the other side of the clearing where a paved road stopped about fifty yards from the edge of the altar. Prentiss and the girl would be coming in by van very shortly, and their trip to the ceremonial grounds was going to be strictly one-way.

THE VAN LURCHED to a stop and Jessica shivered. Next to her, Jed pressed his shoulder against hers. It was all the comfort he could give her, and damned little, under the circumstances. If Michael Rome was coming to rescue them, it had better be soon. They had almost reached the end of the line. "I'm sorry I got you into this," he whispered.

Jessica pressed back for just a moment. They were shackled together leg to leg and arm to arm. But fear, not the chains, made even the simple movement stiff. *Michael,* she thought. *Michael, where are you? Oh, God, Michael.*

After the first shock of seeing Jed, she had tried not to look at his body. Like her he was almost naked and painted with a carefully symmetrical design. Simone had shaved the thick hair on his chest to make the application smoother. Only the orchids were missing.

There were more wardens than passengers in the van. One got up and threw open the doors at the back. The drums had been growing louder during the short trip from the clinic grounds into the jungle. Now, with the back open, the noise seemed to boom inside the vehicle, almost like a physical assault. Jessica shrank back, but strong arms seized her wrists and pulled her onto the pavement. Jed lurched along with her. In a moment they were standing with a semicircle of armed escorts around them.

Her legs were rubbery so she stumbled against Jed. She knew from her laboriously spelled-out conversation with him that they had been practically starving him to make him weak. Nevertheless, his body tensed, his gaze darting about the clearing, seeking an escape route.

Moonshadow was standing before them, flanked by two tall attendants dressed in linen loincloths. The dark skin of their bodies had been oiled so that it glistened in the light of the torches they held. Behind them was another shadowy figure, holding a bowl.

Though still garbed in white, the priestess had exchanged the simple shift for a long ceremonial robe gathered just under her high breasts. In the flickering light, Jessica could see that she had painted heavy black, almost Egyptian, lines over her lids and extending beyond the corners of her eyes. The space above them was filled in with a brilliant, iridescent jade. There was no resemblance between this woman and the friend of Jessica's youth.

The priestess intoned an order, and the man with the bowl stepped into the small circle of light. Whatever was in the container smelled foul.

"You will drink this," Moonshadow commanded her captives.

"Drink it yourself," Jed spat out.

One of the wardens behind him grabbed his head. Another held his mouth open. As they poured the liquid down his throat, he gagged.

When Jessica's turn came, she didn't fight. What was the use? The vile-tasting concoction burned all the way down.

Moonshadow looked at them with satisfaction. "Now we are ready," she pronounced.

With two escorts walking behind them, two in front and two on either side, they started toward the altar, the chains clanking as their legs moved.

IN THE DARKNESS of the jungle, Holcroft grasped Michael's arm. The other man nodded, although he suspected that the gesture went unseen. Dressed in black, their faces and hands smeared with carbon, they were crouched in the deep shadows behind an oleander. The three islanders who had come around the clinic wall with them were fanned out in a semicircle guarding their rear. Michael could see the other recruits among the dancers in the crowd. They looked pretty into it. He wondered if they were really going to be of any help once the action started.

But at least part of the operation had gone off smoothly. As no one was expected to have the audacity to sneak in from this side of the ceremonial ground, the approach was only minimally patrolled. Michael had taken out two guards, and Holcroft had brought down another.

Since sunset, the two agents and their local commandos had silently carried out their own preparations for the ceremony. At a dozen locations to the north and west of the ritual clearing they had planted plastic explosives, molding them to the trunks of trees and hiding them with foliage. Each charge was equipped with a blasting cap and a fine-gauge antenna. The small transmitter that would set them off one at a time rested on the ground between them.

Yet Michael was far from sanguine. He and Holcroft could cause a diversion, but they had no control over what would happen after that.

The prisoners were coming. Michael suppressed a gasp. He'd thought years of fieldwork had prepared him for anything. But he watched in stunned silence as the captives were led forward to the front of the altar. Jed was still holding himself alert. Jess stumbled and one of the guards jerked her up roughly. Three wooden stakes had been set up facing the audience. As Michael watched, the captives' hands were lashed to rings at the tops of the posts. Only then were the leg chains and handcuffs that held them together released. A guard tested the bonds and nodded with satisfaction. Michael had to stop himself from crashing out of the bushes, his automatic blazing.

The drums began a new beat. The frenzied movement of the worshipers slowed slightly. All eyes were riveted to the altar and the two captives immobilized between the wooden posts. Up till now a tall man dressed in a feathered costume had been holding sway. With a little bow, he stepped aside in deference to a stately woman clad in a white gown. As she ascended the steps to the altar, her head high and her back straight, Michael barely suppressed an exclamation.

The woman from New Orleans! The one with the shop. Jess's friend Simone! She was here. It didn't make sense. Or did it? The scene in the garden Jessica had related—the *hungan* replaced by a woman. Simone. *She* was the voodoo priestess! He'd had a bad feeling about her from the start, and now she was getting ready to preside over two murders.

Chapter Eighteen

The armed escorts moved to the background, giving the priestess center stage with her victims. Michael was calculating the moment when he would set off the first explosive charge and stun the crowd so he could make the rescue.

But the priestess had other plans. With no forewarning, she pulled a silver dagger from the folds of her gown. He heard a low exclamation rise from the worshipers. Without further preamble Simone raised the knife in an arch above her head. It plunged into Jed's painted chest, piercing the skin above his heart. As she withdrew the blade, dark blood spurted and the agent slumped, his lifeless body held up only by his bonds.

Michael watched in frozen horror. He had expected rituals, chanting, *something* to let him know that the moment was approaching. It had simply happened before his eyes like an ax murderer leaping unexpectedly out of a closet in a third-rate horror movie. But this was not make-believe. It was hideously real.

The woman held the bloody knife up for the crowd to see, then she turned toward Jessica. God, no. With a curse he was on his feet. There was no thought of the plan he'd worked out—or his own safety. He had to save Jessica. He had just reached the edge of the crowd when a blast tore through the jungle, sending bark and wood flying.

Holcroft must have detonated one of the charges. Farther to the right, a second explosion erupted, a flash of light followed by a concussion in the darkness. A moment of shocked silence among the worshipers erupted into mass panic. As a date palm crashed across the clearing, men and women screamed, almost stampeding each other trying to get out of the way.

A wave of human flesh hit him, knocking him backward. He was going in the wrong direction through a sea of people. It was almost impossible to struggle forward, yet he made the desperate effort, focused all the while on the altar.

The priestess looked up in disbelief. Though chaos reigned, her mind was clear. She saw the *hungan* start toward Jessica, a long dagger in his hand. He must be intent on finishing the sacrifice despite the sudden shambles. She couldn't allow that. Without hesitation she pushed the tall, feather-clad man out of the way and raised her arm again, bringing her own silver knife down into Jessica's chest. Her second victim uttered a muffled scream and collapsed between the wooden posts.

Jessica's gasp was echoed by Michael's gut-wrenching cry of anguish. Redoubling his efforts, he surged forward like a madman. More blasts ripped through the jungle, causing the ground to tremble as though from an earthquake. The air was filled with the acrid smell of the explosives. Wood and bark rained down on the clearing.

A QUARTER MILE AWAY, the blast sent a retort crashing to the floor of Gilbert Xavier's laboratory. The chemist's eyes swiveled to the burner where a large beaker of highly volatile chemicals was heating. It vibrated on the stand, and he jumped back. God, he wasn't going to be able to pull it off. Simone had asked him for an explosion. The stuff was going to blow while he was still in the lab! Another shock wave hit the building. This time a bottle tumbled from a side shelf sending a spray of acid across the room, searing his face. He didn't notice. A few drops fell into the open beaker. No! Xavier could literally see the chemical reaction taking place before his eyes, but there was nothing he could do to stop it. Run! his mind shouted.

BENEATH THE feathered mask, Piers Lavintelle's features registered pure hatred for the foreign priestess. How dare an interloper shove him aside! His fingers contracted around the handle of the dagger he still held. Raising his arm, he brought down the steel blade. In the next instant it had buried itself in Moonshadow's back. She uttered a curse and sank to her knees. Another wicked jab and she pitched forward in front of the man and woman she had offered up to the gods.

Holcroft had pulled out his gun, but he couldn't shoot. Rome and their local recruits were still in the middle of the crowd. As he watched, one of them shouldered his way toward Blackstone's director.

At the side of the altar Talifero was on his feet shouting orders over the din. No one paid the slightest heed. The worshipers were too intent on flight, trampling each other as they struggled to evacuate the clearing. Gorlov had climbed below the platform at the side of the altar and flattened himself against the ground, his hands over his head. Their man reached the director's side and tried to grab his arms. From inside his jacket, Talifero pulled a small pistol. The recruit grabbed for the gun. They struggled and there was a sharp report. Talifero went down.

Michael was only yards away. Ignoring Talifero, he leapt onto the altar. The priest grabbed his shoulder and their eyes locked. The urge to strangle the man with his bare hands was almost overwhelming. Instead he settled for a vicious abdominal jab that sent Lavintelle flying off the platform and across the clearing. He hit a running woman and landed like a broken doll. Michael didn't even look to see what had happened. Quickly he untied Jessica's hands and lowered her limp body gently to the rough stones.

He felt as if someone had plunged a dull knife into his own chest and twisted the blade to increase the pain. God, why had this happened? Jessica had come down there to help him. He should have alienated her so completely that she wouldn't have wanted to be on the same continent with Michael Rome, let alone the same Caribbean island.

He touched one of the white orchids still clinging to her hair, then smoothed his hand across her brow. The skin was already cold and gray. He could feel no breath from her nose or mouth. If she had a pulse, it was too weak for him to detect. He cursed, then bent to examine the wound where the knife had gone in. It seemed to have sealed itself up, the blood no longer flowing freely. He remembered the disembodied presence that had come to him last night over the water. It had promised that Jessica and Jed would only appear dead. He hadn't really believed it then. He certainly couldn't believe it now. He was probing gently, trying to assess the internal damage, when the devil priestess stirred beside him. He wanted to stay with Jessica, but something compelled him to turn to the other woman.

Savagely he rolled her over. Her eyes were open. As he watched, her face contorted with effort and her lips formed words. Whatever she wanted to say must be terribly important. He bent so that his ear was inches from her lips. "Not dead."

He stared at the woman. The voice in his head. Simone. Was it possible?

"Jessica. Jed. Not dead. Drugged," she repeated.

He stared at her, his heart starting to pound but his brain still not daring to believe. He had seen her stab them, could still see the congealed blood on their bodies.

"Last night. I came...to you...Xavier and I...a plan."

He grasped her shoulder. "Tell me what you've done!"

"I—"

He saw the life force slip from her body. There was no use wasting any sympathy. He pried the silver knife from her limp hand. Just as he was cutting Jed down, another explosion rent the jungle night. Much more powerful than anything they had set, it came from the direction of the clinic. The sky to the west was lit as if by a second sunset. Then flames shot upward toward the heavens. The heat was intense. Even at this distance, Michael could feel it licking out toward him. If the priestess was right, he had to get Jess and Jed out of there. They could find Xavier later.

Holcroft and two of the men materialized at his side. The CIA agent looked toward where Talifero and Gorlov had been viewing the ceremony. The Russian was gone. But there was still the chemist to consider. "What do we do about Xavier?" he questioned.

"We can worry about Xavier later. We've got to get Jed and Jess out of here."

"But they're dead!"

"The priestess said they're not. I hope to God she was right."

Holcroft looked incredulously from one ashen body to the other. He'd seen them killed.

"You can carry Jed, I'll take Jess," Michael ordered.

"What's the use now?"

Michael's hand went to his gun.

Holcroft appraised the deadly look in the man's eyes. He meant what he said. Arguing with him might be suicidal. Silently, he reached for Jed's body.

He reached for Jess. Slipping off his shirt, he pulled her hands through the sleeves. Then he slid his arms under her limp shoulders and hips. Despite the wound in her side, she didn't move or groan. For just a moment he pressed her slender body close against his chest. Then he slung her over his shoulder so that he could carry her more easily.

Flames licked through the underbrush. Fanned by the wind, they headed in the direction of the ceremonial clearing. There was an acrid smell in the air.

Chemicals, Michael thought. Had the lab gone up? Right now it didn't matter. He looked around for the best escape route. Alone they could have easily outrun the conflagration. Carrying two limp bodies, they would be slowed down considerably.

Maybe they could get to the van that had brought the victims in. But when one of the men went to check it out, the vehicle had disappeared. Their own truck was out of the question. It had probably already gone up in the fire.

"The boat," Holcroft shouted.

I hope it's there, Michael thought, but didn't waste the breath to voice the uncertainty.

With the fire at their backs, they slogged through the thick vegetation, one of the islanders leading the way. Thorns and tangled undergrowth grabbed their clothing and tore at their flesh. Pushing on, they disregarded the impediments.

Every step Michael took was agony. Jessica's inanimate body sagged over his shoulder. Her skin was cold and clammy. It was almost impossible to believe she was really alive.

Finally the little group broke from cover to confront the moon reflecting a silvery path along the water. Holcroft set Jed down. The agent took a deep breath and wiped his forearm across his brow. Then he pulled out his gun and fired two signal shots. From the darkened water came an answering flash. Thank God. They were there.

The cabin cruiser maneuvered in closer. It took several trips with the small boat; but twenty minutes later the party had been transferred to the *Star Fish*. Miraculously, they had only lost one man in the melée.

"You'd all better come with us to Jamaica," Holcroft told the islanders, "until we find out how hot it is on Royale Verde."

Bequi, the island recruit, peered back at the flames consuming the peninsula. "Right, mon."

Holcroft set a course for his home port and one of the islanders took the helm. When he came down the companionway, Michael was already below in the lounge with the couple they had rescued. Each had been laid out on one of the bunks. Holcroft turned on the cabin lights.

"The priestess swore they're alive," Michael muttered. As he spoke he pulled out blankets, covering first Jessica and then Jed.

Holcroft shook his head. Rome still wasn't acting rationally. Was he deluded? Or desperate? He remembered the way the man had put a threatening hand on his gun. Right now the safest course was to humor him. He held up a flashlight and peered into Jed's face.

"What should we do for them?" he questioned.

Michael shook his head. "Damn it, she didn't tell me that. All we can do is keep them warm. Sponge this goop off. How long before we get to a hospital?"

"From this side of the island, two or three hours."

Michael knelt and pressed his fingers against the artery in Jessica's neck. At first he felt nothing. He was about to give up when he detected a faint throb. Twenty seconds later there was another.

"I've got something. It's unbelievably slow. But—"

Holcroft turned to the sink and filled the kettle. When the water was hot, he and Michael each took a bowl and a towel. Holcroft worked on Jed. Michael took care of Jessica.

"His color's better," Holcroft remarked, his voice sounding as if he still didn't believe the evidence of his eyes. "And I'm feeling a pulse. Very slow, but getting stronger. It's weird."

Michael bent closer to Jessica for a better look at the knife wound. It was slanted precisely to follow a black line painted on her skin; it seemed as if the priestess had used it for a guide and worked with a surgeon's precision.

"Check out where the knife went into Jed's chest," he directed. "Is there a black mark?"

"Uh-huh." Holcroft's brow wrinkled. "Do you suppose she could have put the blade in so it would miss vital organs?"

"I hope so." Michael pressed his fingers against Jessica's neck again. Her pulse was stronger and more regular and her skin was warming. She was coming back to life under his touch! Hope swelled in his chest. God, let her be all right, he prayed silently as he tenderly sponged the hateful paint from her body.

They continued to work in silence. Michael pausing every few minutes to check Jessica's pulse. It was still far below anything approaching normal, but it was getting steadily stronger.

Twenty minutes later a startled exclamation from Holcroft brought Michael across the lounge. The CIA agent was staring down at the man on the bunk in disbelief. As Michael watched, Jed's eyelids fluttered. His lids opened, closed, and then opened again. His eyes were dilated, but they swung toward Michael. His lips moved but no sound came out.

"Easy. You're safe."

"Rome. You old coyote. What took you so long?" The voice was barely above a whisper.

Michael looked at Holcroft. "He's his usual cheery self."

"Jessica told me—" He stopped abruptly. "Is she?"

"Right here," Michael assured him. "Not quite as far along as you."

Jed closed his eyes.

"Just rest," Holcroft told him. "We'll get you to the hospital."

The man on the bunk seemed to be drifting for a moment. Abruptly his eyes snapped open. "That bastard Talifero?"

Michael shrugged. "I saw him go down."

"Good," Jed spat out.

"The clinic went up in an explosion. I think maybe Xavier—Talifero's chemist—blew up the lab."

"What makes you think so?" Holcroft questioned.

"The priestess. She mentioned Xavier. Told me they had something cooked up together."

Jed stirred restlessly.

"Do you need something?"

"Water. Nothing to eat and only a little to drink in days."

Holcroft swore vehemently and turned toward the sink. He could only imagine what this man had endured. He was back quickly with a cup of water. "Better take it easy," he advised as he supported Jed's shoulders and held the cup to his lips. After a few swallows the weakened man closed his eyes.

"Thanks," he whispered.

Michael and Holcroft exchanged glances.

"I'm sorry. You were right," the CIA man acknowledged.

"Yeah. Forget it."

A low exclamation from the other side of the cabin made them both turn.

"Michael." Swiftly he crossed the deck and knelt beside Jessica again. He could see she wasn't quite awake. But she was calling him. After everything that had happened, she was still calling for him.

"Michael . . ."

"Right here." He took her hand, chafed the cool flesh. She still didn't seem to know he was there and moved restlessly on the bunk.

Leaning closer, he pulled the blanket tenderly up around her shoulders and smoothed back the wreath of auburn curls around her face. His voice was low, murmuring soft, reassuring words.

She calmed under his touch, but for several minutes she continued to struggle toward consciousness. Then her lids fluttered open. Like Jed's, her eyes were dilated.

"Jess, oh, Jess. Thank God."

She tried to raise her arm toward him.

"Don't move, baby." He knelt closer, gathered her in his embrace, held her tightly. Tears filled his eyes as he brushed his lips against her cheek, her forehead.

"I thought I wouldn't get a chance to tell you I love you," she whispered. Every word was an effort, yet she had to speak.

"I thought that too, baby." His voice was husky. "I thought I'd lost you. I love you, too."

She closed her eyes, hugging the words to herself. Then her lids fluttered open, and she searched his face. "Was it that hard to admit?"

"Yeah. A Herculean task. I've never said that to anyone before." He bent again to nuzzle his cheek against hers and trail his lips across her forehead, feeling her skin warm even as he caressed her.

Her hand came up to touch his shoulder. He knew how much effort it must have cost her and pressed his fingers over hers. Everything he'd said to her about his life was still true, yet the idea of giving her up made him feel as desperate as he had when he'd awakened in that tomb. Could they really work things out? Finally he had admitted to himself how much he wanted to.

Holcroft stared at the emotional scene with sudden understanding. He'd caught tension between Rome and Jessica but hadn't associated it with a personal involvement. Now it explained a lot about Rome's losing his cool. Turning, Holcroft tiptoed up the stairs to the deck, giving Michael and Jessica privacy. Besides, he still had work to do. He needed to get a message to the backup team Rome had put on alert. They were going to have a lot of cleaning up to do on Royale Verde—like finding out what had happened to Talifero, Gorlov, and Xavier.

JESSICA LOOKED OUT the floor-to-ceiling windows of the solarium. On the wide lawn at the back of the Aviary, Michael and a much-improved Jed Prentiss were tossing a football back and forth. The mid-October day was warm. Though both men had come out in sweatclothes, they'd soon discarded their hooded jackets. Once again Jessica admired the ripple of muscles in Michael's arm and back as he reached up to snag a high pass. Just watching Michael Rome stirred her senses in a way she'd never felt before.

He caught her appraisal and waved, motioning her to come out. She opened the door and stepped onto the terrace, feeling like a student stealing a few minutes of relaxation between final exams. She'd already had several extensive debriefings with Connie in which she'd given her accounts of the events on Royale Verde the week before. She'd also learned some of the aftermath of their last night on the island. Both the lab and clinic had burned to the ground, but the staff had been able to evacuate most of the patients. Inland waterways had contained the fire to Devil's Point.

Jed jumped to catch the ball and missed. "You're getting old, Prentiss," Michael gibed good-naturedly.

"Not too bad for a zombie," Jed retorted.

"Speak for yourself," Michael advised, "but Jessica's no zombie." He put his arm around her and pulled her close.

"Maybe not, Michael old man. But what about you? I'll bet you're the only Peregrine agent who's ever been encrypted."

Michael snorted. "How long did it take you to think up that one?"

"All week, or you would have heard it sooner."

"You two are beyond belief," Jessica marveled. She turned to Jed. "What you need is some lunch. Connie asked me to come and get you."

"I'll go for that." He'd been industriously putting back on the weight Talifero had starved off him.

They all started toward the house, the two men still tossing the football back and forth.

"We'll change and meet you in the dining room," Michael advised her.

As the men turned away, Jessica thought about the zombie remark. They might never know exactly what Simone had given them, but the Jamaican doctor had offered a theory. The potion she'd forced them to drink had apparently intensified the body's natural reaction to injury. Under normal circumstances, the knife wounds would have sent both her and Jed into shock. The drug had magnified that reaction a thousand times—closing down functions so that they had been catapulted into a state of catatonia.

Jessica shuddered. The ruse had saved her life, but it had been a terrifying experience she'd never forget.

Shaking the unsettling thoughts from her head, she watched the two men head for the stairs. It was hard not to be envious of their easy camaraderie. They knew where they stood with each other. Despite the emotional conversation on the boat and the joy of their lovemaking this past week, she and Michael still hadn't been able to talk about the future.

After lunch the Falcon suggested that they adjourn to the library. "I'm sure you're all eager for the latest intelligence on this case," he surmised.

There was a chorus of agreement around the room.

"Well, let's start with unfinished business. I have confirmation on the identify of Talifero's body. But Gorlov is still missing. He could be among the bodies burned beyond recognition. We do know, however, from intelligence reports that the advisors and arms in Cuba have been shipped home. Apparently Moscow has abandoned their plans for a Royale Verde takeover.

"Xavier was another unknown," the Falcon continued. "But the forensic unit has finally confirmed the identify of the body found near the lab. The chemist isn't going to be processing any more Dove. His last actions ensured that no one else will either. Everything went up in the explosion, including his notes."

"Simone Villard won't be dabbling in voodoo medicine either," Connie added.

Next to Michael on the couch, Jessica shuddered. He reached out for her hand and squeezed it reassuringly.

"She was so mixed up," Jessica murmured. "She's the one whose betrayal almost got Michael killed. But in the end she saved Jed's and my life. She wasn't all bad."

"We've uncovered some of her involvement with Talifero," Connie continued. "It goes back more than ten years. She was too young to know what she was getting into at the time. Once he had a hold on her, she couldn't break it. At first she saw Xavier's discoveries as a way of getting Talifero off her back, but it just got her in deeper."

The Falcon looked over at Jessica. "Lonnie Milstead got away too, but he surfaced in New Orleans thinking that he could call in some favors. He was wrong. The drug community works strictly on a cash-and-carry basis. Lieutenant Devine picked Milstead up a few days ago."

"Thank God he's off the streets."

"Talifero was powerful enough to set him up in business and give him some protection. With his sponsor gone, he was left twisting in the wind. When they booked him on murder one for his buddy Joe Valenchi's death, he decided to plea bargain."

"What's he had to say?" Michael questioned.

"He's supplied names and addresses of a major portion of the Dove distribution ring in the Crescent City. He's also revealed his connection to Bergman at the university. According to his statement, the chairman of the chemistry department was the one who asked him to take care of Aubrey."

Jessica's fingers tightened on Michael's. "I hope they lock them both up for good."

"Devine's working on it." The Falcon went on to give some more details. When the meeting finally broke up, the Peregrine chief asked Jessica to stay for a moment.

She glanced at Michael. "I'll be out back," he told her.

When they were alone, Gordon leaned back in his leather chair. "Do you have any idea what I want to ask you?"

She laughed nervously. "You've been broadcasting it at me all afternoon."

"You have a unique talent that the Peregrine Connection could make good use of. I know that your recent experience has been pretty traumatic, but I wonder if you'd be willing to consider joining us as a consultant."

"I have to think about it."

"The offer is open." Though he wanted to, he wouldn't press her harder now.

"I'll let you know."

When she closed the door to the library, she took a deep breath. The Falcon had spoken of her talent. She'd spent years trying to deny that special ability. Now that was impossible. She was never going to step back into the shoes of the person she'd been a month ago. Where did that leave her? And more specifically, where did it leave her with Michael?

Outside she found him leaning against an oak tree and looking out toward the mountains, a pensive expression on his face. His hands were jammed into the pockets of his jeans and one snakeskin boot was propped against the tree trunk. She smiled, knowing she was seeing the real Michael Rome and not one of the personas he so often portrayed. Then her expression sobered. Maybe now was the time for the talk they'd been avoiding.

He looked up as she approached.

"I could go the conventional route and offer you a penny for your thoughts," she began. "Or I could play Mr. Spock and try a Vulcan mind meld."

"I'm not sure I'm quite ready for that."

"I didn't think so."

They regarded each other for a moment. "Michael, I can't turn it off. For years I repressed that part of myself. That doesn't work anymore. I think I can come to terms with it. Can you?"

His words weren't exactly the answer she wanted. "Jess, how would you feel if you never knew whether I was going to be peeking into your mind, catching some thought you didn't want me to catch?"

"I don't know. I suppose it would be difficult, require adjustments. It would mean I'd always have to be honest with you."

She was the most honest person he knew. "Baby, I want to be. Just don't be disappointed if I fall short of the mark sometimes." His face became more gentle. "But being open to you does have its compensations. Like when my shoulders hurt and you come over and rub the exact spot that needs attention. Or when we're making love, and I feel as if your soul is merging with mine."

"That's when you're most open to me—when we're making love."

"Being close to you then is very precious, Jess." He pulled her into his arms and wrapped her tightly against his body, his hands moving up and down her back. His lips slid along her cheek, found her mouth. He brushed them back and forth against hers, then settled, drank more deeply. "I don't think I can get along without you anymore."

She sensed the promise in his mind, yet she needed to hear the words. "So what do we do?"

"Love each other." His voice was gruff.

"Is love enough?"

"It's supposed to be."

"But for us?" she persisted.

"Jess, I think I've finally freed myself from the past. We'll just have to work on the future together."

He found her lips again, and for a few minutes they didn't speak, both wanting to show the other how strongly they felt. But there was another question she needed to ask. "How would you feel about my working for Peregrine? Gordon's asked me to be a consultant. I suspect that's his way of easing me into it."

"He told me he was going to speak to you. It would mean you'd have the right clearances. But I still can't be sure how I'm going to handle it."

"I know. I'll worry about you when you're out on assignments. But I won't try to stop you from doing your job."

"I told you once that you were an extraordinary woman."

"You were trying to get rid of me then."

"Not now, baby." He looked at her and grinned. "At least you don't know everything I'm thinking. I'm due a month's leave and plan to head back to Texas to see if my ranch is still there. I want you to come with me."

"I'd like that." She knew the ranch was his alone. To be asked there meant he was letting her into his life. "But I do need to make a slight detour to Annapolis and see how my business is running itself."

"Fair enough. Besides, I'd like to see where you live too." A devilish expression came over his face. "Can you guess what I'm thinking right now?"

She moved her hips against his. "I don't have to read your mind to guess that."

"Uh-huh. I'm wondering whether to take you down into the woods and make love to you there, or whether we can sneak back up to bed without getting corralled by someone for another debriefing session."

She grinned. "Let's take the safest route." She slipped her hand into his. Together they walked away from the house and toward the orange and gold of the autumn splendor.

Chapter One

With an effort, Jed Prentiss kept a smile plastered on his face. But as he gazed across the crowded room at the woman with the upswept golden curls, his fingers tightened around the tumbler of planter's punch he wasn't planning to drink. When he realized he was in danger of shattering the glass, he eased up on the pressure.

Was that Marissa? Here to screw things up for him?

He kept talking in his excellent Spanish to the minister of Economic Development while he tried for another look at the blonde.

She turned her head gracefully as she put a champagne flute down on a passing waiter's tray, and he knew he'd been right. He'd recognize Marissa Devereaux's silky hair anywhere. It crowned a heart-shaped face with innocent-looking blue eyes, a petite nose and a mouth that could twist facts and half-truths together so adroitly, you didn't know you'd been had until the middle of the next week.

In fact, she was almost as good at undercover work as he was himself. Except that she took foolish chances. As if she had nothing to lose.

Damn! She was the last person he wanted to run into at Miguel Sanchez's townhouse—as San Marcos's commander in chief referred to his thirty-room Spanish colonial mansion.

After promising that he'd talk with the minister about mining loans early in the week, he excused himself and made his way across the room.

The nearer he got to Marissa, the more burningly aware of her he became. He couldn't possibly be close enough to smell her perfume. Yet he imagined the scent of gardenias drifting toward him. She was wearing a little black dress that she probably didn't think of as sexy, but it emphasized her narrow waist and sassy little hips. He hadn't seen the front, but he knew the way it clung to her high, firm breasts.

He scowled. He'd better keep his mind on business.

He could see she was just finishing a conversation with Thomas Leandro, the outspoken university professor who'd made his reputation with pie-in-the-sky blueprints for turning the Central American republic into a socialist paradise. The professor was on Jed's list, too. But he could wait.

When Leandro went off toward the buffet table, Jed stepped into Marissa's path.

Her cheeks took on a hint of heightened color, and her blue eyes widened and darkened, but the momentary lapse was her only betrayal of surprise—or anything else.

No matter how many times they met, he was never prepared for her reaction. As if she were suppressing strong emotions she didn't want him to read. Or couldn't acknowledge. When he'd tried to find out what was going on below the surface of those beautiful blue eyes, they had iced over. The rebuffs had hurt his ego. He'd vowed never to let it happen again.

"Jed. How nice to see you. Are you here on behalf of the Global Bank?"

Smooth, he thought. Like they were just friendly colleagues who traveled in the same business circles.

"Yes."

They studied each other carefully.

What was she planning for the evening? he wondered. Did she already know he'd be prowling the same turf? Or was she as unpleasantly surprised as he'd been? Only one of them was going to leave the capital city with the evidence they'd come to steal. He was going to make damn sure it was him.

"You're a long way from Baltimore."

"Yes."

"So what brings you to San Marcos?" he asked conversationally.

"Oh, you know. My usual. I'm scouting out off-the-beaten-track vacation locations for Adventures in Travel."

Latch on to anything exciting?"

"I think I'll be able to set up a jungle trip to some partially excavated Mayan ruins. And there are excellent snorkeling and diving opportunities along the coral reef. I think I can guide visitors to a stingray feeding location."

"Sounds dangerous."

"Not when you know what you're doing."

"Be careful."

"Oh, I will."

He was enjoying the subtext inlaid into the conversation and was about to ask if she wanted him to introduce her to General Sanchez when one of the uniformed staff approached them. "Señorita Devereaux?"

"*Sí.*"

"*Teléphono para usted.*"

She gave Jed an apologetic look. "I'll see you later."

"Expecting an important call?"

For a split second, she looked as if she weren't sure how to reply. Then she simply shrugged and followed the man who had delivered the message.

As Jed watched him lead her toward a back hall, he wondered if there were some way he could listen in on the phone conversation.

He memorized the floor plan of the house. There was another access to the hall, from a door in the enclosed patio.

As if he had nothing more important to do than get a breath of the fresh air, he wandered casually toward the French doors.

When he stepped onto the stone terrace, the tropical night, rich with the scent of flowers, enveloped him. It took several moments for his eyes to adjust to the darkness. As they did, he went very still. Marissa had come out the side door he'd been heading for and was walking rapidly toward the far wing of the house where the office complex was located.

The office complex that was strictly off-limits to everyone except Sanchez and his hand-picked staff. Jed had heard stories of summary executions of suspected spies caught there.

My God, didn't Marissa know the risk she was taking? For that matter, didn't she know there was a guard out here? Jed's gaze probed the darkness.

There was *supposed* to be a guard. He didn't seem to be here. Had Marissa taken care of him? Lord, this was just the kind of audacious maneuver she was so good at pulling off.

Jed was about to follow her. Before he could, however, he saw a figure ooze out of the shadows like a night creature crawling out from under a rock. Without making a sound, he slunk after her.

The hair on the back of Jed's neck stood on end as if a cold breeze had just blown across the patio. Marissa was in deep banana oil. Unless he could stop her before she reached the office wing.

* * * * *

*Don't miss this next 43 LIGHT STREET tale—
#318 Till Death Us Do Part—
coming to you in April 1995.
Only from Rebecca York and Harlequin Intrigue!*

COMING NEXT MONTH

#309 BODYGUARD by Leona Karr
Dangerous Men

Damas Silva was watching her...but there was something so mysterious and compelling about the man who claimed to be her bodyguard that Alexa Widmire soon wondered if her heart's deepest secrets were safe....

#310 VEIL OF FEAR by Judi Lind

When a stalker began trailing Mary Wilder, preparations for her fairy-tale wedding became a nightmare. But Mary soon discovered she was more at risk under the paid protection of bodyguard Trace Armstrong—especially since her fiancé was out of town.

#311 SUSPICIONS by Connie Bennett

Holly McGinnis had never gotten over her ex-fiancé, but the savvy marine archaeologist sure didn't trust him. Still, when Logan Tate was accused of murder, Holly was startled to find herself rising to his defense...and falling back into his arms.

#312 STAND BY YOUR MAN by B.J. Daniels
Woman of Mystery

Denver McCallahan had vowed to find her uncle Max's murderer...but why were the two men she loved most so bent on accusing each other? Denver was forced to choose between them—would she stand by the man who had stood by her, or by the man who'd broken her heart?

Take 4 bestselling love stories FREE

Plus get a FREE surprise gift!

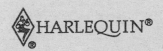

HARLEQUIN®

Deceit, betrayal, murder

Join Harlequin's intrepid heroines, India Leigh
and Mary Hadfield, as they ferret out the truth
behind the mysterious goings-on in their
neighborhood. These two women are no milk-
and-water misses. In fact, they thrive on

MISCHIEF & MAYHEM

Watch for their incredible adventures in this
special two-book collection. Available in March,
wherever Harlequin books are sold.

HARLEQUIN®

I N T R I G U E®

HARLEQUIN INTRIGUE BOOKS ARE MOVING!

Your favorite Harlequin Intrigue books have been available at your local retail store in the last two weeks of every month. Intrigue is moving!

Starting with February 1995 publications, Harlequin Intrigue books will be available two weeks earlier at your local retailer.

Look for all Intrigue titles in the first two weeks of every month, and happy reading!

HARLEQUIN BOOKS—NOT THE SAME OLD STORY!

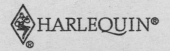